Scorpius

JAMES BOND

IN
JOHN GARDNER'S
Scorpius

Stoddart

in association with

Hodder & Stoughton

The extract from 'Down by the Salley Gardens' taken from *The Collected Poems of W. B. Yeats*, which appears on page 120, is quoted by kind permission of A. P. Watt Limited on behalf of Michael B. Yeats and Macmillan London Limited.

First published in 1988 by
Stoddart Publishing Co. Limited
34 Lesmill Road
Toronto, Canada
M3B 2T6

Published in Great Britain by
Hodder and Stoughton Limited
47 Bedford Square
London, England
WC1B 3DP

Canadian Cataloguing in Publication Data

Gardner, John, 1926–
  Scorpius.

ISBN 0-7737-2197-5

I. Title

PR6057.A63S28 1988   823'.914   c88-093370-4

Printed and bound in Great Britain

This book is dedicated to –

Alexis & John,
Simon &
Miranda

Contents

1

The Longest Mile

At exactly ten minutes after midnight the girl stepped from the train, pausing for a moment, surprised at the newspaper poster in front of the closed kiosk: PRIME MINISTER CALLS GENERAL ELECTION - JUNE 11th. Now she knew why they had been given the orders, and why she had, instinctively, refused to stay.

It was not until she got outside the main concourse of Waterloo Station that she realised it was raining. Badly in need of help she went back into the station, trying three public telephones before finding one that was not vandalised. She dialled the 376 Chelsea number and waited as the ringing tone went on and on, reading the graffiti with only a small part of her mind – scrawled telephone numbers next to girls' names offering unspecified services; the occasional morsel of crude wit. At last, knowing the call was not going to be answered, she replaced the receiver. He was out, or away from London. She thought she would faint, or cry. He would never have lectured her. He would have understood and helped – advised. But now there was only one option. Home.

And home was the last place she wanted to go, but there was no really safe alternative.

There were no taxis, and the rain had turned into a fine drizzle: par for the course in May. Thank God it was not far to walk. The longest mile. What made her think of that? A song – 'The longest mile is the last mile home.'

She threaded her way down from the station into York Road, then over onto Westminster Bridge. Crossing to the far side she saw that County Hall was still illuminated, looking more like a luxury riverside hotel than a battleground for the capital's politics. Traffic and pedestrians were sparse now. Three cabs went by with their signs switched off. Odd, she thought, that in London as soon as it rained cabs seemed to be either heading home, or were occupied by very small people.

She reached the far end of the bridge and turned right into Victoria Embankment. Across the road, behind her, Big Ben rose triumphant, while the sinister black statue of Boadicea in her war chariot loomed over her right shoulder, a dark blotch against the sky.

The apartment was less than ten minutes' walk away, and she now wondered how her parents would take the unexpected arrival. That part of her which remained stubborn revolted against returning home.

There would be the inevitable recriminations, but, as they had tried every trick in the book to get her back, they would at least show some relief and happiness. Her problem was having to admit that they had been right all along.

As she turned onto Victoria Embankment, she became suddenly alert. For a moment she realised that her guard had been down during the walk across the bridge. People *were* looking for her. That was as certain as night followed day. So far she had taken precautions. They would have people at Paddington Station, for that was her most likely place of arrival. The journey had taken several hours longer than necessary, changing trains and taking a bus so that her entrance to London had been Waterloo and not Paddington. But they would also be watching the building in which her parents lived, she had no doubt about that.

Just as all this crossed her mind, two figures stepped from the shadows into the pool of light thrown across her from the street lamps.

'What we got 'ere, then?' The first one to speak had a drunken slur in his voice. She wrapped the thin white raincoat around her as though it afforded some kind of protection against them.

As they came near, she realised these were not the type to have been sent after her. This pair wore jeans, bomber jackets studded and hung with chains, while their hair was spiked and dyed – one red and orange, the other pink and blue.

'Well, you on your own, darlin'?' asked the larger of the pair.

She took a step back, one hand going out to the wall behind her. Somewhere, she knew, there was an opening, with steps leading down to the little mooring platform used during the summer for the tourist pleasure boats that plied up and down the Thames.

It was irrational, but there was hope she could escape that way.

'Come on, darlin'. No need to be scared of us.' Their voices were similar, both of them ragged with drink.

'Nice girl like you wouldn't refuse a couple of beautiful fellas like us, would you?'

Slowly they moved nearer. She even thought she could smell the drink on their breath. Almost safe and this had to happen – muggers, or worse.

The latter thought was immediately confirmed.

'Course, you'd have a lie down with us, wouldn't you?' The wolfish grin was clear in the diffused light.

The other one gave an unpleasant drunken giggle. 'She'll lie down, even if we has to 'old 'er down.'

As they lurched forward, she found the gap in the wall. She turned, almost falling down the steps towards the river, one hand clutching her tote bag, with its strap around her shoulder, terror like a bright light in her head which seemed to make breathing difficult and caused her stomach to churn in a butterfly roll.

They were following, their boots noisy and heavy on the broad steps. Then she smelled the water, and fear became panic. There *was* no escape. Not across the water, for she could not swim. There was no pleasure boat on which she might hide, only the short metal poles joined together with chains.

They were almost on her and she turned again, determined to fight back if she could. Purity. Purity mattered. They all said so. Father Valentine said so. At all cost she must keep herself pure.

She backed away, and the chain touched her behind the knees making her cry out, stumble and jump. In that moment she lost her balance, shoes slipping on the damp stone, legs caught for a moment in the dangling safety chain, so that she seemed to be held upside down. Then she fell, and the water was everywhere, black, filling her mouth, nostrils and clothes, the raincoat ballooning around her, the weight of her clothes and bag dragging her down. She could hear someone screaming, then realised it was herself coughing, choking and spluttering as she thrashed around, hands hitting the water, her body cloaked in terror.

From a long way off she heard the voice of her old PE teacher, the sadistic one who had tried to teach her to swim by throwing her bodily into the pool. 'Come on girl, don't flap about! You're like a pregnant pelican! Get control of yourself! Come on you stupid girl . . . girl . . . girl . . . girl . . . gir . . !'

The darkness took over. She felt a terrible, yet soothing, weakness. Panic gave way to a kind of serenity. She stopped struggling, as though overcome by an anaesthetic, and dropped into an endless sleep.

2

The Floater

M really had too much on his mind to see the man from Special
Branch, and the loyal Miss Moneypenny knew it. Within the headquarters building which overlooks Regent's Park they were going
through a period of unpleasantly complicated and time-consuming
housekeeping and housecleaning. The auditors had been in for a week,
inconveniently taking up much-needed office space, checking and
rechecking the accounts of each department, and severely cutting into
the working time of a number of senior officers.

The Audit was a serious disruption that took place every two or
three years. Eventually the auditors would return from whence they
came – under stones near The Long Water in Kensington Gardens,
if you were to believe M – but that would not be the end of the
business.

In three months' time the Audit would have been studied by a select
number of people, including the Chancellor of the Exchequer and the
Foreign Secretary who would put the figure of the Secret Vote before
the Cabinet, and from there to the Treasury.

The Secret Vote was M's lifeblood – the financial allotment with
which he had to run his Service: the hard cash to pay for everything,
from the salaries of officers under his command to the funding of
agents in the field, the satellite costs, research, and a hundred and one
other items, right down to the paperclips and staplers here on the
eighth floor where M had his suite of offices.

The Audit was a time of strain, and now a further tension had been
added by the announcement of a General Election. In less than a
month, M would be working for the same masters in the Foreign
Office – for governments come and go, but the mandarins of Whitehall
go on for ever. Yet emphasis on the kind of work carried out by M's
Service might alter drastically should a government of a different
political colour sweep into power. Changes of government, even *possible*
changes, set the chief of the Secret Service's mind on a knife-edge of
anxiety. That very day he had a crammed diary, which included five
top-level meetings and lunch – at Blades -- with the Chairman of the
Joint Intelligence Committee.

The officer from Special Branch had said it was urgent: M's ears
only. Moneypenny glanced at her watch and saw the policeman had
already been kept waiting for nearly an hour. He had arrived, without
warning, only ten minutes before M returned from lunch. Moneypenny

took a deep breath and buzzed through on the inter-office line.

'Yes?' M growled.

'You haven't forgotten that Chief Superintendent Bailey's still waiting, sir?' She tried to sound brisk and efficient.

'Who?' M had lately taken to his old habit of side-stepping issues by feigning a sieve-like memory.

'The officer from the Branch,' Moneypenny tactfully reminded him.

'Hasn't got an appointment,' M snapped back.

'No, sir, but I put the memo from Head of the Branch on your desk before you got back from lunch. His request *is* rather pressing.'

There was a pause. Moneypenny heard the crackle of paper as M read the memo.

'Head of the Branch can't get away himself, so he's sent a lackey,' M grumbled. 'Why us? They usually bother our brethren in Five. Why doesn't he trot over to Curzon Street, or wherever the Security Service hangs out these days?'

Though Special Branch often work with MI5, at the latter's request, they are not the overt mailed fist of the Security Service. They have even been known to turn down a request to assist Five, for they tread with care. They are answerable, not to some faceless men in Whitehall, but directly to the Metropolitan Police Commissioner. Rarely did the Branch make any approaches to the Secret Intelligence Service which was M's fief.

'No idea why us, sir. Just that Head of Branch wants you to see this officer PDQ.'

M made a strange tch-tching sound. 'Old-fashioned expression, Moneypenny – PDQ. Pretty Damned Quick, eh? What you say he was called?'

'Bailey, sir. Chief Superintendent Bailey.'

'Oh well.' Another sigh. 'Better wheel him up, then.'

Bailey turned out to be a tall well-groomed man in his middle thirties. His suit was of a conservative, and expensive cut, and M could scarcely fail to notice that he wore the tie of a much admired Cambridge college. Bailey's manner was pleasant enough. He could easily have passed for a young doctor or lawyer. Wouldn't be out of place in Five, either, M thought.

'We haven't met, sir. My name's Bailey.' The police officer came straight to the point extending his hand. 'The HOB sends his apologies, but he's going to be tied up all day with the heads of A11 and C13.'

A11 is better known as the Diplomatic Protection Group, body-guards to politicians and royalty – visiting or permanent. C13 is the police Anti-Terrorist Squad which has strong links with MI5 and the Secret Intelligence Service, as well as C7, their own Technical Support Branch, and D11, the 'Blue Berets', Scotland Yard's firearms department, within which a squad of élite specialists is always at the ready for a serious incident.

'Bit pushed now the PM's gone to the country, sir.' Bailey smiled.

'Aren't we all?' M did not smile. 'Not your usual happy hunting ground, this, is it, Chief Super?'

'Not normal, sir. No. But it's a bit special. The HOB thought it best to approach you personally.'

M paused, looking up at the younger man, his face betraying nothing. At last he waved towards a chair.

Bailey sat.

'Come on, then,' M said quietly. 'Haven't got all day, either of us. What's it about?'

Bailey cleared his throat. Even experienced police officers do not always throw off the habit, born of giving evidence in many court-rooms. 'Early this morning we got what, when I was a young copper, we called a "floater".'

'Body recovered from water,' M murmured.

'Exactly, sir. Picked up by the River Patrol near Cleopatra's Needle. No press release as yet, but we've been on the case all morning. VIP. The Head of Branch himself broke it to the family. It's a young woman, sir. Twenty-three years of age. Miss Emma Dupré, daughter of Mr and Mrs Peter Dupré.'

'The financier? Merchant banker?' M's eyes flashed, as though interest was only just aroused.

Bailey nodded. 'The same, sir. Chairman of Gomme-Keogh. Impeccable merchant bank, beyond reproach. I understand that the Foreign Office sometimes borrow their very senior people for special audits.'

'Yes. Yes, they do.' M wondered if this young man knew that a member of the Gomme-Keogh Board was in the building at this very moment, working on the Audit. 'Suicide?' he asked – his face blank – not even the most experienced interrogator or police observer could have divined what might be going on in his mind.

'Don't think so, sir. They've carried out a post mortem. Death by drowning. The body wasn't long in the water – six, seven hours at the most. Appears accidental. I've seen the report. But there are one or two interesting things. The girl was recently weaned off heroin. Within the last couple of months, according to family friends, if you see what I mean. We haven't taken it up with her mother and father yet.'

M nodded, waiting for the police officer to go on.

'You heard of a religious group – bit cranky – calling themselves the Meek Ones, sir?'

'Vaguely, yes. Like the Moonies, eh?'

'Not really. They have a religious philosophy, but that's very different to sects like the Moonies. For instance, the Meek Ones got her off drugs – the deceased, I mean – there's little doubt about that. They put a premium on morality. Won't have people living together within their community. They have to go through a form of marriage, followed by a Register Office ceremony. Very big on old values, but they do have some exceptionally strange ideas once you get out of the moral area.'

'Look, Chief Super, what's this got to do with me, and my Service? Funny religious groups aren't much in our line.'

Bailey raised his head, mouth opening for a second, closing and then opening to speak. 'The young woman, sir. Miss Dupré. We found at least two strange items on her. She was pulled out of the Thames still clutching one of these tote bags that girls carry around, filled with everything from a Filofax to the kitchen sink. It was a good one – the bag – zipped tight, and no water damage.'

'And you found the "odd" items in the bag?'

The Branch man nodded. 'The Filofax, for instance. All the pages of addresses and telephone numbers had been removed, except for one – a telephone number scrawled across a page of this current week. My impression is that it was noted down from memory. One digit's been crossed out and the correct one inserted in its place.'

'So?'

'The number belongs to one of your officers, sir.'

'Indeed?'

'A Commander Bond, sir. Commander James Bond.'

'Ah.' M's mind ran through a number of possible permutations. 'Bond is out of London at the moment.' He paused. 'I can get him back if you want to speak to him. If you think he can help you with your enquiries – as they say in the press.'

'He could very well be of help, sir. Though we do have a couple of other things as well. For instance, I believe Lord Shrivenham – also of Gomme-Keogh – is working in this building, on a temporary basis. I'd like a word with him.' He saw M's eyebrows twitch slightly. 'You see *his* daughter – the Honourable Trilby Shrivenham – was one of Miss Dupré's close friends. She has had similar drug problems, and she's also a member of the Meek Ones. I gather Lord Shrivenham's rather cut up about it.'

'You want to see Shrivenham here? On these premises?' M asked, his agile mind already working on how he could possibly be of assistance to Basil Shrivenham. Some little favour might be useful when it came to the Secret Vote.

'I'd rather like to have a word with Commander Bond first.' Bailey's face was blank. 'Depending on what he has to say, there's another matter we might have to talk about – with Lord Shrivenham present.'

M nodded, reaching out to pick up the telephone. 'Moneypenny, get Bond back to London in double-quick time, would you? And let me have his ETA as soon as you know it. I'll wait in the office until he arrives. Even if it means being here until the wee small hours.'

He replaced the receiver, frowning slightly. Bond's lifestyle had changed drastically over the past few months, and any changes in 007 made M a shade nervous – even when the changes appeared to be for the best.

In the outer office, Miss Moneypenny picked up the red scrambler telephone and dialled an unlisted number. The area code was 0432 – the code for Hereford.

3

The Crossroads Incident

James Bond could not recall the last time he had felt so completely exhausted. Every muscle ached; fatigue seeped into his bones like some pernicious poison; his legs felt like lumps of lead so that each step forward was a conscious effort, while his feet seemed to burn inside the usually comfortable DMS boots; his eyelids drooped, and it was difficult to concentrate on more than one thing at a time. On top of it all, he felt unclean from the sweat that had collected under his clothing, dried, then collected again. The sight of the Bedford RL four-tonne truck parked on the road below him was like an oasis to a man who had spent days in the desert with little food and less water. But Bond had been in no desert; quite the contrary. For the last ten days he had been taking part in a survival and endurance exercise with 'The Regiment' – as those familiar with the Special Air Service always call it – working out of the 22 SAS Regiment base: Bradbury Lines Barracks, Hereford. M had called it 'A nice little refresher course'.

For nine of those days he had been up before four o'clock in the morning, in a truck by five, kitted out in combat gear, a heavy Bergen pack on his back, other equipment slung around him, and one hand clutching a rifle – the so-called IW (Individual Weapon) XL65E5.

Each day, together with seven other officers from various branches of the armed forces, he had been dropped from the back of the truck, somewhere on the edge of the wild and rugged countryside around the Brecon Beacons, alone and with a map reference shouted at him as he went. Each night he, like the others, had been briefed on the following day's work.

Sometimes that map reference simply meant he had to beat the clock, arriving at the designated point in a certain amount of time; on other occasions he had to evade being spotted on the way by regular SAS officers, NCOs and troopers – still within a strict time limit. If caught, he would be subjected to intensive and humiliating interrogation.

Bond had not been caught on the two occasions he had been assigned to this exercise, but twice he had failed to beat the clock – on both times it was the fourth map reference of the day, for these operations seldom ended by reaching the first given point. The survival course demanded much more – other map references which had to be reached while spotting and 'killing' hidden targets; or retrieving an extra heavy load hidden at a predetermined point.

Back in Bradbury Lines at night, kit and weapons had to be cleaned before a session which usually included a swingeing criticism of the day's work, and collecting orders for the next morning. Now, on the tenth day, Bond had just taken part in the most gruelling and shattering exercise which is a regular feature of SAS selection and training – the forty-five mile endurance march, to be completed in twenty-four hours, carrying a 50lb pack, 12lbs of other equipment and an 18lb rifle (hand-held, for no SAS weapons are fitted with slings).

The march follows a route straight across the Brecon Beacons – wild, rocky and mountainous terrain, and the test is treated with great respect even by the most hardened professional and élite members of the Special Air Service. In bad weather expert men have died on the endurance march, and, given the relatively good conditions of this late May – gusting low winds and drenching drizzle – the exercise had been, to quote most of those who took part, 'a right bastard'.

All Bond wanted, now he had reached the final reference point, was to be taken back to Hereford in the truck, followed by a shower, food and sleep for around twenty-four hours before reporting back to London. But this was not to be. He sensed it when he saw the adjutant walking towards him from the parked truck.

'Your CO telephoned.' The adjutant was a tall, bronzed SAS captain – a matter-of-fact soldier who had long since learned that economy of words communicates unpleasant news with greater force than an involved explanation. 'You're wanted back in London, fast as a bullet.'

Bond cursed. 'Playing more games are we, Adj?' He tried to grin.

'Sorry.' The adjutant did not return the smile. 'This is for real. Seems your lot has a flap on. I'll give you a lift back to barracks.'

Only then did Bond see the adjutant's car parked behind the truck, and realised this was truly not another of the sometimes almost sadistic tricks with which SAS refresher courses abound.

As they made the journey back to Bradbury Lines, the adjutant suggested – a shade strongly, Bond thought – that it would not be wise for any man just off the endurance march to drive himself from Hereford to London, a journey of roughly two hours. 'Sergeant Pearlman hasn't got much to do. Good driver. Get you there fast and in one piece.'

Bond was too tired to argue. 'Whatever you say.' He shrugged. 'Sergeant Pearlman can drive the bloody thing, but he'll have to make his own way back.'

'You'd be doing him a favour. He's due on leave tonight and wants to get to London anyway.'

Back in his quarters, Bond showered, retrieved his personal hand gun – the 9mm ASP – from its hiding place in a sliding compartment of his suitcase, changed into a pair of casual slacks, soft leather moccasins, a comfortable shirt and a raw silk jacket made for him by his favourite tailors in Hong Kong – *Bel Homme*. He then returned the military gear to the Quartermaster's Stores, picked up his case and made his way to where the Bentley Mulsanne Turbo stood, immaculate in its British Racing Green, parked outside the Officers' Mess.

Sergeant 'Pearly' Pearlman awaited him, also in civilian clothes – a broad-shouldered, big, almost thuggish-looking man, with dark hair worn longer than would be allowed in most crack British regiments. 'Ready for the off, boss?' His tone was casual – another convention of the SAS.

Bond nodded. 'Mind if I curl up in the back, Pearly? Bit knackered to tell you the truth.'

The sergeant grinned. 'It's a swine, the endurance march. I've no love for it myself. Sleep away, boss. I'll wake you when we get into the London area.'

Bond made himself comfortable on the soft leather of the rear seats, while Pearlman started the car and drove off past the famous SAS memorial clock tower. Near the base of the tower a large plaque commemorates the names of SAS officers and men who have failed to 'beat the Clock' – the SAS synonym for staying alive in action or training. The clock tower is collapsible and portable, something which says much about the flexible attitude of 'The Regiment'.

As they whispered through Hereford to follow the main road to the M5 motorway – which in turn would give access to the M4 and London – James Bond closed his eyes and surrendered to a deep, dreamless sleep. He had no idea how much time had passed before he was wakened by Pearlman shouting loudly, 'Boss? Come on, boss! Wake up!'

Bond struggled up through the unconscious darkness, like a man half drowned, reaching towards light on the surface. At first he imagined they had reached London. 'Wha . . .? Where?'

'You awake?' Pearlman asked loudly.

'Yea . . . Yes. Just about.' Bond shook his head as if to clear his brain.

'In the land of the living, are we?'

'What's up?' Gradually he was adjusting to the car and its surroundings.

'Would you ever expect surveillance?'

'Why?' He was now more alert.

'Just would you? Don't know your line of business, boss. Don't want to shout wolf, but in your line would you expect surveillance?'

'Sometimes.' Bond had straightened himself out in the spacious rear of the car, leaning forward so that his head was close to Pearlman's left ear. 'Why?'

'May be nothing, but I get the distinct feeling we're in a mobile "box".'

'How long?' Bond was fully awake.

'I reckon from Hereford itself.'

'And where are we now?'

'Just come off the M5 and onto the M4. North-west of Bristol.'

'And?'

'There was a grey Saab that picked us up in Hereford. A 900 Turbo. Didn't take much notice, but he wouldn't let go. Then a light-coloured BMW – a 735i, I think – took over. Just before we skirted Gloucester there was the Saab again, ahead of us. He's behind us now – back two cars. The BMW's leading us, well ahead.'

'Coincidence?' Bond suggested.

'Thought of that. Tried the usual. Sudden slow, letting the BMW overtake, giving this heap a bit of welly. They've maintained station nicely. I even went off at Junction 13 and did a bit of round-the-houses, but they're still there. It looks like a full box – there's a light blue Audi, and a nasty little red Lotus Esprit as well. They're pro, I'm pretty certain. Dead middle-management, though. Yuppie cars, all of them.'

Bond murmured, 'You're sure it's not just coincidence?'

'Doesn't look like it to me. I've done all the business and they're still in tow. Mean anything?'

Bond did not reply immediately. A mobile surveillance 'box' was a tried and true technique: one in front, one behind, and a couple to left and right – in parallel streets in towns and cities; hanging around to run interference on open stretches of motorways. All would be in radio contact, probably pretending to be taxis, using code phrases that would sound innocuous to the police or anyone else picking them up. In reality, they would be passing precise instructions, one to the other, regarding their target. Why, though? Why him? Why now? M running a little surveillance test with some of the novitiate? Unlikely.

Pearly was driving with skill and confidence, fast and very accurate, sliding from middle to outside lane, sashaying through traffic like a dancer.

'Let's give 'em another go round-the-houses. What's the next exit?' Bond asked.

'Seventeen, boss. Chippenham to the right, Malmesbury left.'

'Know the roads?'

'Know the Chippenham side best. Nice lot of country lanes around there. Narrow. Very difficult, those lanes.'

'Let's give them a run, then. Stop them if we have to.'

The traffic on the motorway was heavy, but, glancing back, Bond could clearly see the shape of the grey Saab, outlined by other vehicles' headlights. It stayed on station, a couple of cars behind them. 'You carrying?' he asked Pearlman.

'Not so's you'd notice. You?'

'Yes. There's a spare in the map compartment – a Ruger P 85: solid and a stopper. I've been testing it for friends on your range. Full mag and one up the spout. You'll need the spare keys.' He passed them forward.

'How're we fixed legally?' Pearlman's tone was of one who was not particularly bothered, but neither was he completely disinterested.

'Don't honestly know,' Bond said, his brain still clicking away at the possibilities. Only three people at the Regent's Park HQ knew where he had been – M, Bill Tanner, his Chief of Staff, and the faithful Moneypenny. If the surveillance was a genuine hostile operation against him, the information could only have come from inside Bradbury Lines, and people there were usually as silent as deaf mutes, for they knew the necessity for secrecy as far as work was concerned. Their lives often depended on discreetly closed mouths.

Ahead the junction was coming up and Bond saw, with some pleasure, that the BMW - also holding station three cars ahead – swept past the turn. Pearlman signalled at the last moment, accelerated up the exit ramp, moving onto the big oval roundabout, cutting in on two slow-travelling cars and swerving onto the Chippenham road. A mile or so further on, he pulled off the main highway. Soon they were slowing to a slightly safer speed with which to negotiate the dark country lanes – trees and hedgerows black in the strong headlights.

'We lost them?' Pearlman muttered the question, pumping the brakes to take a tight corner.

'Don't know.' Bond swivelled to look behind them into the darkness. 'Certainly no lights, but that doesn't mean a thing.' He had been through surveillance routines like this himself, and knew that if he was doing the following his lights would have been dowsed as soon as they hit the minor roads of the countryside. From that point he would rely on luck and a sixth sense – or the use of night goggles – to get him safely behind his target. No lights followed them, yet he felt a cold sense of concern.

By now they had travelled some six or seven miles. If the surveillance vehicles were on their heels he should at least be able to see something.

Bond glanced forward as they rocketed through a village. He caught a glimpse of the shocked white face of some local by the side of the road – just a sudden face, contorted in horror or anger at their speed.

There for the blink of an eye, then gone. A pub. Then a church. A lurching right-hand bend, and out of the other side, down a long straight hill.

Suddenly an oath from Pearly, and the judder of brakes being pumped violently.

Ahead there were two sets of lights – not coming towards them but streaming out from either side of the road.

In the blur of speed, Bond realised several things. The lights were flooding from the right and left of a crossroads some twenty yards ahead. Yet, as the facts slid through his mind, the twenty yards closed almost to zero. Two cars emerged from left and right; Pearlman clicked on the Bentley's main beams and the cars were caught, stationary, serrated, bonnet parallel to bonnet in the classic roadblock formation – a red Lotus Esprit and a blue Audi.

Pearlman was still pumping the brakes and veering left as the cars grew in the windscreen. The Bentley touched the grass bank, bounced slightly and they were on top of the cars.

From where Bond sat there appeared to be very little room between the roadblock and the left – 90° – turn, but Pearlman handled the large car like a rally driver, moving in his seat to use the handbrake, his feet dancing on accelerator and footbrake.

The Bentley's tyres protested, screaming as the whole vehicle skidded, side on, then straightened, and gathered speed, brushing the hedge to the left, but clearing the Esprit's boot by what must have been less than an inch.

The road into which they had turned was overhung by trees, still with their stark winter look, the fresh buds and leaves of spring invisible in the car's headlights. It was like driving through a tunnel overhung with scaffolding, and its width would barely allow two cars to pass with ease.

As he looked back towards the diminishing tail-lights of the Esprit, and the full beams of the Audi, Bond automatically ducked. A series of tiny blue flashes flared briefly in the darkness, and, above the whisper of the Bentley, he felt rather than heard the bullets that sprayed around them.

'Christ!' Pearlman muttered, edging up on the accelerator, and dragging the car around a long right-hand bend, leaving the roadblock cars out of sight. 'What's your real job, boss? Guinea-pig for the National Health Service?'

'The Audi'll come after us, Pearly. Better give them a run for their money.'

'What d'you think I'm doing – Sunday afternoon sightseeing?'

They appeared to be in open country now, and Bond expected the distant lights of the Audi to appear behind him at any second. He had the ASP out and his hand on the window button ready to try and take out the pursuers should they suddenly leap from the darkness.

'Any idea where we are?' He peered into the blackness, wishing there was a set of Nightfinder glasses in the car.

'I can get us into London if that's what's bothering you.' Pearlman's voice was taut with concentration. 'But I'm going by the scenic route. Best keep well away from any motorways.'

'Good . . . Hell!' Bond pressed down on the switch operating the rear offside window. With a dazzling blast from full-beamed headlights, the Saab which had been following them on the motorway seemed to come from nowhere, tucking itself in close behind them. 'Put your foot through the floor, Pearly!' he yelled, crouching close to the door, lifting the ASP, feeling the rush of cold air on his face and hand.

The Saab still clung on as he fired two shots, low and fast, in the hope of hitting a tyre. Pearlman was throwing the car through the narrow lane at around eighty, rising to an unsafe ninety. In the back, Bond bucked and rolled with the big machine, clinging to the door, attempting to get a clean shot, eyes narrowed against the ferocious blinding glare of the lights.

He fired again, and one of the Saab's headlights went dead. As it did so, the car veered sharply as though its driver was momentarily out of control, rolling right, then hard left, coming square into Bond's line of sight. He fired twice, two quick double shots, and saw the windscreen shatter. He also thought he could hear a scream, but it was just as likely that it was the wind rushing past, cold and fast into the Bentley.

The Saab seemed to hang close to their rear bumper then drop back, faltering before it swerved violently to the left. Bond had a perfect view as the car mounted the bank. For a second he saw it poised almost in mid-air before it was lost in darkness. A moment later a plume of flame shot upward. The crump came only a finger-click later.

'I think we should put a fair amount of distance between that wreck and ourselves,' Bond muttered.

'What wreck?' Through the driving mirror Bond could just make out the smile on Pearlman's lips.

Presently he asked if Pearlman had managed to get a make on the other cars. The SAS sergeant quietly repeated the registration numbers of all four cars then went through the makes and colours once more as Bond committed them to memory.

'Didn't notice what the drivers were wearing, by any chance?' Bond's face was creased in a grim smile.

'Wasn't paying all that much attention.' He knew Pearlman was also smiling, but none of this helped solve the question of why they were under surveillance, and by whom.

Bond was still puzzling over it when they pulled up in Knightsbridge and changed places, Pearlman retrieving his own gear from the boot and thanking Bond for what he called, 'An interesting ride home.'

'You want my telephone number, boss? Just in case?'

Bond nodded from the driving seat, and the sergeant ran through the digits. 'Any time I can be of help, it'd be a pleasure.' Pearlman nodded and, closing the window, Bond put the car into drive and drew away from the kerb, heading in the direction of Regent's Park and his Service's headquarters.

4

Avante Carte

'Glad you made it so quickly.' M's sarcasm seemed to pass over Chief Superintendent Bailey's head as the introductions were made.

'Traffic, sir. Absolute murder on the motorways coming down.' Bond was more than a little put out. He had expected to meet M alone. Even Moneypenny had not warned him of the police officer's presence – a fact that was decidedly disturbing.

M grunted, waving Bond into a chair. 'Probably best if Bailey here puts you in the picture.' He looked both men square in the eyes, before adding, 'Especially as we've become involved partly because of you, Bond.'

Bailey gave the bare outline – girl dragged from the Thames in the early hours. He left out the name of the victim until the end. 'The deceased was twenty-three years old, and she carried your telephone number in her Filofax.' He paused before adding. 'Actually it was the only telephone number on her.'

Bond's body ached from the hard march over the Brecon Beacons and the events during the journey into London. He was aware that unless he got all the salient facts quickly there was a good chance that his mind would begin to drift from the essentials of the case. Apart from that, a whole section of his tired brain still wrestled with the how and why of the surveillance and attack. He needed to spend time with M to make his report. At last he began to take in the seriousness of what the police officer was saying. '*My* telephone number?' he queried. 'Who is it? Who's the victim?'

'We're not classing her as a victim,' Bailey told him. 'But the girl's name is Emma Dupré.' Both the Branch man and M watched for any signs of distress from Bond, who merely shook his head in disbelief. 'Young Emma,' he said, quietly. Then, 'Emma Dupré. Poor girl. Why, in heaven's name . . .?'

'You did know her, then?' from Bailey.

'Only very slightly.' He sat calm and upright in his chair. 'Haven't seen her for a couple of years. Though I did get an odd telephone call from her last November.'

'What do you mean by slightly?' Bailey, like many police officers, had that blunt, suspicious tone, even when asking seemingly innocent questions.

'*Very* slightly.' Bond was firm, his voice acquiring a sharp cutting edge. 'Two years ago I was invited to her twenty-first birthday party.

I've known Peter and Liz Dupré for a long time. I think they asked me to the party as a kind of makeweight. As I recall it, somebody dropped out at the last minute.'

'And you got on well with the girl?'

Bond took a deep breath, held it in, then slowly exhaled. 'She's a shade young for me. I don't want to sound . . . well . . . she had a kind of crush on me. In the end it became embarrassing. I took her out to dinner a couple of times.'

'You didn't . . .?' The Branch man left the remainder of his question hanging in the air.

'No, Mr Bailey, I certainly did not. In fact I did nothing at all to encourage her. It really was difficult. She never stopped telephoning me and writing notes.' He paused for a moment, remembering Emma – dark, fine looks, grey-eyed. The eyes he could recall almost too well. They were large and very clear.

The final dinner with her came tip-toeing back into his mind, unbidden, but there in its entirety. Rather than store it up, he told them, keeping to the important points. 'When it really got difficult I took her out to The Caprice, fed her and gave her the Dutch uncle routine. Told her I was already heavily involved with someone else . . .'

'Were you?' M asked, looking bland. 'A couple of years ago, one forgets.'

'Yes, there *was* someone at the time,' Bond managed to stop himself from snapping at his chief. 'I offered to be her friend – to be Emma's friend, I mean. Told her that if she found herself in any spot of bother she could call me.'

M gave a long sigh. 'Never understood women myself, Bond, but I would've thought that kind of talk would have encouraged her.'

'It depends how you do it. I think I used some finesse. At the time I was due to be out of London for a while – on Service business, sir. The thing with Rahani, you might recall it?' The last said with a heavy touch of sarcasm.

'Yes, yes, yes.' M made a sweeping movement with his right hand, as though trying to flick some unpleasant insect from the air.

'And you didn't hear from her again?' Bailey asked.

'Only the telephone call last November.'

'You said that was odd.'

'Yes.'

'In what way, odd?'

'I'd more or less forgotten about her – well, not forgotten, but put her out of mind. I still see Peter and Liz Dupré from time to time.'

'You move in exalted circles, Bond,' M muttered.

'Not really. I was at school with Peter's brother, years ago. He got himself killed in some damn-fool episode with a motorcycle. I met Peter at the funeral. He gave me pieces of advice now and again . . .'

'Nothing under the counter, I hope,' M snapped.

Bond frowned, looking at him, then – 'Oh, you mean "insider dealing" and all that kind of thing. No, sir. Just common-sense advice. It was when I came into that little legacy.'

'That's alright then.' M seemed to drift off into a semi-comatose state. The old boy was always at his most dangerous when he performed that trick, Bond thought to himself.

'The telephone call?' Bailey prompted.

'Yes. She rambled on a bit. Said she was in some kind of hospital. Then asked me if I had been saved. Religious talk, you know.'

'And you told her?'

'What?'

'Whether you'd been saved or not.'

'I think I was a touch flippant. I said I thought I'd been saved, but it had been a damned close thing.'

'How did she take that?'

'She didn't. She seemed not to notice, just talked some drivel, then suddenly put the phone down.'

'That concern you?'

'Thinking back, yes. Yes, it did. I remember feeling that she'd been interrupted, or that the phone had been snatched from her hand.' He scowled, wondering why he had not followed through on his instinct at the time.

'When you knew her – a couple of years ago – would you have said she was the kind who'd get mixed up with drugs?'

Bond looked at the Branch man, cold-eyed. 'How can you tell these days? Was she?'

'Mixed up in drugs? Yes, she was. Badly. Heroin. We know what happened about it. The family have been most co-operative. She wouldn't accept help from them. They were worried stiff. Then poor drowned Emma got religion. Religion of a kind anyway. The Meek Ones. Heard of them?'

Bond nodded. 'Who hasn't? Do good, yet seem to do a great deal of bad at the same time. Anti-promiscuity, anti-drugs, but all for a new world. The world of equality, that's their phrase, isn't it?'

'You've got them.' The Branch man nodded. 'On the surface these people appear to be ultra do-gooders: purity; sanctity of marriage; beware excess – they run a very successful detoxification unit, catering for drug and alcohol abuse. Great, but scratch the surface and there's something a shade more sinister.'

'For instance?' Bond asked.

'For instance they draw on the most extreme views of a number of religions – equal belief in the Bible, the Old Testament *not* the New, in particular the Torah. And they use the Koran as well.' Bond nodded; he knew enough about comparative religions to be aware that the Torah consisted of the first five books of the Old Testmant which made up the strict Jewish Law.

Bailey continued. 'They set great store by their religious ceremonies. Very theatrical and taken from Lord knows how many different liturgical traditions. You follow me?'

Bond nodded again. 'You mean they have rituals and religious ceremonial stolen from many periods in history and belief.'

M looked at Bond with patent disbelief. The chief was always surprised when his agent revealed interests or information outside the normal business of their trade or his excellent knowledge of food, wine, women and fast cars – which was grossly unfair to Bond's intellect.

'That's right.' Bailey seemed to have settled himself, leaning forward in his chair, elbows on knees, hands together. 'All this is combined with politics, of course. Their religion is really based on the ideal of a revolution. Very immature, of course, but, for the young or impressionable mind, it's heady stuff. The meek shall inherit: you know the kind of thing. All men are equal, and that equality must be attained, even if through the most bloody kind of revolution. A large number of wealthy young people're members, and have donated their entire fortunes to the Society – that's their full title, the Society of the Meek Ones.'

'You're telling me that Emma Dupré was a fully paid-up member?' Bond frowned.

'Exactly. She inherited a couple of million when she was twenty-one. Some of it went on an extravagant life-style and that nasty little habit she acquired. The rest was made over to the Society when they got her off the junk.'

'When Father Valentine got her off it,' M said sharply. 'Let's try to see things in their right proportions, Bailey – especially now we know Bond's relationship with the dead girl was slight and quite proper. Y'see Bond, we've got a small problem here. Dead girl, daughter of a merchant banker – Chairman of Gomme-Keogh. She'd become a dedicated member of the Meek Ones. We – this Service – have a connection. Basil Shrivenham, Lord Shrivenham, is on the Foreign Office Special Audit panel. He does the books of this Service regularly. He also has a daughter – the Honourable Trilby Shrivenham. Trilby was an old chum of the deceased. Trilby is also a member of the Meek Ones. She's handed over *her* birthright, a cool five million sterling. And who actually gets this wealth? The grand guru of the Meek Ones, who calls himself Father Valentine.'

'Sounds like one of these American TV evangelists.' Bond made a humourless grimace. 'I understand our connection because Lord Shrivenham casts his eye over the books every few years, but surely this is a Police and Revenue job, sir?'

'Under normal circumstances, yes. But we've got some abnormalities. Our brothers in Five have, it seems, also been keeping an eye on the Meek Ones. Matter of possible revolutionary activities, but now we've been invited to share in the product – in particular where it's concerned with Father Valentine. So far the popular gutter press have had to confine any of their more sensational comments to the leader of the sect – Valentine. The Meek Ones themselves appear to be beyond reproach with the dogmas of morality, purity and the like. Valentine himself has a reasonable standing. He alone is responsible for getting a large number of people off drugs like heroin and even derivatives such as crack. We know from the Duprés that he had undoubtedly brought Emma back from the edge of death. So the only press attacks are with regard to his finances. Where does all the money go? One newspaper has said that Valentine's worth several billion. The impression is that a large percentage of the revenue from the Meek Ones goes into Valentine's personal coffers, giving him a pretty extravagant life-style which has been well hidden until now.'

M nodded towards Bailey before continuing. 'Our friend here from the Branch came to me because your telephone number was found on the poor lass. He also told me that old Basil Shrivenham's girl was mixed up in it. I sent for you, and while we waited something quite out of the ordinary occurred.'

'Yes?' Bond's mind was needle-sharp now, even though his body still appeared to be preparing him for a lengthy period of unconsciousness.

M talked for some time. Two things had occurred between Bond being sent for and his arrival. The first was a request for a private interview by Lord Shrivenham. 'Bailey here was good enough to step outside for a moment. I've known old Basil Shrivenham for years. Even so it took the poor fellow a lot of courage to come in here and bare his soul, so to speak.'

Lord Shrivenham had, according to M, been in a terrible state, having just heard, via the offices of Gomme-Keogh, of Emma Dupré's fate.

'Came in here almost blubbing.' M's granite face actually appeared to soften. 'Never seen him like it, ever. Then the whole thing became a touch embarrassing. Fellow all but pleaded for help. All the stuff we already know: young Trilby – damned silly name that. Always felt it was Dorothea's idea, Lady Shrivenham, you know. Old Basil married beneath himself. Trade, really. Her father was in some kind of patent medication, name of Porter, made a mint out of Porter's Pick-Me-Up

Pills. Supposed to give you vitality and keep you regular, that kind of thing. Not the right sort of background.

'Anyhow, Basil admits to Trilby being recovered from the wretched addiction, but she has parted with her birthright, and he hasn't had a word from her in over a month. He asked me – begged me – if I could use influence, within the Service, of course, to get her back. Even suggested some kind of kidnap. All a bit emotional really, but I must admit that he got to me. Old friend and all that.'

'You promise him anything?' Bond asked, and there was a long pause before M answered.

'Not specifically. No. Just said I'd make some enquiries. Possibly do something unofficially.' He gave Bond a sidelong look.

'Such as having a word with our brothers in Five?' Bond asked.

'At that point, no, not exactly.' This time M did not even look his agent in the eyes.

'Ah. A deniable operation?'

'Well. At the time I did think . . .'

'The kind of thing that gets the Service a bad name. Sort of operation that comes out years later in the memoirs of a retired officer unhappy with his pension?' Bond looked at his chief with a blandness learned only in the hard school of secret dissembling.

'Well, maybe it crossed my mind. Possibly. For a moment. Anyway, not necessary any more. That's the next thing that happened.'

Shrivenham had just left when David Wolkovsky arrived in reception. Wolkovsky was the CIA's liaison officer at Grosvenor Square – which meant the American Embassy.

'Too smooth by half,' M said, biting each word as though he was a predator stripping the flesh from carrion. There was, Bond knew, a long-standing feud between M and Wolkovsky.

'You saw him?'

M nodded. 'Straight away. He said it was classified Cosmic, and needed setting up last week.' Suddenly his demeanour changed and both Bailey and Bond were treated to a beam which lit up the whole of M's face. 'Our cousins in Grosvenor Square, and Langley, Virginia, are also interested in Father Valentine. So interested that they've managed to make it a priority Anglo-American operation. The DGSS came on the scrambler soon after Wolkovsky left.' Another beam – by DGSS, M meant the Director General of the Security Service. In plain language the Head of MI5. 'Files coming over in the morning, but, in essence, the US Internal Revenue Service want a word with Valentine who is suspected to be a wolf in sheep's clothing.' He paused again, this time for effect. 'A wolf called Vladimir Scorpius, would you believe?'

Bond heard himself suck in breath sharply through his teeth. '*The* Vladimir Scorpius?' he asked.

'None other. Scorpius, Armourer – gun-runner – to just about every terrorist organisation known to man, and a few others nobody's yet discovered.'

In his mind's eye, Bond could see the Scorpius file now. It was as thick as the entire London Telephone Directory, and even then everyone knew it was incomplete.

'I suggest,' M continued, 'that you, 007, re-acquaint yourself with what we have on Scorpius. That's what they'll be doing over in Grosvenor Square, and at wherever Five are holing up, not to mention the Revenue in Bush House, the Chief Superintendent's people and the US Internal Revenue Service who, I gather, have the power of God.'

Bailey coughed. 'A word, sir, before we get deeply involved in any possible connection with Scorpius, who is not unknown to the Branch as an international arms dealer of almost unique and evil calibre.'

'Yes?' M was sharp. He obviously wanted to get on with what appeared to be a link of pressing importance.

'It's the other thing I wanted to talk about with you, and, possibly Lord Shrivenham.'

'Well?'

Bailey reached into his briefcase. 'Miss Dupré carried only a little money on her, and, if she had passed on all her assets to the Society of the Meek Ones, none of us could understand why she also carried credit cards – which she did.'

He paused, his hand still inside the briefcase. 'Her father and mother say they did not receive or pay any credit cards on her behalf. Yet we found these in the tote bag.' He produced a small leather wallet from which he extracted an American Express Gold Card, a Barclays Premier Visa, a Mastercharge and a Carte Blanche. He dealt out the credit cards in a neat row on the desk, directly in front of M.

'There is one more.' Bailey sounded like a magician doing some complicated legerdemain. 'This!' – he put the small piece of plastic next to the other cards as though playing an ace on a king.

The card was of the same quality and texture as the others – white and gold with the name *Emma Dupré* in the left-hand bottom corner, followed by start and expiry dates. The card number was embossed along the centre, and to the right was a small silver square holding a hologrammatic logo, a Greek A and Ω intertwined. 'Alpha and Omega.' Bailey touched the hologram. 'The Beginning and the End.' Then his finger moved to the top half of the card. In gold embossed letters were the two words, AVANTE CARTE. 'Not a credit card I've come across,' the Branch officer said. 'We're having it run through the computers, of course, but it's an oddity. I thought Lord Shrivenham might help us with it.'

Without taking his eyes from the card, M picked up his intercom phone and asked Miss Moneypenny if she could locate Lord Shrivenham and ask him to come into the office. 'I don't care if he's dining with the Prime Minister, or even if he's at Buck House. This is a matter of some urgency. Just get him here.' M looked up at the two men. 'I think you'll find that Basil Shrivenham *will* have something to say about this.' His eyes were as bleak as the North Sea in winter.

While they waited, Bond – deciding that Bailey was safe – told the whole story of his drive into London from Hereford. He left nothing out.

All three men looked very concerned by the time Lord Shrivenham arrived.

5

The Meek Shall Inherit

Lord Shrivenham's name belied his appearance. When people spoke of Basil Shrivenham, others who had never seen the man, pictured him as a sleek, distinguished peer of the realm. In truth, he was large, ungainly, with big, very clumsy hands, and a clump of greying hair which stood on end. In his late fifties, Lord Shrivenham looked troubled, tired, harassed and untidy.

After the initial introductions, M addressed his old friend as Shrivenham, while the peer was very correct, punctiliously referring to Bond's chief as M.

'Wanted you to see this, Shrivenham.' M passed the *Avante Carte* piece of plastic across his desk.

His Lordship took the card and examined it as though it might explode at any moment. Eventually he said, 'Good grief!', turned it over again and exclaimed, 'Well, well. The fellow did it after all.'

'What fellow did what?' Chief Superintendent Bailey began, but M held up a hand and turned to Basil Shrivenham, taking the card from him.

'I'd like you to repeat to these gentlemen what you told me during our discussion earlier,' M said quietly.

'About the Valentine man?'

'Yes. Especially about his approach to you at Gomme-Keogh.'

Shrivenham nodded, looked over at the card on M's desk and shook his head as though he still could not believe his own eyes. 'Do they know?' he asked.

'About your daughter? About Trilby and the Meek Ones? Yes, they know all about it. Everything about it. No need to worry yourself, Shrivenham. Just tell them of your own dealings with the so-called Father Valentine.'

'Well.' He placed his big hands on his knees then decided that was not right so he folded his arms. He looked very uncomfortable. 'You know my daughter had problems?', he began, stopping as though he really did not want to go on.

Bailey stepped in to ease him through the difficulties of facing the truth and spitting it out in front of strangers. 'The Honourable Trilby Shrivenham became addicted to heroin, sir. She received help from Father Valentine, the leader of a religious sect known as the Society of the Meek Ones. He treated her and she recovered. Came off the drug.'

'Yes.' Shrivenham hesitated again, then launched into a lengthy, somewhat halting monologue. It appeared that Trilby had come off heroin about seven months before. She had returned home for a long weekend and told her parents that she would be joining the Society of the Meek Ones. Leaving home. 'Wife and I thought it was a fad – a phase, you know?'

'But it wasn't?' Bond prompted gently, backing up Bailey.

'We didn't know at that time – 'course not. Both of us were just glad to see the girl fit and well again.' He pronounced 'girl', 'gel'. 'Trill – that's what we call Trilby, sort of pet name, eh? Trill. Always called her Trill.'

Inwardly, Bond sighed. If he was nothing else, Lord Shrivenham was a terrible bore.

'Well, we'd have done anything for Trill at that time. Looking so well, and in control of things. Couldn't refuse her a favour. She told us about this priest, or whatever he is. Calls himself Father Valentine. Naturally we were very grateful to him – for what he'd done. Understand?'

'Of course, sir,' from Bond.

'So when she said this Valentine man wanted some advice – banking advice – I agreed to see him.' For the first time that night, Shrivenham smiled. When he smiled Bond was reminded of a Hallowe'en pumpkin.

'Thought he was out to borrow money, to tell you the truth.' He looked around the room almost aggressively. 'And I'd have lent him money at the time. At reasonable interest as well. Felt I couldn't do enough for him.' He paused again, and they all thought he had run out of steam, but it was only to catch his breath. Shrivenham continued, as slowly and long-windedly as before.

Valentine had come to see him in the Gomme-Keogh offices in the City, and he did not want to borrow money. He wanted advice about the financial arrangements of setting up a credit card company. Shrivenham pointed out that it would be very difficult. The major companies were operated from huge financial institutions, banks, and conglomerates, even chain stores which allowed credit on purchases.

'Seemed he wanted to give members of his religious sect certain financial facilities. Very hot on the sanctity of marriage – said he had both rich and poor in the Society, but insisted that everyone had the same start in their married lives. He showed me some – and only some – of his banking arrangements. America; Cayman Islands; Hong Kong; Switzerland, of course. Seemed sound enough – if they were genuine. Yet I told him plainly – I mean you have to be damned plain speaking as a merchant banker. I told him he would fall very foul of government financial policy, not to mention the law.'

'You obviously didn't convince him,' Bond said with a half laugh.

Shrivenham gazed at him without humour. 'Obviously not,' he said. 'But I must admit I've never heard that this *Avante Carte* thing had got off the ground – in my position I pride myself on knowing most of the world's credit card facilities. Worrying. Very worrying.'

'Did he actually mention what he was going to call his card?' Bailey asked.

'Oh yes.' Shrivenham stared at the Special Branch man as though he was looking at a half-wit. 'Oh yes,' he repeated. 'That's the shock of it. Couldn't believe my eyes when I saw the thing on M's desk. Yes, he said he would call it Avante Carte.' At last he seemed to have dried up completely.

'Tell them what else he said.' M stirred in his chair.

'Well, he isn't the kind of man who shows pique, or temper. But, as he left, he said to me that one day *his* credit card idea would be more powerful than all the other credit cards put together. Those were his exact words – "more powerful".'

'Did you take to Father Valentine? Did you like him?' asked Bailey.

'Can't say I did really, no. There was something just not quite right about him. Odd, couldn't put my finger on it, but he seemed, well, somehow sinister. Quiet, calm, unassuming, but sinister. Doesn't really add up.'

'I've known murderers who were quiet, calm and unassuming,' Bailey said. 'They were cold-blooded killers, nevertheless.'

'And, even though you tried to put him off, he still appeared to be intent on going ahead with the credit card thing?' Bond probed.

'Oh, yes. Most certainly, yes. He seemed a little obsessive about it. Maybe that was the thing I found sinister. Never thought he'd do it, though.'

'Apart from this obsessiveness, you didn't detect anything abnormal?' Bond once more.

Shrivenham frowned, screwing his face up. He reminded Bond of a small child going through the motions of trying to remember the answer to a tricky question. At last he said no. The man had been very soft-spoken, rational – except for the determination about *Avante Carte*. 'He had eyes, though,' Shrivenham said, as though this was something unusual in a human being. 'I mean, one was taken by the eyes. Clear. Piercing. Very striking, those eyes. Looked right through one, if you see what I mean.'

'Colour?' barked M.

'What?'

'Colour of the man's eyes? D'you recall the colour?'

No pause this time. 'Black. Black as night.' He halted suddenly, looking puzzled. 'Wonder why I said that? Black as night. If something's really black I usually say "jet black".'

Probably Father Valentine had that effect on you, thought Bond.
Father Valentine sounded more than sinister to him, what with the
night-black eyes and the soft voice. Father Valentine sounded a fair
old charmer. 'You only saw him the once?' he asked aloud.

Shrivenham nodded. 'Just the once. Then old Trill went back to
the Society. Heard from her twice. Written a hundred times. She
doesn't reply. Dorothea gets very down about it. I do as well, of course.
Funny lot these Meek Ones. Last people I'd want Trill to subsidise.
But she's done it. Every last penny.'

'Well.' M cleared his throat. 'Well, thanks for coming in, Shrivenham. I wanted these officers to hear your story. I should tell you we'll
be following up on the credit card thing – the Fraud Squad will as
well. But I think you can be certain we're all going to have a closer
look at your friend Valentine and the Meek Ones.'

'They have this place near Pangbourne – Berkshire. Used to belong
to Buffy Manderson . . .'

'Sir Bulham Manderson,' M translated.

'Yes. Buffy's country place. Had to sell, of course. Upkeep beyond
any fellow's means nowadays. Beautiful place. Hundred rooms. Acres
of land. Good fishin'. Buffy's moved into some poky little flat in
Mayfair – seven rooms and a balcony. Roughing it a bit. See him
sometimes at the club. I often . . .'

'Shrivenham, thank you.' M cut him short before he could continue
reminiscing about poor old Buffy roughing it in a seven-roomed flat
in an exclusive Mayfair block. 'Thank you for coming in. I'll be in
touch.'

'Ah, time I was off.' Lord Shrivenham appeared to wake from a
snooze of nostalgia, and, at that moment, M's intercom telephone
rang. Moneypenny - who usually left at around six in the evening –
was still there. It was now well after midnight.

M spoke to her in a low voice after his initial rather curt response.
'When?' he asked. Then, 'Yes. I see.' His eyes slid towards Bond who
thought he detected uncertainty or concern in the brief look. 'Yes,' M
said again. 'Yes, you can leave that to us. I'll tell him. Bond and the
Chief Super'll do the rest. Good.' He put down the telephone and
looked at Basil Shrivenham. 'Got a bit of a shaker for you, Basil.' It
was the first time he had used his old friend's first name.

'For me?' Shrivenham's face went a little less ruddy, and his eyes
showed even more anxiety. 'Bad news?'

'No. No, I think probably good news. Your daughter's turned up.'

'Trill? Where? She's alright?'

'She's at home. At *your* home. Bit shaken, I gather. Needs a doctor,
but at least she's there – away from the Meek Ones.'

Basil Shrivenham looked as though he was going into shock – his face beginning to grey out. 'Well, I'd better get on back.' He clung to his chair, as though in need of support. 'Better find out what's happening. Doctor and all that. If you'll excuse me . . .'

'No,' M said with the kind of commanding tone nobody – not even a Prime Minister – would have disobeyed. 'No. You'll go with these officers.' He looked up as Moneypenny came quietly into the room. 'First go with my good Miss Moneypenny, here. She'll give you coffee, tea, or something stronger if you want it. I shall talk to Bailey and Bond, then they'll accompany you home. I think you'll find that best.'

'Oh, well, if you say so, but shouldn't I ring Dorothea or something?'

'Just go, Basil. Everything will be fine.'

Looking more dazed than ever, Shrivenham allowed Moneypenny to lead him from the room.

As soon as the door was closed, M began to talk. About twenty minutes before, Trilby Shrivenham had been found by a patrolling police constable in the doorway of the Shrivenhams' house near Eaton Square. She was, to use the officer's own words, 'in a semi-conscious condition'. He had put it down to either drink or drug abuse and was about to call into his local station when Lady Shrivenham, hearing the voices at the door, had come to investigate and identified her daughter.

'Sorry, Bond. I know you've had a tough day, but I think we're onto something. I'd like both of you to go with Shrivenham, see the girl – and her doctor. He's going to wait until you arrive. Size up the situation. Report back to me, then we'll see what has to be done. I'm going to need someone down at the Meek Ones' HQ as soon as possible, and I'd also like you both to read this file on Scorpius/ Valentine – that is the old file, and some updated stuff Wolkovsky brought over.'

'I need sleep at some point.' Bond's voice was that of a very tired man. 'Don't think I can go down and act as look-out in Berkshire straightaway.'

M gave a cross little scowl. 'No. No, you're not superhuman, I suppose. Anyway, I'll probably need you for something else I have in mind. We're desperately short-handed at the moment. Question is who can I spare to watch the Berkshire place?'

'Can we use safe outside talent?' Bond asked.

'What kind of talent?'

'The SAS sergeant who drove me down. He's trained. Keen. Knows all the tricks. We've used their people before now.'

'Yes.' M was not enthusiastic. Then – 'You got his name, number and all that?'

'Naturally.'

'Leave them with me. Name of Pearlman, or something, you said earlier?'

Bond recited the telephone number Pearly had given to him when they parted.

M nodded. 'I'll have a word with his CO. When one gets strapped for bodies on the ground, as this Service is at the moment, we have to use other resources. It might be possible.' He looked unhappy as he said it. 'I shall be here all night. You two go off with Shrivenham and report in as soon as you can.'

Chief Superintendent Bailey gave a small cough, then a charming smile. 'With respect, sir, I'd better get the HOB's sanction on this.'

M flapped a hand, 'It'll be alright. I'll take care of the Head of the Branch. You can be sure of that.'

The Special Branch man was obviously uncertain, but nodded and followed Bond from the office. Lord Shrivenham sat in the anteroom, which was Moneypenny's domain, nursing a very large whisky. Moneypenny hovered.

'Ready, sir.' Bailey took the lead.

'She is alright? I mean young Trill, she's not . . .? Well, not . . . You know . . .?' Shrivenham suddenly looked much older, as though the news of Trilby had taken some terrible toll on his stamina. Natural enough, Bond thought, especially coming hard on the heels of her friend Emma's death.

Bailey was very calm. 'The Honourable Trilby is under the influence of something, sir. You should know that before we go. Doctor's with her and we don't know if she's gone back to her old habit – the heroin – or if it's merely alcohol. The main thing, Lord Shrivenham, is that she's at your home, which means she's beyond Father Valentine's influence. Let's go and see what we can do for her.'

As they left the building, Bailey muttered to Bond that he hoped to heaven the girl *was* beyond Valentine's influence. Bond nodded and wondered if he had the same troubled expression as the Branch man.

The Shrivenhams lived in one of those pleasant white Regency houses which you can see all around the Belgravia area. There were two unmarked cars outside, and the lights blazed within. A uniformed policeman stood guard over the front door and Bailey flashed his ID. Inside, a female servant of uncertain age fluttered around the hall, ready to be of help to anybody and everybody. She showed them in to an elaborate room stuffed with Victoriana, the mantelpiece alive with antique china pieces.

Sitting together on a velvet-covered buttoned Chesterfield were a large woman in a floral dressing gown which made her look like some grotesque bush in bloom, and a small man who bore all the marks of a doctor whose practice was in the heart of a well-heeled area. His hair was sleek, and he wore the uniform still expected of a doctor in this part of London – striped trousers, black jacket, waistcoat with watchchain, and a stiff white collar set off by an immaculate grey silk tie.

Shrivenham pounced into the room like a big bear. The floral apparition rose and the two met in the middle of the room. Bond almost winced with amusement at the collision, but, as the unlikely pair embraced, he became embarrassed. Lord and Lady Shrivenham vied with each other for speech, and as they talked they used pet names – 'Oh, Batty,' said Her Ladyship on the verge of tears.

'There, Flower, there,' Basil Shrivenham soothed. 'Flower, how is she?'

The scene was almost ludicrous, but information came pouring out. Trill was unconscious. The doctor thought it was drugs – not heroin, but something else.

Bailey nudged Bond and they detached themselves from the melodrama being played out on centre stage, turning to the doctor. 'You've called a consultant?' Bond asked after they had introduced themselves. The doctor's name was Roberts, and at the question he seemed to lose the power of speech. He simply nodded.

'What's your opinion?' from Bailey.

'I think we should wait. I am professionally bound by certain . . .'

'Not the time for ethics, I'm afraid,' Bond said sharply. 'Not with people like us. So tell us, doctor. Your personal opinion.'

'I'd say someone fed her a cocktail of drugs. I have a nurse with her now.'

'She's going to live?'

The doctor looked down at his highly polished shoes. 'I've got her on a drip, and given her mild anti-toxins . . .'

'She said anything?'

'In a kind of delirium, yes. She comes in and out of it. Repeats one sentence again and again. "The meek shall inherit. The meek shall inherit."'

'Can we see her?' Bailey asked, and the doctor was poised to stand on ethics again, then thought better of it and led them from the room. They were aware of Lord and Lady Shrivenham in their wake like a pair of dreadnoughts.

The room was cool and silent, with a slightly less fussy decor and furnishings just visible from the standard and bedside lamps. A nurse, dark, crisp, efficient and giving away nothing from either face or stance, monitored a drip by the bed on which a young woman was lying, covered by a blanket. The doctor moved over to her and began a conversation, conducted *sotto voce*.

Bond could make out the contours of the body under the blanket.

Unlike her father and mother, Trilby Shrivenham was obviously tall and slender, her oval face placid, as though she was in normal repose, the head on the pillow surrounded by a mass of untidy blonde hair. Bond and Bailey stood, for a moment, looking down at her, then Bailey saw a large tote bag on the floor near the bedside table. He asked if it belonged to the patient and the nurse gave him a curt nod, then moved to stop him picking it up, but the doctor restrained her, muttering on as he had done since they entered the room.

Bailey began to go through the bag while Bond could not take his eyes off the face on the pillow. After a minute or so, Bailey tapped him on the shoulder. Bond turned to see that the Special Branch officer was holding an *Avante Carte* card in his hand. This one was made out simply to Trilby P. Shrivenham.

They looked at one another and Bond raised his eyebrows, then the girl on the bed started to stir and moan.

The hairs on the nape of Bond's neck rose, for from this beautiful creature came a voice that could have somehow scrabbled its way up from the grave – hoarse, cracked and sneering, as though wrapped in evil – 'The meek shall inherit. The meek shall inherit the earth,' the voice croaked, and Bond knew there and then that it was not Trilby Shrivenham speaking as she went on and on – 'The meek shall inherit . . . The meek shall inherit the earth.' Then a laugh which seemed to come from far away, so horrible that both doctor and nurse reflexed, stepping away from their patient. 'The meek shall inherit the earth,' it said again. Then, for the first time the eyes opened, staring and wide, flooded with fear. It was as though Trilby was looking at something nobody else could see, there in the bedroom. Again the laugh, and – 'The blood of the fathers will fall upon the sons!' the voice said. To Bond it was as though the words were crawling up through a slimy dark pit, filled with a pile of decomposing bodies. Later he was to remember the picture as it came into his mind at that moment.

Behind them Lady Shrivenham gave a little sob, and they all shuddered as though a curse had come from somewhere beyond the girl's lips and vocal chords.

6

Two of a Kind

Bond tried to rationalise the sense of horror that shrouded the room with the unnerving, other-worldly voice coming from the undeniably attractive young woman lying on the bed. In that moment of sorting through the filing system of his mind for the many possible causes of the phenomenon the fatigue and exhaustion seemed to leave his body.

He took two swift steps towards the doctor, placed a hand firmly in the small of his back and said, 'A word in private, please.'

The man gave him a sharp, puzzled look, then nodded and followed him out of the room and onto the small landing. 'This consultant you've sent for,' Bond began.

'Yes?'

'Who is he?'

'A man I've used many times.' Doctor Roberts now appeared to be more comfortable with Bond. Initially he had a wary look in his eyes, which was now replaced with confidence. 'Harley Street, naturally. Name of Baker-Smith.'

'And he specialises in?'

'Drug and alcohol abuse and addiction, of course.'

'You really think that's what the girl needs?'

'Mr Bond,' the doctor said, with pained weariness, 'Trilby Shrivenham has a history. I think you can safely leave this side of things to us medical men.'

'After the performance in there?' He cocked his head in the direction of the bedroom. 'You really think that all she needs is a skilled de-tox clinic? You believe that?'

'You have some better suggestion?' Roberts' tone was now patently condescending.

'As a matter of fact, yes.'

'I see. You are a medical practitioner as well?'

'No, but I work in a world in which we have our fair share of this thing. Wouldn't you agree that the girl is more likely to be stoned out of her mind with hallucinogenics and hypnotics?'

'Possibly.' There was no real commitment from Roberts. 'Even so, it's a drug problem. She's got to be brought down. Then weaned off them to regain her equilibrium.'

'Don't you see it as a little more complex than that, doctor? The centre of that girl's mind has been tampered with, under the influence of things like Sulphonal, LSD and the like. Her soul's been stolen from her. She requires more help than a simple de-tox clinic.'

'We'll see. Wait until Mr Baker-Smith gets here.'

'No, doctor, I'm sorry, but the authorities which Mr Bailey and myself work for will probably not allow that.' Bond's mouth was set in a hard stubborn line. 'I must take instructions from my own superior, but in the meantime you will be good enough to leave your patient where she is. I don't want ambulances whisking her off to Mr Baker-Smith's clinic wherever that happens to be.'

'You can't . . .' Roberts began.

'Do this to *your* patient, doctor? Oh, I think you'll find I can.' Bond turned on his heel and went down the stairs quickly, opening the front door and instructing the uniformed constable that nobody – not even a doctor – was to be allowed in until there were further instructions. The policeman nodded and took the orders. He had seen Bond arrive with Lord Shrivenham and Bailey. He had also seen Bailey's ID, so naturally assumed he was receiving instructions from on high.

Bond closed the door and crossed the hall to the telephone which stood on a heavy oak table just below the stairs. He punched out the code for M's private line.

M answered immediately, grunting as soon as he recognised Bond's voice. 'This isn't secure, sir, but we need to take action fast. Does the Service still keep that tame trick cyclist on the books?'

M gave an irritated sigh. ''007, I wish you wouldn't use these slang expressions. He is an eminent neurologist, and the answer is yes. Yes, we do still have access to him and the clinic – but only in cases of extreme urgency. The fact you haven't been sent back to him for treatment in no way indicates that we have ceased to employ him. Now, why do you ask?'

Bond told him in a matter of seven fast sentences. When he finished, M grunted again. 'See your point, 007. But you must have a word with Shrivenham first. On no account can we upset the doctor in charge of the case. But make sure it is *Shrivenham* who gets the GP out of the house. I'll talk to our man now, and then have one of our own units pick up the patient. Standard operating procedure. There should be an ambulance with you in half an hour at the latest. Just make sure they know the day's code. I certainly believe this is a case for our friend, and the sooner the better.'

Bond thanked him. The Service had often used Sir James Molony in the past. He was probably the world's most eminent neurologist, and a Nobel Prize winner for his book *Some Psychosomatic Side-Effects of Organic Inferiority*. On several occasions, some years ago, he had even treated Bond himself, when he had been under great stress.

Trilby Shrivenham was just the sort of case in which Molony would be interested. Putting down the telephone, Bond went quickly back up the stairs and coaxed Basil Shrivenham from his daughter's side. She was quiet again now, as though the half-waking delusions had never happened. She lay, still and placid, silent in deep sleep. It was unthinkable that, only minutes before, an horrific, demonic voice had issued from her lips. Bond thought the girl must look stunning when fit, well, and in her right mind.

On the landing again, he faced Lord Shrivenham, giving him a slightly expurgated version of his conversation with M. 'I'm afraid you're going to have to break it to your own GP, sir,' he ended. 'M is adamant that Trilby should be moved, as soon as possible, and put under Sir James Molony's care. We all know what happened to Emma Dupré, and none of us wants anything to go wrong with Trilby. With Sir James she'll have the best medical care – surely *you* must want that. You must be terribly concerned about her state of mind, sir.'

Shrivenham nodded several times. 'I'll do it. If old M says it's the right thing, who am I to argue? I'll do it now.'

Roberts left the house a few minutes later, cutting Bond dead, his face set in a fury of irritation.

As promised, within the half hour a Service team arrived with an ambulance, complete with paramedics, a trail car and a couple of unidentifiable men on powerful motorcycles. The transference of Trilby Shrivenham to the ambulance took around fifteen minutes, and soon the small convoy was rolling softly away in the direction of the Service's safe clinic near Guildford in Surrey.

At three in the morning, Bond returned to Regent's Park where M told him to get some rest on the camp bed usually used by the Duty Officer. That night the DO was obviously being kept very busy.

'In the morning,' M said, 'I want you to read the Scorpius file, and then take a look at *Avante Carte*'s offices.' Seeing the look of surprise on Bond's face, he allowed his lips to form a brief smile of pleasure. 'Oh yes, 007, we haven't let the grass grow under our feet. We've tracked down the centre of their credit card operation, and I've seen your friend Sergeant Pearlman. Stout fellow. He's off to the Pangbourne place at first light, and they'll keep him busy enough. We've leaked the Dupré girl's death to the press – including the fact that she was a member of the Meek Ones, and details of the considerable funds she provided. That should put the cat among the pigeons.' He nodded brusquely towards the door. 'Rest well, Bond. I'll put in a call for you at six o'clock. Early start's always the best thing. Goodnight to you. Sleep well.'

Bond dreamed of some great temple – he did not know where – with a huge white-robed congregation chanting an incomprehensible mantra. He was in the middle of the temple and looked up to see a girl being carried towards a block of granite that served as an altar. He could not see her face, but she was screaming in a croaking voice as they tied her to the stone and stood back to make way for a gigantic insect. The creature crawled forward, and he saw that it was a massive scorpion. It raised its tail, the sting like a long rapier, ready to plunge it into the girl on the altar. The chanting became louder and louder – 'Si-si-si-si-si-si . . .' – and as he looked, Bond saw the girl had changed into a man. The man turned his terrified face towards the waiting congregation and Bond realised it was himself. The long steel needle that was the scorpion's sting started to come down. 'Si-si-si-si-si . . .'

'Si . . . Six o'clock, Commander Bond, sir.' Harper, one of the senior messengers, an ex-Royal Marine commando, was shaking his shoulder.

Bond realised he was awake and sweating – the nightmare still fresh and real in his mind.

'Nice cup of coffee, sir. Just how you like it.'

He thanked Harper, who had known him and his idiosyncrasies for years. The hot brew tasted good, and seemed to set Bond's life forces flowing again. Slowly he got out of the bed and began his usual morning routine – the hot and cold shower, exercises and some new breathing controls learned from one of the SAS PTIs. It was just after six thirty when he presented himself in M's anteroom. Moneypenny's deputy – an autocratic and unapproachable harridan known through- out the whole Service simply as Ms Boyd – sat at the 'receipt of custom', as Moneypenny's desk, with its two computer VDUs, and complex telephone/intercom unit, was known.

'Would M be expecting you?' The dragon-like Ms Boyd gave Bond a look indicating that, to her, he was but riff-raff.

'He would indeed.' Bond seldom bothered to engage Moneypenny's deputy in conversation, and never in banter. She rarely took over the coveted anteroom, and it was said that Moneypenny had personally hired her because of her unfortunate lack of charisma. Moneypenny wanted nobody usurping her domain.

The light above M's door came on as soon as Ms Boyd gave Bond's name over the intercom.

M had obviously remained in the office all night, for there was a camp bed, recently made up, against one wall. He was in shirt-sleeves and needed a shave – most uncharacteristic for an old sea dog. He waved Bond forward, indicating that he should wait, standing in front of his desk. It took M a couple of minutes to finish going through his papers. 'Right, 007,' he said, finally. 'I've arranged that Registry should have the file in Room 41. As it's flagged Cosmic, since Wolkovsky added to it yesterday, there will be a guard on the door.

You'll leave all writing materials – your pen, notebook, diary and whatever else with the guard. I trust you, but we should abide by the rules, eh?'

Bond nodded and asked how his chief had got on with the Special Air Service sergeant, Pearlman.

'Seems to be the right stuff.' M glanced at his watch. 'He's on his way down to Berkshire now – together with half of Fleet Street, I shouldn't wonder.'

'And Trilby Shrivenham?'

'What about her?'

'Just wondered if you'd had any news about her condition, that's all, sir.'

'Mmm. Well, she's in a bad way. Sir James tells me she'll pull out of the drugs thing. Someone fed her a pretty lethal dose. He's more concerned about her mental state.'

'Mind tampered with while under the influence of this infernal concoction?' Bond was anxious to check out his own theory.

'Something like that. Now, off you go to Room 41. When you've finished the file, get back up here fast. There's a great deal to be done.'

Bond nodded, said, 'Aye aye, sir,' which brought a nostalgic glance from M who added, 'I've had both the *Avante Carte* things sent down to Q Branch. The Armourer's Assistant is giving them the once-over.' He meant the delectable Ms Ann Reilly, expert in both weaponry and electronics, known to most members of the Service as Q'ute because of her role as Assistant to Major Boothroyd, Armourer and Head of Q Branch.

As he took the lift down to the second floor, where Room 41 was located, Bond wondered what had prompted M to let Q'ute pass her experienced eye over the *Avante Carte* plastic.

Like the famous CIA Headquarters at Langley, Virginia, the doors to left and right along the passages of the second floor were of differing colours. There was nothing arcane or sinister about this. The fact was that, when it came to paintwork, the Maintenance Section worked to a strict colour chart. When they ran out of red they moved on to blue, etc. The corridors of the Service HQ were often nicknamed after the predominant colour.

The door of Room 41 was pink. A Service tough stood over it looking as though he would rather kill than let anyone enter. Though the man knew Bond well by sight he still insisted on seeing ID, and he removed all possible writing and copying materials with above-average enthusiasm. Inside the room there was one chair and a table on which lay the thick file. Bond sat, looked at the cryptonym sellotaped to the front cover – BONK – an apt cover name for a man like Vladimir Scorpius, he thought, turning the cover and starting to read.

The bulk of the dossier was old material which Bond had read many times before – the scant details of one shadowy man's life. Vladimir Scorpius, thought to have been born in Cyprus of a wealthy Greek businessman and a renegade white Russian – possibly Evdokia, daughter of the mysterious Prince and Princess Talanov who, with their daughter, had escaped the Bolshevik Revolution in strange, and almost unbelievable circumstances.

Vladimir Scorpius had first come to the attention of the British Secret Intelligence Service in the late 1950s during the guerrilla warfare waged – for independence – against British military forces in Cyprus by the Greek Government, the Communist Party and the guerrilla army, EOKA. Scorpius was suspected of supplying arms to EOKA – the so-called terrorists. Since that time his name had cropped up again and again – always as the supplier of armaments and military matériel, usually to terrorist groups around the world.

While Scorpius' name ran like a crimson thread through shipments of weapons and explosives in every trouble spot on the globe, no firm traces led back to the man. There was page upon page of lists – rifles, hand guns, ammunition, grenades, plastique, fuses, detonators, missile launchers and even more sophisticated machinery of war – yet none of them could be completely and convincingly traced back to Scorpius. It was obvious to anyone, even with scant knowledge of the twilight world of illegal arms supplies, that Scorpius was behind hundreds of illicit consignments. But the man – and the evidence – became a tangled will-o'-the-wisp thread, which ran out once investigations appeared to be almost complete.

Bond concentrated on the realities – what was known fact about the man. First, he was certainly ruthless. In the past twenty years or so, no fewer than sixteen people who were known to be in a position to betray him had died in odd circumstances – four in freak road accidents, three in shootings, four by poison, two beaten to death by supposed muggers, two in possible suicides, and one drowned bizarrely in a motel shower. The file also showed that another twenty people who were suspected of being in Scorpius' employ had also died in either straightforward murder or suspicious suicides. It was not healthy to get on friendly working terms with the man.

Secondly, he was something of a hypocrite. For a large part of the sixties and seventies he had lived with his extravagant and beautiful wife, Emerald, aboard his magnificent 280-foot ocean-going yacht, *Vladem 1*, powered by two 3,000 hp diesels – Bond winced at the sheer bourgeois taste of the name – yet managed to keep the press, particularly the paparazzi, off his back. He gave several interviews, by telephone, to both newspapers and magazines – they were all there in the bulky file – in which he claimed to eschew the world, preferring to live on his boat with the love of his life. Constantly he stressed marital fidelity, yet there in black and white were transcripts of long-range surveillance watches with details of his multitude of mistresses, and nauseating facts about his unslakable sexual appetite, appeased only by weird and imaginative tastes.

So, he had lived like a luxurious hermit, travelling the world in *Vladem 1*. People visited him – there were hundreds of photographs of men and women being shown up the yacht's gangplank – dubious politicians and ambassadors, known terrorists, identifiable underworld figures, and, paradoxically, famous names from the worlds of theatre, opera, and, predictably, the leech-like glitterati.

Scorpius entertained on the yacht, and, on the occasions he ventured ashore into the real world, it was always with a retinue of guards and thugs who made certain nobody lurked in the shadows to watch or photograph the living enigma.

Where the press had failed to get near Scorpius, various security agencies had gained limited access, though, while they had evidence of his hedonistic tastes on tape and in transcript, they were never able to snatch a fragment of evidence concerning his arms dealing and the terrorist underworld which they were certain he inhabited.

The file contained dozens of sneaked photographs, all bad, giving no detail of clarity – except one, caught by a CIA surveillance unit who had suddenly got lucky in 1969 with an infra-red camera outside a house in Portofino. The picture, blown up, occupied a whole page and Bond sat staring at it for several minutes.

It showed Scorpius as a sleek, slightly overweight man, going heavy at the jowls which spoiled his once obvious good, somewhat Italianate, looks – thick lips, a mane of greying hair, patrician nose, head tilted upwards in an arrogant manner. He was dressed for the evening in a white tuxedo, and with what looked like a heavy and expensive watch on his left wrist and a gold chain on the right. The man's eyes were revealed, in the fast exposure of the film, as those of a man who reeked of ruthless power – though Bond knew, from experience, that the camera could, and often did, lie.

Below the photograph was a list of tiny details: the exact time and place; the estimated cost of the jewellery; details of the gold chain ID bracelet with the inscription Vladimir Scorpius, followed by some numbers which were lost to the camera. The watch was a pure gold, hand-made digital timepiece with a normal set of hands which ticked off the minutes and hours by passing twelve small flawless diamonds. Taste, Bond considered, was not Vladimir Scorpius' forte. Yet that wristwatch had cost a king's ransom. Not only had the varied digital functions been installed long before their time on the international market, but also the object had an extra value, for it had been made by a Japanese craftsman whose name was later to become a legend. It was a one-off piece of intricate workmanship known as the Scorpius Chronometer.

He read on. In 1972 Emerald Scorpius had died, tragically, in an accident at sea. Almost immediately Vladimir went missing from his usual way of life. There were traces of him – mainly in connection with larger and larger arms supplies to terrorist groups in all parts of the world – but the great yacht lay, deserted, in a dry dock near Cannes in the South of France. There were occasional sightings of Scorpius, but most were insubstantial. One minute he seemed to be there – in Berlin, Tehran, Tel Aviv, Beirut, Belfast, Paris or London – then he had gone: a shadow; a wraith. In 1982, he disappeared completely. The secret watchers and listeners of every Western intelligence and security agency heard no sound, picked up no trace, sensed no whisper of this once and only uncaught king of the arms dealers.

Bond turned the page to find the new material, provided the night before by David Wolkovsky of the Central Intelligence Agency's London desk. Bond could hardly believe his eyes. There were several pages of typed detail, but the photographs which littered the new section spoke rather more than the words.

Father Valentine, leader of the Society of the Meek Ones, had never been averse to having his photograph taken – in fact, there was an obvious vanity about the man. This, Bond immediately saw, could well be his downfall. The Americans, with their reliance on high technology, had stumbled over a gold ingot in the shape of their filched picture of Scorpius and the many photographs of Father Valentine. During the testing on pieces of new and sophisticated equipment, they had put the two together, and so spent their days examining, measuring and taking detailed digitised computer analysis. From these experiments they discovered several facts concerning the measurements of Father Valentine's facial bone structure.

Even in close-up, Valentine bore absolutely no resemblance to Scorpius, for he was slim-faced, with an almost retroussé nose and thinning hair, dark and well kept, swept back from his forehead. Yet the analysts had placed photograph upon photograph, showing clearly how both men could quite easily be the same, for the basic bone structure matched perfectly. They had even managed, by enhanced computer images, to show exactly how Vladimir Scorpius' face could have been cleverly altered by a skilled plastic surgeon.

There were, however, two clinchers: a pair of pointers which clearly confirmed the experts' suspicions. The first piece of evidence – though inconclusive – filled two pages, consisting of blown-up photographs of the left wrist, from the one old Scorpius print; and the same left wrist from one of the many pictures of Father Valentine. In the entire world, the experts said, there was no duplicate of the fabulous Scorpius Chronometer. Yet here it was, on Scorpius himself, at seven thirty in the evening as he stepped swiftly into a car in Portofino in 1969; and again, on the wrist of Father Valentine, in London during the August of 1986.

The convincing evidence, though, lay in the ears. In his vanity, Scorpius had obviously – and probably arrogantly – refused to have his ears touched by the surgeons. Indeed, why not? He was 99% certain that nobody owned a photograph of the old Scorpius. Valentine's and Scorpius' ears were identical, and the proof ran across eight pages of medical notes, diagrams, photographs, and measurements. This was proof positive.

'Vanity of vanities,' Bond quoted under his breath. 'All is vanity.' In that moment he knew he was looking at one and the same man – the man responsible for Emma Dupré's death, and the devilish voice which had come from Trilby Shrivenham.

God alone knew what other terrors Scorpius/Valentine had in store.

Slowly, Bond closed the file and stood up. M had more work for him. Deep down, he hoped the work would lead him face to face with this man of double identity. Scorpius/Valentine. Valentine/Scorpius.

7

Mr Hathaway & Company

'You believe the American evidence?' Bond studied M's face as though he were trying to read the man's future from the lines in his leathery skin.

'Absolutely. One hundred per cent. To my mind, there's no doubt that Father Valentine and Vladimir Scorpius are one and the same person. A fact which makes our task more urgent than ever.'

Bond raised his eyebrows.

'Nobody's ever proved a thing against Scorpius – nothing that would stick, anyway.' M made it sound as though this was Bond's personal fault. 'Yet we know the man is responsible for thousands of deaths – mostly innocent victims. When terror strikes – a bomb in Ulster; a nightclub wrecked in Germany; an air terminal or train station shattered; a burst of machine-gun fire in a Paris street; a lad on a motorcycle loosing off a dozen shots into some politician's or police chief's car – they're all down to Scorpius as the provider of the material.' He began to thump the desk in a heartbeat rhythm. 'The leopard never changes his spots. Scorpius knows everything there is to know about dealing in terror and not getting caught. He probably salves his conscience by telling himself that he is not responsible for what the end user does with the weapons or explosives. But he *is* responsible. And now he's Father Valentine, running a sect which, on the surface, appears to dwell on purity, the sanctity of marriage, and the exclusion of all substances foreign to the human body – nicotine, alcohol and the other, more sinister, forms of drug. There has to be an angle, Bond, and the angle has to be connected somehow to terrorist forces and their supplies. It's all the man knows. Weapons and women.'

'No clues regarding specific aims and objects?' Bond asked. 'I agree that, knowing what we do about Scorpius, the Society of Meek Ones must have a main objective – and an unpleasant one at that.'

'I hope you'll be the one to discover its direct aims.' M looked at him, no trace of humour around mouth or eyes.

'The credit card offices?'

M nodded, pushing a five-by-three filing card across the desk. In M's neat hand, written in green ink, was the address of one of the many new office buildings that had risen in the streets that emptied into Oxford Street, once you got north of Oxford Circus. The telephone number had a matching 437 prefix. 'It's all legal,' M said. 'Cleared by the Bank of England. *Avante Carte* – though it does not appear to advertise, and has no services list as yet – is a fully blown, one hundred per cent legal credit company with assets of ten million pounds sterling.'

'I suppose your connections in the City supplied all that?'

'No,' M allowed himself the ghost of a smile. 'No, my connections with Q Branch, right here. The Assistant Armourer's still working on the two pieces of plastic we gave her. They're apparently "Smart Cards" – kind of thing we use here to get in and out of restricted areas, and to keep track of files. Little electronic brains embedded in the plastic. They're trying to unscramble them now, but it's going to take some time. They came up with the telephone number which was, apparently, simple. I followed that lead. You can see where it took me.'

'I suppose I'm just expected to walk in there and apply for membership or something?'

'That's it.' M was deadly serious. 'No good ringing them up, Bond. Nothing like walking in and facing the beast head on. Might learn something . . .'

'Might catch a nasty dose of what they used to call lead poisoning as well.'

'Occupational hazard.' M nodded towards his door. 'Get out there and do your best.'

'No backup, sir?'

M shook his head. 'I think not. Just play it as it comes. Walk in and say you want to sign on. I can't imagine a better approach.'

Half an hour later, Bond paused at a point directly across the road from the front of the high anonymous office block, which stuck out like a tall sore finger among the terraced houses and shops between Oxford and Great Marlborough Streets.

He had taken a cab to Broadcasting House and walked back to Oxford Circus, then, by a circuitous route, to this place. All the time he had gone through those obvious, though necessary, routines to make certain nobody had – as they said in the trade – got a make on him.

He had been clear for the whole trip, yet now he had reached the building, Bond felt that sixth intuitive sense – born of long experience – telling him he was no longer alone. He did not loiter, just a pause and glance at the building, with its semicircular glass frontage through which a reception desk and several scattered chairs and settees were visible. He walked on, trying to find a good reflecting point, or a street crossing which would allow him to look back and make a quick scan of the entire façade. He knew someone had their eyes on him.

About thirty yards up the street he could cross and take a turning which he imagined would bring him back to Oxford Street. In his mind he decided this would be the best way. Go back and make a second approach.

He paused, as though checking for traffic, his eyes lingering slightly longer than usual on the street nearest the building. There was a small van parked illegally almost opposite. Nobody in the driver's seat but that meant nothing as far as small vans went. The only thing that consoled him was that this one had no aerial or antennae visible. Aerials are dangerous for they can conceal a multitude of devices, including fibre-optic lenses transmitting a clear 360° picture onto an internal monitor.

In the swift glance he also spotted one man further down the street. He was pacing to and fro, occasionally looking at his watch, as though waiting for a date who was never going to show. There were other cars and pedestrians of course; it was only that Bond's highly tuned senses reacted to these two. The van and the waiting man were obvious suspects.

He crossed and headed into the turning, only to find himself in a cul de sac. There was no other way than to play the game of looking for the right address. He drew an empty black notebook from the inside pocket of his jacket, feeling the comforting hard butt of the 9 mm ASP automatic in its holster.

Slowly he walked back into the main thoroughfare again, stopping, consulting the pages of his notebook as he went. A man uncertain of his whereabouts, looking for an address. He even stopped a harassed-looking young woman wheeling a pram to ask directions to the building now staring him in the face. She laughed, told him he was almost outside the place, and pointed.

Consulting the book again, Bond walked confidently towards the large glass doors. From the corner of his eye he could see the man was still waiting for his date to stand him up, and the van remained in position, still apparently unoccupied and illegally parked.

The semicircular lobby was light and airy; now inside, Bond was aware of large numbers of potted plants as well as the furnishings he had seen from outside. The place had style and elegance. It also had a reception desk with an elderly commissionaire sporting two rows of WWII medals on the left breast of his navy-blue uniform.

'I be of help, sir?' the commissionaire asked with a brief welcoming smile.

'*Avante Carte*,' Bond exchanged smiles.

'They're fourth floor, sir.' He indicated a double bank of lifts in a small passageway to the right of his desk.

Bond nodded his thanks, pressed the call button between the lifts, then began to study the board which listed a number of companies and businesses. Actiondata Services Ltd 1st Floor; *The Burgho Press (Editorial)* 2nd Floor; *Adams Services Ltd* 3rd Floor. There were seven floors altogether. A firm of solicitors appeared to occupy the fifth; what could only be an advertising company – *AdShout Ltd* – on the sixth; while the top floor seemed to be inhabited by one of those ambiguous companies which went under the name of *Nightout Companions*. There, opposite the fourth-floor marker was what he wanted – *Avante Carte Inc* and below it, in smaller letters, the words *Avante Carte is part of the Society of the Meek Ones Charity Trust*. The lift doors opened with a soft sigh and Bond stepped inside, pressing the button for the fourth floor.

At least the Muzak was different – not the usual sickly strings playing romantic popular standards. This was very much Bond's style. He could even date it – Gertrude 'Ma' Rainey, accompanied by a very rough unnamed jazz group, the 1927 re-recording of her 1924 New Bo-Weavil Blues. Bond had the recording on an old 78rpm in his own collection. This one had obviously been enhanced. 'Ma' Rainey still came out on top – wry humour combined with pathos. They could have known Bond was on his way by piping this kind of jazz through the system.

> 'Don't want no man puttin' sugar in my tea,
> 'Fraid that old man might poison me.'

'Ma' Rainey sang, and the words hit him like a warning shot. He remembered the cars and surveillance during the return from Hereford. For a few seconds, the old good noise of traditional jazz had lulled him. Now Bond was as alert as ever. The indicator showed 4 and, as the doors slid open, so the Muzak system cut off. He stepped out to find himself in another large, airy, semicircular reception area. This time nobody stood at the desk, but the whole of the wall behind it appeared to be made of toughened glass, through which he could see a long sterile room stretching back into what seemed infinity, but that, he knew, would be a trick of the glass and mirrors.

The room beyond was filled by a long row of computer workstations, while to left and right, behind these, were more sparkling glass screens, dividing rooms in which the huge databanks of a mainframe were visible. Nobody manned the workstations. Where, he wondered, were the men and women who should be answering credit queries, accessing the obviously large database, sifting information, entering in onto accounts, authorising credit, and doing all that work associated with a company such as this?

Cautiously, he approached the reception desk, his shoes seeming to sink into the deep-piled claret carpet. At the desk, he coughed loudly.

Then he saw a small bell push, set into the smooth acrylic surface. He pressed in two short, sharp jabs.

Seconds later there was movement at the far end of the long room behind. A young woman was making her way past the rank of empty desks.

It took the best part of a minute for the woman to reach the door between the working area and reception, giving Bond time to make a fair appraisal of her appearance – wearing a severe black skirt and white shirt, with a black ribbon tied at her throat, she had an elegant, long-legged stride which spoke of a sense of purpose. The slim figure was attractive, though with slightly large breasts. Her face was not handsome nor pretty in the accepted sense, but one that bespoke humour from mouth and eyes. Somehow the black hair, neatly cut fashionably short, seemed wrong. Bond wondered for a second, as she opened the door into the reception area, if it was a wig, or had been recently dyed, for its depth of darkness struck him as slightly unreal.

'Good morning, sir. Can I help?' She was American, the accent more Boston than the harder dialects. The mouth crinkled, and he saw he had been right about the humour – little laughter lines at the eyes and around the mouth. The eyes were light grey, and again he wondered about the hair.

'I wonder if you can. I rather wanted to apply for an *Avante Carte*.'

'Ah!' she smiled. 'I'm sorry, but I don't think I can help you.'

'Oh?' He let his eyes stray behind her, through the toughened glass into the deserted working area.

She glanced back in the direction of his look. 'Yes.' Another smile. 'Yes, I know. No staff. I'm the only one, and I'm afraid I have as yet to receive instructions. Did you get an invitation to have a card?'

'No. Not exactly.'

'Well, even if I had the authority, I couldn't let you apply. Application is by invitation, and I'm told that only people who belong to the Society of the Meek Ones, or are charter members of the Meek Ones Charity Trust are being invited – to begin with anyway.' She added the last quickly, as though wanting to make certain she did not turn away a potential future customer. 'Where did you hear about our card in the first place, sir?'

Bond shrugged. 'An old friend of mine has one.' He paused, wondering what impact it would make now the details had been released to the press. 'A Miss Emma Dupré. She's got one.'

'But . . .' the girl started, her eyes widening a fraction. Then she remembered herself. 'Well, she must be one of the privileged number. Could I, perhaps, take down your details so that we can get in touch should the membership open up?'

Bond smiled at her, aiming smack into her face, and was pleased to see her give an uncomfortable little blush. 'Boldman,' he said. 'James Boldman.' He added an address that would cover him should the name be followed up.

'All I can do is make a note, Mr Boldman. You see . . .' She paused again, as though weighing her words. 'You see, I'm really as much in the dark as you are.' She took a pace back towards the door, as though expecting him to follow, which he did.

As she spoke, they moved into the work room. 'To tell you the truth, you're the first person to come into the office. I've only been here a couple of weeks, and, as far as I can make out, I'm the only hired help.'

'You're in charge?' Bond tried to make it sound off-hand.

She nodded.

'Monarch of all you survey? In charge, and responsible for all this?' His hand traced a half-circle, taking in all the smart little workstations with the VDUs and telephones and the great mainframe databanks behind the sterile glass.

'Yep,' she nodded again. 'Scary, isn't it? There must be a million pounds' worth of IBM hardware in here.'

'Didn't they interview you?'

'Oh yes. Two very nice young men took me through my paces.'

'When?'

'About a month ago. One long interview – there were several applicants. They wrote to me saying I'd got the job and would I start on Monday. That was two weeks ago. Salary in advance, a couple of telephone calls telling me to stand by, that I was to interview applicants for work – good knowledge of advanced IBM software; at least a year's hands-on experience; good character refs. You know the kind of thing.'

Bond nodded. 'Where did you find the job advertised?'

She mentioned a couple of business magazines – *Fortune, Business Life* – and three daily newspapers: *The Times, The Guardian* and *The Financial Times*.

'And they interviewed you here?'

'Yes.' She looked up at him and he thought he could detect concern flecking the grey eyes. As if to mirror the look, she said, 'To be honest, I'm a little worried. They have all this lay-out: a lot of money invested, yet they don't seem to be doing anything about it. The whole thing's crazy.'

'What's your name?' The question sounded casual enough, but Bond wanted to check this girl out on the magic machines back in the Regent's Park HQ.

'Horner. Harriett Horner.'

It sounded like an alias, but Bond had enough varied experience to know that real names were often like that.

'Harriett Irene Horner, if you're worried by the alliteration,' she added, as though reading his thoughts.

'Well, Harriett, if I were in your shoes, I reckon I'd be worried. It's a very weird set-up.'

'You've got reason to be worried, both of you!' The voice, unpleasant, menacing, came from the doorway.

They both turned towards the voice. It came from a muscular young man, dressed in a dark blue pinstripe suit that looked possibly Aquascutum. Behind him, stood two more men. They were bigger, broader, taller, and looked as though they dressed courtesy of *Soldier of Fortune* magazine. Both had those mean, brutal faces one associates with the SS torturers in more extravagant war movies.

'Mr Hathaway?' Harriett gave a small gasp of surprise.

'You know him?' Bond half whispered.

'Mr Hathaway's my immediate boss. He gave me the job.'

The smart young man smiled, and it was obvious that smiles did not come easily to him. 'Mr Hathaway gave you the job, Ms Horner. Mr Hathaway giveth, and Mr Hathaway taketh away. We know about you. We have a fair knowledge of your friend Mr Bond here, as well.'

'His name's Boldman. James Boldman. That's what he told me.'

'I lied,' Bond said easily. 'Mr Hathaway's got it right.'

'But . . .!' She was obviously nervous.

Bond caught the tension in her coming off in waves. He looked straight at Hathaway. 'You going to introduce us to your friends, Mr Hathaway? Who are they, Mr Shakespeare and Mr Marlowe?'

Hathaway motioned to the thugs as a dog-handler will gesture to a pair of wolfhounds. They began to move forward. They made three paces before Bond moved, leaping to his right, the ASP automatic up and in both hands.

He did not see Hathaway move. The man was very fast, and he cursed himself for concentrating on the hoodlums more than their master. One minute, Hathaway was standing in the doorway looking elegant in his £500 suit, the next he was crouching, something appearing from nowhere – an unexpected and very loud explosion followed, and around ten IBM computer workstations became useless piles of plastic, glass and silicon chips.

'Drop the catapult, Bond, or the next one's on you.' The smoke cleared and Bond could see that Hathaway was holding a short, wicked-looking combat shotgun. He did not dwell on the type, though the name SPAS Model 12 crossed his mind – a weapon of awesome power, for it is semi-automatic and can fire off its seven 12-gauge cartridges in under sixteen seconds. Depending on the load and scatter selector, the shot will do a great deal of damage. Bond only had to glance at the devastated IBM hardware for proof. Reluctantly he dropped the pistol, placing his hands on his head.

By this time one of the hoods had the girl in a neck hold, pushing her in front of him, towards Bond.

'That's better.' Hathaway was not smiling any more. He gestured for the spare thug to take Bond in a similar manner. The man turned Bond around, like an unarmed combat instructor doing a demonstration with a dummy. In a second there was a forearm around Bond's neck and a large hand on the back of his head. He knew that a quick, sharp pressure would cause a broken neck at the least, instant death more probably. The man smelled of something Bond had not sniffed for years – bay rum – that oldest standby of long-gone hairdressers.

'So what do we do now?' He found speaking difficult, for his captor had a tendency to increase the pressure on his windpipe.

'We go and visit friends, and we go very carefully and quietly.' Hathaway had moved closer to them, facing Bond and the girl, who were to his left and right, respectively, with the toughs behind them.

'We go down to the foyer, where we all walk out looking like friends. If anyone tries to be clever, well . . .' He hefted the lethal combat shotgun in his hand – it had a pistol grip at one end and measured no more than thirty inches, if that. Hathaway could easily conceal it under his well-cut jacket. 'You'll behave, right?' He looked from one to the other.

Bond tried to nod. Finally he muttered, 'Yes,' and heard a similar noise from the girl called Harriett.

Hathaway nodded to the men. The pressure relaxed, but the thugs stayed in position behind their victims.

'I would suggest that you go first, Ms Horner and Mr Bond. My associates will be behind me, but I shall be directly behind you, and I can tell you that this thing will make a very nasty mess of you both. Now . . .' He did not finish the sentence, for something amazing happened. For the second time that day, Bond did not fully appreciate the moves, though he knew who was performing them.

The man behind Harriett gave a squeal of pain. Bond was aware of Harriett doubling up, and of the hoodlum suddenly catapulting over her head, straight towards Hathaway.

In a reflex action, Hathaway loosed off another cartridge, but his own man was almost on top of him as he fired – a spray of blood and clothing seemed to fill the air, and by that time, Harriett had stepped behind the other thug.

Bond saw her grasp the man's wrist, then the big hoodlum appeared to be whirling around, as though Harriett was swinging a small child in a circle. Finally she let go and, with a shriek the man went head on into the other bank of IBMs. There was an awful crashing and splintering sound, followed by the popping of fuses and flashes as small electric fires began in the terminals. But, by then, Bond was diving for his own automatic.

Hathaway was sprawled on the floor trying to disentangle himself from the body of his henchman and grab at the shotgun.

'Don't even consider it.' Bond had his pistol up and pointing at the man who called himself Hathaway. But Hathaway took no notice and finally threw the body from him, one hand already on the shotgun.

He was bringing it up when Harriett seemed to materialise behind him. Her hands moved like sharp-bladed lawn edgers, down very hard on the sides of the man's neck.

Hathaway gave a grunt and collapsed, his head lolling like that of a rag doll.

'Where did you learn to do that?' Bond could not conceal his admiration.

'Probably in a similar place to you. I was better positioned, though.' She was straightening her skirt and blouse, checking the seams in her stockings.

'Harriett, I really think I should make one telephone call, then we should get out of here. I've no doubt that Mr Hathaway has friends.'

She nodded and glanced around at the thousands of pounds' worth of destruction. A dangerous little electric fire was starting to get hold of the carpet. 'Damn,' Harriett said. 'This is going to take a lot of explaining. Your name really is Bond?'

'Bond,' he acknowledged. 'James Bond. And yours?'

'I told the truth, but that hasn't helped me much. If you're what I think you are, then your superiors are going to get very cross with me.'

'Not half as cross as Mr Hathaway's superiors.'

She agreed, and Bond picked up the nearest telephone. One quick call to Regent's Park and the so-called 'Disposal Unit' could be here in no time, clearing up the mess – or at least the dead and injured. But the telephone was dead, and he realised they had probably blown most of the electricity in the building.

'I think we'd better go very quickly.' He saw her grab at a handbag and jacket, which matched her black skirt.

'I think you're right,' she nodded.

At the doorway, they paused and Bond looked back. 'Pity,' he said. 'There's an awful lot of incompatible hardware in here now.'

They moved to the lift which was, miraculously, still working.

'Never did take to that man Hathaway,' Harriett said as they reached the main foyer, both of them looking as though they were on their way out to lunch.

'Wasn't happy about his associates either,' Bond smiled. 'Remind me to thank you sometime, Ms Horner.'

'Certainly will.' She grinned back.

The smoke detectors on the fourth floor triggered the fire alarms just as they left the building. The white van was still there, but the man waiting for his date had gone. Bond hustled the girl to the left, and then down towards Oxford Street, his head swivelling in search of a taxi. He kept one hand firmly on her elbow. He could not afford to lose this one.

'James, what do you do?' she asked as a taxi with its light on came into view.

'Sort of Civil Servant.' Bond gave the cabbie an address in Kilburn.

'An armed Civil Servant?'

'That's right.'

'Security Service?'

'You're getting warm, Harriett, but I'd like to know your job. And I'd like the truth, please. No fibs.'

Her eyes were a warm grey, not that cold seascape kind. 'Well,' she began. Then she took a deep breath. 'Truth is, I'm an undercover investigator for the United States Internal Revenue Service.'

'I wouldn't like to underpay my taxes with someone like you around.'

'No? James, I have a small problem.'

'Yes?'

'I'm working in Britain under cover, and nobody's asked your authorities for permission. You've sort of caught me on the hop.'

Bond raised an eyebrow. 'And you hop with great agility, and exceptional talent,' he said with a warm smile.

8

The Blood of the Fathers

'I'll flay Wolkovsky alive for this!' M brought his fist down onto the desk, an action which seemed to make the pictures of his predecessors shake on the walls of his office.

Bond thought he had seldom seen his chief this angry. 'I really don't think David Wolkovsky knew anything about this.' He spread his hands in a gesture of placation.

'Don't be silly, Bond. Wolkovsky knows *everything* the Americans are up to, and I for one won't have their people trampling around our turf without even as much as a by your leave.' He snatched at the intercom phone and began issuing instructions to the indefatigable Miss Moneypenny. 'First, my compliments to Mr Wolkovsky at the US Embassy. I would like to see him here at five o'clock this afternoon. Next . . .' he continued forcefully.

Bond's mind slipped back to the events of the morning. He believed that, in situations such as the current one, it was often better to take action first, then ask permission later. He had taken Harriett Horner to the safe house which the Service kept in Kilburn – usually for debriefings, or field agents just back from an operation and in transit to the so-called convalescent home in Hampshire.

On arrival, he discovered the place was empty, but for a pair of very heavy minders, armed to the teeth. The first priority was to telephone the Disposal Unit, putting them on to the mayhem in the *Avante Carte* offices, alerting them to the possibility that fire services and police might well be already there. Once this was done, he gave the minders instructions concerning Harriett. 'Don't let her out of your sight. I'll get a female officer down here as quickly as I can. In the meantime, treat her as though she was a sister in grave danger.'

'I've got a sister in grave danger if I ever catch up with her,' one of the minders said grittily.

But they took instructions from Bond who then told Harriett he would soon be back. 'Just stay here, out of sight. I'll fix our authorities. You'll be okay. Just don't worry.'

'It's all very well for you to say that, but I'm as illegal as a Russian agent in place.'

She was certainly right on that count, but Bond thought he could probably talk his way around it by using charm and logic with M. They had managed a brief conversation in the taxi and, once Bond had shown her his ID, and she had produced her own bona fides,

Harriett spoke of the operation she was running. 'The Charity Trust, so-called, run by the Meek Ones is a front. Their leader, Father Valentine, has millions salted away, and the Society itself originated in the United States. We have a team of six people trying to unravel dummy companies all over the world. Valentine owes Uncle Sam billions of dollars, and there are other agencies out to get him. I don't believe you just turned up out of the blue to apply for an *Avante Carte*. You mentioned Emma Dupré. Well, her card was stopped this morning. It's one of the few things I've had to do.'

'Ms Dupré's dead,' Bond said quietly. 'That's how our people found out about the card in the first place. Yes, we've had an idea that this Valentine character isn't all he appears to be. How long have you been working on this?'

'It's taken me two months to get this close, and now the whole thing's blown.'

'Not altogether. We're working on it, and I'll see to the matter of your deniable status.' He gave her a thin smile. 'My superior's a pushover for a pretty face and an even prettier figure. Leave it to me.'

She looked uncertain, then leaned forward as though there was something else she wanted to say.

'I'm taking you to a safe place until I can put my people in the picture.' Bond laid his hand lightly on her shoulder. 'If there's anything else – any further information – best tell me now. We have quite a file on the Meek Ones and their guru.'

'Well.' She was undecided. Then, 'There is one other thing. Have you ever heard of someone called Vladimir Scorpius?'

'Who hasn't, in my line of work?'

'There's a link – and it's a very tenuous link – between Valentine and his Meek Ones, and Vladimir Scorpius.'

'Really? What kind of link?'

'Letters. Some cables. A couple of telephone conversations one of the other agencies monitored. Scorpius is a criminal, and nobody's ever been able to bring proof against him. I don't know all the details.'

'That's okay.' Bond was not going to give anything away. 'We also want Scorpius.'

'They put our section of the IRS in because that's often the only way to get these people. They did it way back in the 1920s with Al Capone. Now we're at it again with Valentine and Scorpius. You know they call him the King of Terror?'

'I didn't, but it's as good a name as any.'

Unless Harriett was, like Bond, holding back information, she had obviously not been briefed about the possibility of Scorpius and Father Valentine being one and the same person, but her current target was certainly the Meek Ones. 'My chief will deal with any problems about

61

your operation.' He kissed her, lightly on the cheek, and gave her what was supposed to be a consoling squeeze.

M's present outburst was the result of Bond's laying the news on him about Harriett – an illegal American IRS undercover agent operating in England with no clearance from Home or Foreign Offices, and no note to M's Service. The old man treated it as an outrage.

'But she's working on the Meek Ones' case, and the Valentine/Scorpius business – even though she might not have all the facts. On top of that she's very good, sir. Saved my life,' Bond had pleaded. That was when M almost exploded.

Now, Bond sat and waited for his chief to complete lengthy instructions to Moneypenny. He had dictated a long memo to the American Embassy, and others to the Home and Foreign Secretaries, carefully covering his own back, just like any other cunning Civil Servant. M was in the middle of a further, Most Urgent: Secret, note to the head of the Security Service, MI5, when Bill Tanner – M's Chief of Staff – came in through the private door that was the only other entrance to the office.

Bond raised a hand in greeting, and his eyebrows in a questioning manner, for Tanner clutched at a signal flimsy and looked a worried man. He held the flimsy so that Bond could read it.

THE SOCIETY OF THE MEEK ONES LEFT MANDERSON HALL, PANGBOURNE DURING THE NIGHT STOP PLACE IS CRAWLING WITH PRESS STOP THERE IS A BULLETIN PINNED TO MAIN GATES WHICH SAYS THE WHOLE SOCIETY HAS MOVED TO SECRET QUARTERS BECAUSE OF SENSATIONAL REPORTS TO THE MEDIA STOP I AWAIT INSTRUCTIONS. COWBOY.

'Who's Cowboy?' Bond mouthed, glancing at M who was still giving his lengthy instructions to Moneypenny.

'Your SAS Sergeant, Pearlman.'

'He's not *my* Sergeant. He drove me down from Hereford, that's all. We had a spot of bother and he proved his worth.'

'Try telling the chief that,' Tanner muttered. 'Pearlman's temporarily on the strength with your name as his backer. If the effluent strikes the windmill, it's you who'll be at the receiving end.'

Bond used a well-known four-letter word not far removed from Tanner's last statement.

At that moment, M put down the telephone, turned and glared at both Tanner and Bond. 'So, what's all the whispering about?'

'Signal from Cowboy, sir.' Tanner handed over the flimsy.

M read it and grunted. 'Well! Bird's flown, eh?'

'Looks like it.' Bond was anxious to get Harriett into the office.

Once there she would probably convince M of her suitability for the job in hand. He asked if he could go and pick her up, receiving an immovable, 'Certainly not!' for his pains.

'Sir, she's had contact with some of these people already. The man Hathaway, for instance, and another one. She'd be well worth talking to.'

'In good time. All in good time, 007. For now I want you to go down to the clinic and see how Sir James is faring with the Shrivenham girl.' He gave a wicked smile. 'At least that has kept her father out of Accounts today. Gives us a small breathing space during the wretched Audit.'

Gives you a chance to manipulate Lord Shrivenham as well, Bond thought. He would not put it past his wily chief to call in a favour or two if it helped with the Secret Vote. Aloud, he said he would obey orders and go to Guildford, adding, 'What about Cowboy, sir?'

'What about him?'

'Well, he's down at the Meek Ones' old homestead. You going to send him off on a treasure hunt?'

'I rather think that's none of your business, Bond.'

'I'm told that I've been named as his sponsor, sir, which means to some extent it *is* my business.' In M's current mood, Bond knew he was pushing his luck.

But M gave a short nod – 'I'll probably send him in to have a look-see and report.'

'Burglary, sir. Tut tut. I thought we'd been in enough trouble over that activity.'

This time M allowed himself a short smile. 'That was our sister service, 007. They can burgle and bug to their heart's content, and I'll be very happy if someone finds out it's not been sanctioned. What Cowboy does *will* be sanctioned – from the highest level, I promise you.'

The clinic, a low white sprawling building, lay near the village of Puttenham, hard by the Hog's Back, that long ridge of downland, now scarred by dual-carriageway roads, which runs west of the pleasant county town of Guildford.

In the Bentley, it took Bond less than ninety minutes to reach the clinic, which was bounded by high walls and a secure entrance staffed by retired Royal Marine Commando NCOs, who – together with former SAS personnel – acted as commissionaires, messengers and security guards at many of the Secret Intelligence Service's main HQ and its outstations.

They were expecting Bond, and once inside the clinic, which felt and smelled like any other well-ordered private hospital, a hard-bitten, uniformed member of the First Aid Nursing Yeomanry – that strange auxiliary women's service which, over the years, has done more than nursing or mere administrative duties – had him signed in, then led him to the second floor. 'Sir James is with the patient now,' she said, in a manner which seemed to show her disapproval of any outsider being allowed into the clinic. 'I understand permission has been granted for you to see him and the patient.'

Bond nodded. Charm or subtlety would never work with this dragon who looked as though she was made of steel, with hinges in the right places. 'You'd better wait here.' She indicated a small area furnished with the usual kind of chairs and low tables – covered with old copies of *The National Geographic Magazine* and the *Tatler* – that one found in Harley Street consultants' waiting rooms. 'I'll inform Sir James that you're here.' And she was off, her back ramrod straight, and manner suggesting that he was a very lucky man for her to even carry a message to Sir James Molony.

Five minutes or so later, Sir James appeared, calm yet his bright eyes dancing with humour. 'James.' He offered a warm hard handshake. 'How nice to see you after all this time. You keeping well?' Those same bright eyes seemed to appraise Bond, as though he could, by mere looking, detect any nervous or psychological problem.

For a moment, Bond felt uncomfortable. Sir James Molony probably knew more than any other man about his secret life – not his life of secrets within the Service, but the hidden areas of fear, the complexities of imagination which dwelt within him, motivated him, kept him happy and on an even keel, or came hurtling from his subconscious to plague him like demons in the night.

'How is she?' he asked, quickly sloughing off the discomfort of being with the great neurologist.

'She'll live.' Molony made it sound as though that was just about all Trilby Shrivenham would ever do.

'Only live?'

'No, I think she'll come back into the normal world again, but it'll take time. She needs medical treatment, rest and a lot of love.'

'She's not said anything else, then?'

'We've pulled her into a more stable state. Somebody – not herself – really took a chance. They filled her up with a cocktail of near death. As I think you suggested, it was a mix of hallucinogenics and hypnotics. Somebody took great pains to implant a lot of hellishly complex ideas in her mind while she was going under.'

Trilby's condition, as described by Molony, was one of increasing stability. 'But she's not out of the wood yet.' He placed a hand on Bond's shoulder, guiding him along a passage towards the room where she lay. 'She comes out of it completely sometimes. This morning, for instance, she was conscious for almost twenty minutes. Weak, but knew who she was and recognised her father – he's taking a rest at the moment; you arrived at a good time.' He went on to say that she could still be manipulated. 'I can bring her into a twilight world. The world as she knew it when they put ideas into her head. I've done it once, and it would be dangerous to go on experimenting. When she speaks in that condition it's like listening to what the Bible calls possession by an evil spirit. It's a condition not unknown to me. I've heard it in others who haven't had their minds tampered with. Even the voice is strange. Bit frightening the first time.'

'Yes.' Bond nodded. 'I heard it, before she was brought down here. Made me go cold. I know what you mean by the evil spirits.'

The room was like any other hospital room – the faint clear odour of antiseptic, an oxygen cylinder with its appurtenances in one corner, a wash basin, louvred blind covering the window, and there, in the small bed, the Hon Trilby Shrivenham, her face pale even against the pillow. They still had a drip in her arm.

A nurse rose from where she had been sitting, near the bed. Molony nodded and asked her to get him 10cc of something Bond had never heard of. 'I'll bring her up a little, just for your benefit. She might answer questions. I don't know though.' The nurse returned and began to prepare a steel kidney basin with everything necessary for the injection. When she handed it to Sir James, he said she should wait outside. 'If Lord Shrivenham returns, don't let him come near. The old fool will break down and start blubbing or something.' He looked at Bond, with eyes that seemed to be made of glass. 'This is the last time I'm going to do this for anyone,' he said. 'As it is, this is a special favour to M. So, if there's anything you want to drag out of her, do it now. She'll probably have lost all memory of the subconscious stuff by the time I bring her back into the real world.' He bent over the girl, going through the business of finding a vein in her forearm. 'There she goes.' He stood up, the injection over.

In his hip pocket, Bond was carrying a Sony Professional Walkman. He took it out, laid it on the bedside table, and undid the little felt bag containing the powerful microphone and booster which he plugged into the correct female jack. He checked the tape, and finally started the machine.

'Trilby!' Molony almost barked, 'Come on. Trilby, there's someone who wishes to talk to you. Trilby.'

She stirred, groaned, and began to move her head restlessly on the pillow, then quickly to and fro, like a child uncertain of itself, wrapped within a dream.

'Trilby?' Bond was softer in his approach.

'You have to get tough.' Molony looked across the bed at him.

'Trilby!'

This time the groan grew louder and her eyelids flickered. Then the loathsome voice came, buried from whatever evil had been soaked into her brain.

'The meek shall inherit the earth.' There was no happiness in that promise. It sounded more like a threat.

'How, Trilby? How will the meek inherit the earth?'

'The – meek – SHALL – inherit – they SHALL – inherit!' The word 'shall' was emphasised, the voice assuming a low growl, neither male nor female.

'How shall the meek inherit, Trilby?'

'The blood.'

'Blood?'

Then, very slowly, as though the words were having to be dragged – each a great weight – from a deep pit. 'The blood . . . The blood . . . The blood . . . of . . . the . . . fathers will fall . . . upon the . . . sons.'

'Go on, Trilby.'

This time it was faster, as though all the slack had been taken up, and the words started to tumble out – 'The blood of the fathers will fall upon the sons. The blood of the mothers will pass also. Thus an endless wheel of revenge will turn.'

'More!' Bond shouted. 'Tell us more. The meek shall inherit the earth. The blood of the fathers will fall upon the sons . . .'

She took up the refrain, 'The blood of the mothers will pass also. Thus an endless wheel of revenge will turn.'

'Go on.'

She groaned again, head moving rapidly from side to side.

'GO! ON! TRILBY!' from Sir James Molony.

'The meek shall inherit. The meek shall go to King Arthur!' At these last words the revolting voice cracked into a great cackle of laughter. 'Yes . . .' Hysterical, other-worldly screeching laughter. 'Yes. The meek shall go to King Arthur. King Arthur. King . . . Arthur.' The voice began to trail away, the breathing becoming laboured, gasping.

'That's it.' Molony was beside her with another injection. In minutes the breathing had become regular again, and the agitation ceased. 'Mean anything to you?' he asked.

'Not a thing.' Bond picked up the Sony and rewound the tape. He did a quick check that the voice had recorded, but switched off quickly. He had no desire to hear it again for the sound would have made even the most hardened person draw back with fear. 'Not a thing,' he repeated. 'I'll take it back to M and leave it to the experts – that is, unless it means anything to you, Sir James.'

66

The specialist shook his head. 'Crazy talk,' he muttered. 'Crazy, but sinister.'

Bond used a telephone in one of the small private offices to call M's personal number. He did not repeat what had been said. The line was certainly not secure enough for that, and the puzzle over the tail that had been on him between Hereford and London still nagged. On the way to the clinic, he had been very alert, yet spotted nothing.

'Come on back, then,' M told him. Then, almost as an afterthought, 'Cowboy's on his way here. Better leave your radio tuned to the usual frequency in case we have something for you. Might want you to detour to Berkshire, who knows.'

It was a little after five in the afternoon when Bond bade farewell to Sir James, who still appeared to watch him with an eagle eye, and then, once back in the car, adjusted the short wave receiver to the Service frequency.

Three-quarters of an hour later he was cruising gently into London on the M3 when the normal odd chatter on the radio frequency altered.

'Predator. Come in Predator. Oddball to Predator. Come in.'

Bond, recognising his call signal, calmly felt under the facia for the mike which was magnetically held in place. Pulling it out he spoke – relaxed, without the knowledge that was yet to come.

'Predator. Predator to Oddball. Receiving strength six. Over.'

The anxiety was about to start. 'Predator. Go to Tango Six. Urgent code one. Magnum. Three slabs and a pick-up. Blues on the way.'

Bond gave a sharp 'Roger,' and began to speed up, working out the fastest route to the Kilburn safe house where he had left Harriett Horner. Tango Six was the Kilburn safe house. Urgent code one equalled 'serious incident'. Magnum signified that firearms had been used. Three slabs and a pick-up meant at least three deaths and one injury. Blues on the way was the most obvious – police, probably the Branch, were on the scene.

As he started to weave in and out of the traffic, Bond wondered if the lovely Harriett Horner was one of the bodies. One thing was certain, death had struck in Kilburn, on Service ground. The blood of the fathers, he thought. Then, the blood of the mothers will pass also. Somewhere there had been betrayal – first the watchers on him driving from Hereford; now a house which had always been very safe.

9

The Pick-Up

Once upon a time, Kilburn, which is now part of north-west London, was a thriving area. Now, Kilburn High Road looks a shade worse for wear. Kilburn Priory was originally built in the fifteenth century, but all that remains of it, in Priory Road, is a small piece of brass portraying a nun. The present church was built in the mid-nineteenth century and occupies some of the site of the old Priory.

Turn right off Priory Road, and you will, eventually, come to Greville Mews which sounds much grander than it really is. The Mews contains no houses, instead there is a series of rented lock-up garages. The scene in this little cul de sac, on a normal afternoon, is reminiscent of times long gone. Some of the walls bear old enamelled signs advertising Castrol and Michelin, and a number of the cars being worked on by proud owners also have a mark of age on them.

What is not realised, even by those who rent these little garages, is that four of them are owned by one man, though those who come down to take cars in or out – even to work on them – are not often seen by local people. The four lock-ups are adjacent, one to another, and stand before the rear of a dilapidated Victorian villa. There are interconnecting doors inside the four lock-ups, and two small doors at the back of the two centre garages.

Those who have the right knowledge and access can operate small digital pads, which control a central lock, on the far side of these two doors – for the doors themselves lead into a small brick room. Once the correct sequence is keyed in, a metal door opens, leading into the rear of the Victorian villa. This is the main entrance to the Service's safe house. The front door of the place is strengthened with steel on the inside, and the people who can be seen coming and going are the regular house minders. The interesting folk arrive through the rear, and are seldom, if ever, seen.

The inside of the Kilburn Priory house in no way matches the flaking stonework and rotting windowframes visible from the front. No windows look out of the rear, for they were boarded up long ago. Locals say that the landlord lets off a couple of rooms by the month. The rest of the house, so the story goes, is falling apart.

Not so. The interior is reinforced, with at least four of the ten rooms soundproofed, and with electronic baffles running constantly. There are two ultra-modern bathrooms; a good kitchen with well-stocked fridge and freezer, and the remaining sitting and bedrooms are comfortable – not luxurious, but as good as any third-class hotel.

It was through the lock-up garages that Bond had taken Harriett Horner earlier in the day. The minders were a pair known to him from the debriefing of a defector, carried out in the Kilburn Priory house during the previous year – De Fretas and Sweeney. Known, rather like two favoured dogs, as Danny and 'Todd', the men were both fully trained members of 23 SAS of the Territorial Army – given a statutory month's leave each year to keep their hands in as part-time soldiers. They had also completed the special bodyguard course, and, while very intelligent, they had that full measure of suspicion which made them ideal for the job.

They had taken to Harriett immediately. Bond had found out her private address, which was in a Kensington apartment block, making a mental note so that a female officer could be sent there if necessary to pick up clothes and any other things needed.

Once Bond had left, the minders treated Harriett with almost touching solicitude, always deferential, calling her Ms Horner, taking no liberties but making sure she was comfortable and had everything she needed.

Their routine rarely varied. One would be stationed in what had once been a large box room, now converted into a house surveillance and operations room. Six screens monitored the street and the whole of Greville Mews, while other interior cameras could announce anything untoward in the house itself. Danny took the first shift after Harriett arrived – Sweeney squeezing in to unplug the monitor which gave a perfect picture of the bedroom allotted to the girl.

Later in the day, when 'Todd' Sweeney took over, Danny walked to the Pakistani newsagent's shop on the corner to buy a pile of magazines and some paperbacks, so that the girl had something other than the television to help her pass the time. To Harriett's amusement he brought back a Judith Krantz and two Danielle Steel's, not her kind of reading at all, for Harriett much preferred the works of Deighton, le Carré et al. Nor did she usually read the kind of woman's magazine he bought for her, not that he would have known, for she thanked him profusely and took them to her room.

At around quarter to six, Danny came up and asked if she would care to have tea in her room, or would she do the honour of having tea with him. She chose the latter, joining him in the downstairs back room, adjacent to the kitchen, which they had elevated to the status of dining room. There, Harriett discovered that tea, for Danny, meant large cups of a very strong brew, kippers with plenty of pepper and vinegar, and bread and butter, though there appeared to be more butter than bread.

Up in the operations room, Sweeney saw the large red Post Office van draw up in front of the house and was immediately on alert.

As he raised the first forkful of kipper to his mouth, Danny's portable radio crackled into life. 'Dan, there's a PO van out front. Looks okay, but it isn't the usual time for either mail or anyone bringing over papers from HQ.'

Danny clicked the button of his radio to transmit. 'I'll take a look,' he said dryly. 'Could be something to do with our visitor.' The bell rang in the hall outside and Danny, automatic pistol drawn and held low behind his right thigh, went through and asked who it was. His actual words were, 'Who is it? That you, Brian?'

He would have expected to receive the answer, 'Special Delivery for Mr Dombey,' to which he would have replied, 'Right, it's his son here.' This was today's pattern of code words.

Instead, the voice outside said, 'I got a registered package. It's this address, but I can't read the name.'

'Check it out and come back in the morning, then.' By now, Danny had the pistol safety off, and raised towards the door. At the same time he stepped back three paces and, as he did so, Sweeney's cry came over the RT – 'Watch it, Dan, there's four of them! I'm coming down!'

Danny motioned Harriett to stay out of the hallway just as the first burst of fire hit the door, doing nothing but spread itself back among the four men who were gathered in the porchway, for the door was disguised with five-inch armour-plated steel.

There was a cry of pain as one of the strangers received a ricochet in the face. Then a steady rain of axe blows began pounding on the door, making little impression.

'Place is like a strong room!' someone yelled from outside. 'Pick him up, we're not going to get in here.'

Sweeney, who was now at the top of the stairs, dashed back into the operations room to check the full situation on the camera monitoring the porchway, but it had been knocked out by the first, ineffectual burst of fire. He banged down on the alert button, which would trigger an alarm in the Special Branch ops room of Scotland Yard, then returned to the stairs and shouted. 'Watch it, Dan. I don't know what the situation is out there!'

Too late, Danny, on hearing the scuffling of withdrawal, clicked back the automatic bolts, threw the door open and stepped forward, raising his automatic in the two-handed stance.

The shotgun blast caught him full on the chest, throwing him back along the hallway. Two intruders had been left at the door. Now they leaped inside, the lethal shotguns at the ready.

But Sweeney, at the top of the stairs, had flicked out the landing light. He put the first man to sleep for ever with a pair of shots taking off the top of his skull. The second attacker lifted his shotgun, but caught two bullets in the chest. The shotgun exploded as he was thrown into a kind of macabre back-flip. A lot of plaster dislodged itself from the hall ceiling.

Harriett leaned into the hall, despite Sweeney's call for her to get back, and helped herself to dead Danny's automatic. The other two men were in the street, one – wounded from the ricochet – being helped into the post van by the other. Sweeney put a pair of shots in his direction, not aiming for a hit – the man appeared to be unarmed – and saw the big dents the slugs made as they went through the side of the red van.

The man dropped his partner, who lay groaning on the pavement, and leaped into the van, taking off dangerously and at speed. In the distance came the wheep-wheep-wheep of patrol cars.

By the time Bond arrived at the scene, carefully, through the rear lock-up entrance, the bodies had been removed, and the wounded man was being treated in a secure area of the London Clinic – often used in an emergency. There were two police cars still outside, while, in the main sitting room, Bill Tanner, together with Detective Chief Superintendent Bailey – who had been the start of the whole business the previous day – were going through the stories of Todd Sweeney and Harriett, who appeared, to Bond, to be in shock. There was a plainclothes SB man in the hallway and a doctor standing by.

'I got here as quickly as I could.' Bond went straight over to Harriett, placing an arm on her shoulder. 'You okay?' he asked, and she gave a quick uncertain nod, followed by a brave smile that suddenly changed Bond's day. If he was not careful he might get very attached to this girl. That kind of thing was not good, particularly as she was undoubtedly still an unknown quantity as far as this investigation was concerned.

'She's given us a very accurate description of what happened.' Tanner sounded more than gruff. 'But this house is blown.'

The Branch man coughed. 'To blazes,' he added.

'And by whom, I wonder?' Bond asked of the air.

Tanner still sounded put out. 'By your good self, in M's estimation,' he said, looking coldly at Bond. These two had a friendship which went back to their Navy days, and it was unlike Tanner to be censorious. 'You, or the young lady here.'

'Don't be stupid,' Bond snapped.

'It's M's opinion, not mine. Though it does make me wonder.'

'I had nobody on my tail when I brought Harriett here this morning. Nobody. We came by taxi, and I walked her around the block to make certain.' He turned towards Sweeney. 'She use the telephone?'

Harriett gave a small cry of alarm. 'James, you don't think . . .?'

'Did she?'

'No.' Emphatic, and again, 'No. No way could she.'

'Good.' Bond turned to Tanner. 'So, I'm to blame, eh?'

'At the moment.'

'What're the orders?'

'When we've finished here, you're supposed to come back with Mr Bailey and myself. Debriefing. Ms Horner and you. Both.'

Bond frowned. 'The message I got said "three slabs". Who were they?'

'Todd got two of the intruders, complete with black jumpsuits and hoods. They got Danny De Fretas.'

'Oh, hell no.'

'I'm afraid so. There's a team coming in tonight. We're clearing everything out, and the office is concocting a press story.'

'"Three slabs and a pick-up," they said. Who was the pick-up?'

'He's down for interrogation. Blast in the face. They fired a damned great shotgun at the door. The shot, and flakes of steel just bounced back and shared themselves out with the attackers. One caught a lot in the face.'

Bond thought for a moment, remembering Trilby Shrivenham at the clinic. 'Bill.' He motioned Tanner towards a corner. 'Listen, where's the pick-up?'

'London Clinic. We've got him mewed up close and tight.'

'Can you do me a favour?'

'Depends.'

'How's my standing with M? Really, how is it?'

'He's convinced that you bringing Ms Horner here blew the cover on this place. You did it first and asked afterwards, James. You know how much he likes that kind of thing. What is it you want?'

'I want to have a crack at the pick-up. Is he receiving visitors?'

'They've removed a lot of shot and splinters from his face. Shock, of course. The doctors say he should be okay for interrogation tomorrow.'

'I want him now.'

'I don't think . . .'

'Bill, believe me. M sent me to Sir James Molony to listen to Trilby Shrivenham. I have the tapes with me. I have an edge. I only need five minutes with this wounded terrorist. Five minutes, then I'll come back and face the music. You can convince M, Bill.'

'I don't know.' Then he gave a quick shrug. 'Oh, well, nothing ventured. Okay, I'll call him. But I can't promise anything.'

Everyone was preparing to leave, and Bond had a hurried word with Harriett as Bill Tanner went off to make the telephone call.

'Small piece of advice, Harriett.' Bond stood close to her. He could smell her hair full of the reek of cordite and feel the bowstring tension in her body. 'You're going to be interrogated by a very cunning old intelligence expert. Tell the truth and we'll all come up covered with rosebuds.'

She gave him a wan little smile. 'Do my best. It's been quite a day. I'm not used to getting myself shot at twice in twenty-four hours.'

'Few of us are. Now the real advice. Do you know an Agency man called David Wolkovsky, who works out of the US Embassy, Grosvenor Square? Truth now.'

There was no hesitation. 'Yes. Yes, I know him.'

'Right. Does he know of your operation?'

'He knows I might make contact. He was there as back-up if I ran into real trouble.'

'Don't kid yourself, Harriett, you *did* run into real trouble. Now, when my chief interrogates you, do not, and I mean *not*, own to knowing Wolkovsky. Any friend of his is an enemy of my superior officer. Apart from that, just tell the truth as I said.'

'Thank you, James. I'll try and remember.'

She sounded very formal, and Bond caught her gaze drifting over his shoulder. He turned to find Bill Tanner there. 'Your wish has been granted.' He gave Bond a friendly, almost conspiratorial grin before continuing, 'But he says five minutes only, and you are to come straight on to HQ.'

Bond nodded. 'See you later.' His hand brushed Harriett's shoulder, fingers squeezing for a second. Then he was taking long strides out of the room, heading back towards the rear of the house and the lock-up garages. Half an hour later, with the Bentley parked nearby, he walked into the London Clinic.

They had the wounded man on the third floor, in a private section enclosed by a ring of bodyguards and police. A senior minder called Orson was in charge and he recognised Bond immediately. 'The doctors don't like it, sir,' he began, 'but M has decreed that you have five minutes with him. That really is all I can give you.'

'Fine. Five minutes with the pick-up is all I asked for.'

There was an armed hood by the bedside who stood up as they entered. 'Stay,' Bond said, casually. 'I want to check one thing out with the man.' He took out the Sony Professional Walkman – the tape had already been wound on – fitted the mike and placed it by the bed. The man who lay there was short and thin, his face covered with dressings and bandages, except for his mouth and one eye, which moved constantly. Bond could see the fear in that one eye. At least he had that going for him.

He turned the Sony to record and leaned forward, speaking with his lips close to the man's ear. 'Listen well, my friend, and nothing bad will happen to you. I come because I know the meek shall inherit the earth.'

The one eye twitched anxiously. 'I don't know what you mean,' he whispered. The accent came from somewhere in the Middle East.

'Oh, but you do. You know the meek shall inherit the earth. Just as the blood of the fathers shall fall upon the sons; and the blood of the mothers will pass also. Thus an endless wheel of revenge will turn.'

'Oh, my God!' It came out in a breathless rush. 'You *do* know.'

'Of course I know. Now, I have one question.'

'What is it?'

'Why are the meek going to King Arthur?'

There was a long silence, and the twitching eye appeared to have become much more steady. 'What is the time, friend?' the wounded man asked. Even his voice was steady now.

Bond glanced at his watch. 'Nine thirty.'

The wounded man's lips formed a tiny smile. 'Then it's too late, whoever you are. The meek went to King Arthur at nine o'clock.'

'I see.'

'You will.' The man's head moved a fraction so that he could bring his one eye to bear on Bond. 'You will see. And you will not see. The meek shall inherit, and not just by going to King Arthur.' He turned away again and closed the one eye, like a prince signalling the end of an audience.

Bond switched off the recorder, nodded to Orson and the hood, then walked to the door. Half-way down the corridor he heard footsteps behind him, moving fast. It was Orson, making little gestures for him to stop.

'Bad news, sir.'

'Yes?'

'Old Lord Mills.'

'What about Lord Mills?' Everyone in the country knew, and loved, Lord Mills, no matter what their politics. Lord Mills of Bromfield, formerly Mr Samuel Mills, had twice been Prime Minister, was outspoken in criticism, even against his own Party when necessary. Still his wisdom and charisma could sway huge audiences, even though he had reached the age of eighty-seven. 'What about him?' Bond repeated.

'Just came through. He's been assassinated.'

'What?'

'About fifteen people dead altogether. Some kind of bomb.'

'How? Where?'

'He was on his way to a campaign meeting in the West Country. He stopped to go walkabout and talk to an election crowd in Glastonbury, sir.'

'It happened *in* Glastonbury?'

'Terrible. Yes. Terrible carnage.'

Bond started to run towards the lifts. Glastonbury, he thought. The meek had indeed gone to King Arthur. The small market town of Glastonbury with its great knoll of a Tor surmounted by a tower, and the ruined Abbey nearby, with the thorn bush supposed to have been grown from the staff of Joseph of Arimathea – the man in whose garden Christians believed that Christ was buried and rose again. Glastonbury, the place many Arthurian scholars singled out as the legendary Avalon – with Arthur himself buried in the Abbey. That was where the much-loved Lord Mills had been assassinated, together with innocents. As he rode down in the lift, Bond felt shocked and numb. The blood of the fathers? The endless wheel of revenge? The meek had gone to King Arthur and killed, violently and with vengeance.

10

Go Find the Devils

'It is difficult to describe the carnage here, by what was once the market cross of this usually quiet and peaceful West Country town. The police and rescue services are still sifting through the wreckage, and, at the moment, the casualty list stands at thirty injured – ten seriously – and twenty dead, including, of course, Lord Mills himself. The Prime Minister has postponed an election meeting due to be held tonight in order for her to come here, to Glastonbury, and then to visit Lady Mills.

'Lord Mills began his long political life in 1920 when he first stood for Parliament and was elected as Member for . . .' Bond snapped the car radio over to short-wave and hit the button for his listening-out frequency. He drove as fast as possible through the evening traffic, a hundred questions invading his mind.

Inevitably, everything went back to the beginning – to young Emma Dupré's death, and what followed. There were massive question marks over so much, not least the other vehicles who had him under surveillance when Pearly brought him down from Hereford. Someone must have known exactly where he was; just as someone knew he had taken Harriett to the Kilburn Priory safe house – which was no longer safe.

Pearly, he wondered. Might it have been him? He could certainly have tipped someone regarding the journey to London, but what was the point? It had been a dangerous ride and Pearly was just as much at risk as Bond himself. As for Harriett and the safe house, he would have to check on whether Pearly fitted the profile there – whether he knew of the safe house, Harriett's existence, and the fact that she was there.

This last was certainly unlikely. Only a handful of people knew, and if they did have a penetration agent – damned if he would call him a mole – then that person had to fit a distinct profile. *Had* to know of the trip from Hereford, and *had* to know where Harriett had been lodged. As far as he knew, the only people who fitted the entire profile were M, Bill Tanner, Miss Moneypenny and himself. David Wolkovsky? He wondered. The CIA London resident rarely missed anything. It *could* just be possible. Though certainly Bond doubted it.

He managed to keep the other demons at the back of his mind – the horror at Glastonbury and the undeniable fact that at least two people had known it was going to happen – even if the knowledge was only in Trilby Shrivenham's subconscious. As to who had carried out the atrocity, Bond was in no doubt that it was Father Valentine/ Vladimir Scorpius, through the agency of the Society of the Meek Ones. Why, was another matter.

At headquarters it looked and sounded as though they were on a war footing. M sat behind his desk, his face lined, eyes sad and tired, a man almost in shock. They were waiting for the most recent reports to come in from Glastonbury in the calm folds of England that form Somerset.

'You are absolutely, completely certain that nobody had you marked when you took the girl, Horner, to Kilburn?' M asked for what seemed to be the hundredth time.

'Positive, sir, as I've already told you. I plead guilty to taking Ms Horner to Kilburn without authorisation. I acted first and asked permission afterwards. But I was very concerned for her safety.' In truth he was certain, but knew that in his trade nothing is totally certain. Was there not an old Italian proverb – 'He who knows the most believes the least.'

'Mmm,' M growled. 'I've asked Wolkovsky to step over from Grosvenor Square again.' He spoke almost to himself. 'So far it looks as though your Ms Horner is genuine, and one hundred per cent safe. But there are aspects that still worry me.'

'There are at least two that worry me, sir.' Bond had yet to tell his chief about Trilby and the surviving member of the raid on the Kilburn house.

He was about to play the tapes when Bill Tanner came in, through his private office door. 'There's a full and detailed newsflash going out on all channels in two minutes, sir.' He crossed the room to the small portable television set that had been brought into the office. Things had to be serious for the TV to be there at all: M regarded television with grave suspicion. He was the same with computers, but they were forced upon him while television was not.

The pictures that came up with the detailed report of the bomb outrage were ghastly. The area around the market cross at Glastonbury looked as though a giant demolition machine had gouged a crater in the middle of the road. There were grotesque and tangled pieces of metal which had once been vehicles, while some of the old houses had frontages blown away. Others had escaped with shattered windows. Explosive blast knows no natural laws in the open. A man standing near the centre was likely to be completely destroyed, though it was technically possible to survive, deaf and naked, but alive. Blast will remove windows from one building, leaving it intact while the structure next to it collapses.

The cameras roamed the streets, bathed in light from the huge arc lamps that had been set up by the emergency services, picking up a bloodstain here, a woman's handbag there, a shoe in what had once been the gutter. The market cross had disappeared altogether.

The commentary was relentless. Lord Mills – Sam to his many friends – had been in a chauffeur-driven Rover and was scheduled to make three stops: one at Shepton Mallet, then a detour to Glastonbury before going on to address a meeting for the Conservative candidate in Wells. It crossed Bond's mind that the old man had still managed to travel and speak in public like someone in the prime of life. Shepton Mallet was well known for its military prison; Glastonbury for its Abbey ruins and the supposed connection with King Arthur, and Wells for its beautiful cathedral. The visits and speeches had been planned only four days before. Whoever had decided on Mills as the target had chosen one of the most peaceful towns in England to carry out the horrible deed. The whole thing had barbarous overtones – target and place, not to mention the fact of innocent bystanders.

A large crowd had turned out to see the famous old man. A local police car had picked up the Rover two miles out of Glastonbury, taking over from the Shepton Mallet car. They had come into the town slowly, the few local police on duty holding back the crowd which threatened to press in on the car. It was all good-humoured, and the police would certainly never have even considered Sam Mills as a terrorist's target.

The cars had finally stopped near the market cross – the whole area cordoned off by the police – and the crowd appeared to be forming an orderly circle around the vehicles. An aide assisted the old man out of the Rover, and, just as the door was closed behind him and he had pulled his body into its familiar tall, unstooping stance – one hand on walking stick, the other raised in salutation, face wreathed in a smile – part of the crowd appeared to break out almost swamping the car, and from its centre came the fireball, ripping forward, then billowing outwards. All had been caught by the cameras, and the public were spared nothing in the viewing.

'My God!' M breathed. 'The evil devils. Sometimes I think these people do it merely for the love of death.'

Both Bond and Tanner, who had seen a great deal of carnage over the years, were sickened by the sight.

When it was over, all three men were shaken. Even M jumped when the intercom phone rang. He spoke, then listened and spoke again. 'Send him straight up,' he said into the instrument, then, replacing it, looked up at Tanner and Bond. 'Bailey, from the Branch, is here. Says he has some urgent information for us.'

The Chief Superintendent also had the haggard look which seemed to be infectious. M ushered him into a chair. 'Nobody claiming responsibility,' he said wearily. 'As yet we just don't know how it happened, but none of the known terrorist groups have come on the line with a code – not even the idiot calls. Usually someone claims one of these within the hour. It's very worrying. To be honest with you, I don't think it's a one-off.'

'I can tell you who did it,' Bond said quietly. 'But I'd like to know how. Was it thrown, launched, pre-set or what?'

'Who?' It was a chorus from M, Tanner and Bailey.

'I was just going to play a couple of tapes for M when the newsflash came on.'

M was tetchy. 'Why didn't you say so, Bond? This sounds essential for any follow-up.'

'The Society of the Meek Ones did it.' He even sounded matter-of-fact.

They listened as he played through the awful, evil tape of Trilby Shrivenham with her strange, witch-like coded prophecy. Then the more obvious conversation with the injured raider of the Kilburn house. 'He knew – knows – some of the details and should be sweated,' he said after the recordings had been played. 'Trilby is different. That's almost certainly her subconscious.' He went on to tell them what Molony had said about the possibility of Trilby not being able to recall anything once he had weaned her off the overdose of drugs still in her system.

'If it *is* the Meek Ones, we should start an immediate operation.' M's crustiness had gone. 'It would be best if everyone combined forces – the Branch, local police forces, ourselves and Five.'

'And the Americans, sir,' from Tanner. 'This Valentine man *is* wanted by our beloved cousins. It's reasonable to bring them in, I think.'

'If we have to, I suppose. Yes. You know how I fell about . . .' They all knew what he was going to say but the telephone cut him off short. He picked up the instrument, listened to Moneypenny, then said, 'Oh! Yes, I see. Put her through, please . . .' His tone was now deferential. Bond and Tanner exchanged glances, and Bailey raised his eyebrows.

The conversation went on for six or seven minutes. Nobody was in any doubt as to the identity of the caller. 'Yes, Prime Minister, yes, I rather think we do know. But it's highly complex . . . Certainly . . . Yes, of course . . . I'll take the action and report . . . At midnight, very well, I shall be there, Prime Minister.' He put down the receiver, glared around him in an almost Churchillian look of belligerence and announced, 'That was the Prime Minister!' Tanner actually stifled a snort at this statement of the obvious, but M was speaking again, steamrollering anybody who wanted to get a word in. 'We shall be performing a combined operation. Even though we're in the middle of a General Election the PM is assembling COBRA. I'm to be there by midnight.'

COBRA is a special committee – taking its name from the Cabinet Office Briefing Room – usually consisting of the Home Secretary as Chairman, the Secretary of the Cabinet Office and several others, mainly representing the Home and Foreign Offices, MI5 and the Secret Intelligence Service, Metropolitan Police and Ministry of Defence. It has the power to co-opt members from other departments or services – particularly when the committee is assembled to deal with a terrorist threat.

'As there is an American interest here,' M continued, 'I propose to move that we co-opt Cousin Wolkovsky. Keep him out of mischief. Also, as we appear to have all the leads, I am going to ask you, Bond, to go out and track this dangerous and wicked man, Valentine – or Scorpius as we know he is – and his nest of killer spiders, the Meek Ones. You may ask for any assistance. I can't stress too strongly that this is a desperate assignment.'

'Where do I start looking, sir? We don't even know how they did this thing.' He glanced at Bailey who merely shrugged and said the forensic people were there, with C13 – the Anti-Terrorist Squad. As soon as there was any news it would be passed on.

'You've seen the television tapes,' he added. 'They tell you as much as we know. They are, of course, undergoing analysis at the moment.'

'You look under every stone.' M spoke steadily. 'You take who you like. For the honour of this service – as well as your country – you get them. Understand?'

Bond thought, yes, for a few more million in the Secret Vote as well. Then he felt ashamed at even having thought it. M was a wise, experienced officer who would go through fire and ice for his country. This one terrible act of killing an old, well-loved, highly respectable politician, plus a crowd of innocents was being interpreted as possibly only the start of some even worse atrocities – or a whole campaign, aimed at disrupting the General Election. Whatever M's other motives might be, his first concern would most certainly be to root out and destroy the evil that had come among them in the guise of a moral, peace-loving religious organisation. 'Has Pearlman come back yet, sir?' he asked.

M nodded. 'He has, but I've yet to hear his report.'

'I'll take him, if I may?' He knew there were dangers, for he could not rule out the possibility of Pearlman not being straight. But those you cannot entirely trust are best kept close, he thought.

'When we've heard what he has to say, yes.'

'And Ms Horner, to represent the United States. She appears to have been on this case for some time.' Harriett was another unknown quantity. Again, he thought, she is best kept close. Watch, observe and be on your guard. He had to remind himself, for Harriett Horner was, in a strange way, playing havoc with his emotions.

'She has, indeed.' M sounded distracted. 'Yes, very well Bond, but take care. I've seen the interrogation reports, and her personal file – at least Wolkovsky allowed me that. She's very good, but we'll have to get clearance from her service. Providing that's agreed, yes, you can take her.'

As M reached out for the telephone again, Bailey asked if he could go. 'I'll be on to you the moment I have some solid news, sir.'

M nodded, an almost arrogant dismissal, then, as though changing his mind, held up a hand. 'I don't even know if Pearlman's got anything for us, but, in the light of Commander Bond's tapes – evidence – regarding these precious Meek Ones, I suspect someone should get Forensic and Scene-of-Crime Units down to Manderson Hall. Can you fix that, or d'you want me to get on to the Commissioner?'

'I can do it, sir. Leave it with me.'

M turned back to Bond as the door closed behind the Branch man. 'Let me get on to Wolkovsky, then we'll have Pearlman in.'

Wolkovsky had already left the Embassy, on his way over to Regent's Park, so M instructed Moneypenny to let them know as soon as he arrived. 'In the meantime, I'll see Sergeant Pearlman, he's been waiting long enough.'

'Pearly' Pearlman looked decidedly the worse for wear. He had not shaved for forty-eight hours, and the clothes on his back looked as though they were more fitted for a tramp than an SAS NCO.

'Good grief, man, do you usually report to your CO in Hereford like this?' M showed a touch of the old sea dog he had once been – 'A terror when you were up before him,' a former Naval rating had once confided to Bond. 'They used to call him the Defaulters' Curse.'

M's tone rolled off Pearlman like water off the proverbial duck's back. 'Well, chief, sometimes one has to, if you see what I mean.'

'I'm afraid I don't see what you mean.'

'Look, chief. I've been press-ganged into this. Certainly I told the boss here that I'd help. But I didn't expect to be standing out half the day waiting for everyone to clear off. Yes, I went down like this to mingle – sit in hedgerows, blend into the landscape. I was called back here and I've been sitting in your padded cell for a long time.'

'All right, all right,' M frowned. 'Let's forget it. As soon as we've finished here I suggest that you go and get spruced up a little. Now, have you anything to report?'

Pearly held his hand in front of him, tipping it to and fro. 'A little. Not a lot.'

'Well?'

'I went through the place as best I could. Had to jemmy open a window round the back, so that was me, if anyone's asking. I left no prints on the place, that's for sure, and I didn't spoil any evidence that might already be there. I can tell you one thing though, they *knew* they were leaving. It was planned well in advance. Looked as though they had known for several days. Prick neat the place was, as my old mother used to say. Prick neat. Everything stowed away shipshape and Bristol fashion. Beds made, nothing in the wastepaper baskets, nor the dustbins. Not a sheet of paper in there. Not a pair of jeans; not a shirt; not even an old pair of drawers. They'd swabbed down and got out as though they had never been there in the first place.'

During Pearlman's little speech, Bond turned away to smile. He had no doubt that, while Pearlman was giving a very clear picture of the state in which he found Manderson Hall, he was adding a few seafaring phrases for M's benefit.

'Commander Bond?'

'Sir?'

'Any questions you want to put to Sergeant Pearlman?'

'Tyre marks? Signs of the way they left?'

Pearlman nodded. 'Yes. Tyre marks round the back, but the cars – about four of them I reckoned – and a couple of small vans went empty. Anyway, there wasn't enough room in that transport for the whole lot.'

'Left empty?'

'Marks not deep enough for fully loaded vehicles.'

'And how many people do you think were at the place?'

'One hundred and fifty, going on two hundred.'

'How d'you work that out?'

'First, the beds. There were doubles and singles. I told you they was made up, neat. All tidy. Shipshape.'

'Yes, yes.' Bond gave him a look to signify that the SAS man had taken the mickey for long enough.

'Even though beds're neat and tidy, you can usually tell if they've been slept in within the last week or so. That is unless they had all the sheets changed – something people in a hurry do *not* stop for, even if they've left everything else tidy, and cleared every scrap of paper, and every last stitch of clothing, every book, every plate, every last thing. They did all that, but they did *not* change the sheets. I went through each bed in the place and I'd swear every pair of sheets had seen at least three to four days' recent usage. Right?'

'Right,' Bond nodded. 'How do you think they left, then?'

'Over a couple of days, I would say. Probably took the heavy stuff out a while ago. Then they'd go in twos and threes. No big rush, just drifting off. Some in cars and vans picking others up. I had a word in the local pub – well, more like I listened out really. I'm sure that's what they did. They just drifted off, all set for either an RV somewhere else, or on a series of operations to be carried out.'

The enormity of what Pearlman had said hit Bond. Aloud, M gave a groan. 'Lord have mercy,' he added.

'Amen to that, chief,' from Pearlman.

The telephone buzzed again and M gave muttered instructions. Then, to Bond, 'You want to give the Sergeant his orders?'

'I can't do that, sir. I can ask him.'

'Well . . . Well, be quick about it, Bailey's back and our friend from up the road is waiting.'

'Pearly.' Bond smiled at the SAS man. 'Will you go on helping?'

'If I'm needed, yes, of course.'

'Nine o'clock sharp tomorrow morning.' He gave a place near to his own flat just off the Kings Road. 'We'll go over the Pangbourne place again.'

'I'll be there, boss. That all?'

Bond nodded, and M raised a hand, gesturing towards the door.

'Bailey first,' M said, when Pearlman had left. 'Says they have evidence of how it was done. He's got a video. It seems his people sent it over here; he hasn't been out of the building.'

Bailey looked even more shocked than before. He lugged a video recorder into the room and set it up by M's television. 'We slowed the tape right down, and our specialists managed to enhance the picture – zoomed in on the vital part.'

'And?' M had watched the setting up of the electronics with a certain wariness.

'And, I think you should see for yourself, sir. First, this is the original tape.' He pressed the Play button and the scene that had sickened them before was replayed on the screen. The cars drawing up, the friendly crowd, the old man being helped out of the car, waving and smiling. Then the sudden break and the explosion.

'Now,' said Bailey. 'I want you to watch this.' He pressed Play again. This time it was as though they had a camera zoomed in on a small section of the crowd who were pressing forward. In slow motion, they moved and the Rover's bonnet came into the frame.

'Watch the young man in the green anorak,' Bailey almost whispered.

They picked him out easily, a dark-haired young man. Bond thought he would be nearly thirty, certainly no older. Suddenly, in this shocking slow motion, they saw the young man leap forward, almost onto the bonnet of the car. As he did so, his hand moved inside the anorak and he was gone in a huge fireball, flesh, bone and blood disintegrating.

'My God!' M was almost out of his seat. 'My God! The fellow detonated himself. That's too horrible. Terrible.'

'But it's true, sir.' Bailey really was whispering now. 'What happened in Glastonbury was that a human bomb exploded himself close to Sam Mills.'

He played it again. This time Bond almost retched.

'Get them, James!' M spoke through clenched teeth. 'Just get them. Kill them, wipe them off the face of the earth if you have to, though I'll deny ever saying that to you if it happens. Go out and find the devils.'

11

Call Me Harry

The buzz-saw of the radio alarm cut into the deep cocoon of sleep like a vandal's knife. James Bond's eyes snapped open, every sense alert to the start of a new day. He could hear his housekeeper, May, already bustling in the kitchen. There was a temptation to lie there for an extra few minutes, even if only to sort facts and intuition into a well-filed order in his mind. But he could do that just as easily during his early morning routine. The time was seven thirty.

As always when he was at his own flat, Bond's morning ritual rarely changed. Once out of bed he went through the twenty slow push-ups, then, rolling onto his back, began the series of leglifts which continued until – as someone once wrote in a confidential dossier – 'his stomach screamed'. On his feet again, this time to touch his toes twenty times, before heading for the shower – as hot as he could stand, followed by turning the control lever to cold, so that the icy spray took his breath away.

May knew his moods, and could tell, instinctively, that today was not a talking day. She served him his De Bry coffee, together with the precisely boiled three-and-one-third-minute egg in the dark blue egg cup with its single gold ring around the top. The usual deep yellow Jersey butter and the pots of Tiptree 'Little Scarlet' Cooper's Vintage Oxford marmalade and the Norwegian Heather Honey stood by the toast rack. Breakfast, as ever, was his favourite meal of the day, an immovable and set feast when he was at home. Apart from a brief acknowledgement of her presence, Bond took little notice of May, who went back into her kitchen clucking to herself about his bad habits of coming in late at night, then acting like a 'Wee bear wi' a sore heed!' the next morning.

Indeed, he had arrived home late. After watching the shocking video of Lord Mills' assassination he had outlined the first steps he would take to track down the Meek Ones and their guru. Then there was Wolkovsky to see, and M insisted on Bond being present – always a difficult situation. Bond got on very well with David Wolkovsky, while the CIA resident was anathema to M.

The meeting was frosty with M making a formal complaint concerning Ms Horner, undercover agent for the US Internal Revenue, being involved in an unsanctioned operation on British territory. M was starchy, while Wolkovsky tried to act in a very composed and relaxed manner.

'Sir, let me tell you, I have nothing to do with any operation mounted by the IRS in this country. You're beating on the wrong melon. If there's a serious complaint, then it should go through the Ambassador to the Court of St James, not through me.'

'I think we can avoid that.' M remained unconvinced.

'That's good, Sir. Saves an awful lot of paperwork.'

'To hell with the paperwork, Wolkovsky. I know you people, and I know you could get the ear of the United States IRS in two minutes flat if we made it worth your while.'

Wolkovsky spread his hands. 'That what you want me to do?'

After a long pause, M answered, 'Yes.' Another silence. 'This ghastly terrorist attack . . .'

'Sam Mills? I heard. Ghastly's the right word.'

'There's some evidence that an American's involved!'

'Jesus!'

'No. An American.' M stared at the CIA officer. His face would have made a fifth at Mount Rushmore. 'I have evidence of this involvement which I intend to put in front of COBRA which has been convened for midnight tonight. I also intend to ask that you, as the CIA's Head of Station in this country, are co-opted onto COBRA.'

'Well . . .'

'You're willing to be co-opted? I have to ask. Nobody has any right to push you. I should add it is our opinion that the Glastonbury business is only the opening shot in something pretty desperate.'

Quietly, Wolkovsky said he would help in any way possible. They allowed him access to a private, secure telephone so that he could talk at length with Washington and obtain permission, first to serve with COBRA, second to allow Harriett Horner to become involved in a British covert operation. M would give no precise details, but left Wolkovsky in no doubt that the operation would be a joint affair, using the SB, the Metropolitan Police, SAS, MI5, the IRS girl, and M's own service.

'I've refrained from telling him that you are to be at the starting gate before anyone else,' M said rather smugly while the American was making his call. 'COBRA – if I know the way those people work – will be up all night, and come to some decision by late tomorrow. By then I would expect you to have made considerable progress.'

Bond did not say that he needed considerable sleep as well, though he did push things along as soon as Wolkovsky returned, bringing with him the news that everything had been accepted in Washington. 'There'll be a coded telex on the line by now giving the okay for the Horner girl to work with you.' He turned to Bond. 'Lucky devil; she's a stunner.'

'I said you knew about it, and I was right.' M's look spoke of

Siberian wastes, or preferably, Camp No. 19 at Lesnoy on the so-called Dubrovlag which has facilities for foreigners.

'Okay.' Wolkovsky sank into a chair and stretched out his long legs. Bond thought to himself that the man must be very attractive to women, with his tall, deceptively lazy manner, the tanned face, sun-bleached hair, startling blue eyes very like Bond's own, and lips in an almost permanent smile. Nothing ever seemed to faze David Wolkovsky. 'You win,' he said, raising both hands. 'I wasn't party to it, though the damned thing went across my desk. If you want the truth, I advised IRS to get your sanction. Obviously they didn't. But I saw the Horner girl's file when she came into the country. You want me to talk with the Ambassador?'

'We'll let it pass.' M now fixed Bond with his most authoritarian look. 'It matters not that Wolkovsky's present, but the cipher for your operation is HARVESTER. I expect a good crop. Now, you'd better take Mr Wolkovsky down to see Ms Horner.' His eyes flicked towards David. 'And *you* had better come straight back here; we'll be going on to COBRA in the hope they'll agree to your being co-opted straight away.'

They rose – Wolkovsky giving a little mock bow – and, as they left, M called Bond back to the desk. 'Don't forget, James, you can have whatever you need. I'm circulating the cipher HARVESTER to all sections. They will know you're in command. For God's sake, wrap them up, if possible before anything else happens.'

The meeting between Harriett Horner and Wolkovsky was brief. Bond excused himself after five minutes to 'Go and see somebody about security'. Harriett had done all the necessary talking and was free to leave, so, when he came back, Bond suggested that Wolkovsky should return upstairs. 'I'm going to see you home, Harriett. I want you to get plenty of rest, and I've already arranged a good watch on your flat. Nobody's going to get near you during the night, that I can promise.'

'Oh!' She gave a little mock pout. 'I was hoping maybe you might try, James.'

He smiled, placing a hand on her left shoulder. 'Thank you for your confidence, Harriett, but I need rest.'

He drove her back to the old, rather gracious, apartment block off Abingdon Road in Kensington, and went up with her, mainly to check that there was nobody lurking inside either building or flat.

It was clean – nobody in sight, while the flat turned out to be small and pleasant. Even though she rented it, Harriett had managed to put the stamp of her own taste and personality on the interior. There were jokey little things like a set of drinking beakers with the KGB crest on them, a poster proclaiming BE CAREFUL. DO NOT DISCUSS NAVAL,

MILITARY OR AIR MATTERS. Side by side with these amusing items – which were mainly in the kitchen area – he saw two good prints which must have belonged to her, for no landlord would ever have left Hockney's *The Panama Hat* etching or Frink's *The Spinning Man VII* in a rented apartment.

He strolled from room to room – all four of them – on the pretext of checking for any signs of entry. True, he was doing just that, but Bond also believed you could read a woman by the way she lived. Harriett Horner appeared to be neat, quirky, tasteful and, almost certainly, very good at her job as an undercover IRS agent. The bedroom proved femininity, from the unfussy sheets and pink pillow-cases, the *broderie anglaise* nightdress draped over the bed's foot to the pile of freshly laundered Reger underwear folded on a chair ready to be stored away, and the sets of Clinique cosmetics and varied scents on the dressing table. One of the closet doors was open, so he swept the clothes to one side, making certain that was all the cupboard contained. He thought that her salary – or the expenses provided for cover – must be exceptional judging by the quality and designer names on the clothes. Earlier in the day, Bond had not missed the attractively severe black suit she wore, and the Kutchinsky watch on her left wrist.

Leaving the bedroom, he caught a glimpse of Eric Ambler's *Doctor Frigo* on top of the unfortunate and dull *Spycatcher*, and considered she had got them in the right order. He also glanced at the telephone and saw that she had carefully covered the number with a white sticker.

'Seems okay,' he said finally.

'Drink? Coffee?' she asked in a voice indicating that she could slip into something loose while he prepared the nightcaps.

He shook his head. 'Big day tomorrow, Harriett. I want us both fresh and raring to go.'

'And where are we going, James?' She moved close to him so that he smelled her hair again. The scent of cordite had gone, replaced by something more fragrant. He questioned silently where she had got it from.

'First, I suppose we'd better get the man we'll be working with to take us on a guided tour around the last place these Meek Ones used as home – in Berkshire, somewhere near Pangbourne.'

'Right.' There was a choke in her voice, and, suddenly, the seemingly poised Ms Horner thrust her face into his shoulder and began to weep, holding on tightly.

Almost automatically, Bond held her close and, against his will, felt his body react to the pressure of her own breasts and thighs. He made gentle patting motions against her back, and murmured into her ear, 'Harriett, come on, what's wrong? Harriett, what is it?'

Still sobbing she pulled him towards the burgundy-coloured leather settee. She still clung to him, and continued sobbing while he felt foolish, making soothing noises.

Eventually, after ten or fifteen minutes, she appeared to pull herself together, releasing him and swallowing hard, using the back of her hand to wipe her eyes. 'I'm sorry, James,' she said in a little voice. Either she was very upset or a damned good actress, he thought. Her face was red and blotchy, the make-up around her eyes ran black in straggling deltas down her cheeks, and her nose had begun to run, reddening like her eyes. She got up, went into the bedroom, returned with a box of tissues, and began to tidy herself up.

Bond felt embarrassed. As a rule, he disliked women who cried, but somehow this seemed different. Once more he asked what was the matter.

Two bright spots appeared on her cheeks, and through the moisture her eyes flashed with a kind of anger – 'What do you think's wrong, James?' It came out with another sob. 'What in hell's name do you think's the matter?'

'It's been a rough day, I really . . .'

She gave a mocking little laugh which disintegrated into a sob. 'That has to be the understatement of all time. Sure, sure, I'm a trained undercover operator. It's taken weeks, months, to set me up with the Meek Ones. Then, in a day, for the first time in my life I face real violence – real death – not once, but twice. Don't you see what that can do . . .?'

'I'm not being callous, Harriett, but it's something . . .'

'I've got to learn to live with! Yes, that's what they tell you in training, and I honestly don't know if I can live with it.' She took a deep, shuddering, breath. 'That man – Hathaway. Did I . . . James, did I kill him?'

'You've been very well trained, Harriett. It was you or him – or me, come to that. You did exactly what anyone of your training would have done.'

'Did I kill him?' The tears were being replaced by something else: anger? conscience? Bond had seen it before, but only in men, not women.

'Yes.' He spoke with firmness, his voice almost etched in cruelty. 'You killed him, Harriett, just as anyone else would have done – anyone in our kind of trade anyway. You killed him, and, to live with it, you have to put it away, close it from your mind, otherwise the next time it will be you, stretched out on a morgue slab. Get it out of mind.'

'How?' she almost shouted.

He thought for a second. Then – 'Earlier today you mentioned the way the IRS once trapped Al Capone. Well, there's a story from that era which might help. Okay, so they were ruthless killers, the old mob, but in our kind of business it's ruthlessness that counts. The famous "Bugsy" Malone – killer, gambling boss, you name it – once turned to somebody who upset him in public and said the two most chilling words I can think of. He said, "Be missing." The man concerned was never seen again. Harriett, you have got to be that cold about things like today. You have to say to Hathaway, "Be missing." Missing from your mind.'

She looked at him, her face blotched and unattractive following the tears. Minutes seemed to tick away, then she took another deep breath. 'You're right, James. Of course you're right. It's just . . . Well, facing it for the first time, it's shaken me up.'

'You must unshake it, Harriett, otherwise I'm going to have you kept in the office, or returned to Washington. *I* can't afford that kind of uncertainty and sentiment, if we're to work together.'

She gave a small nod. 'I'll be okay. Thanks, James,' and she reached forward and kissed him, hard on the mouth, with her tiny wet tongue licking his lips and sliding around his gums. Once more, he pulled away. Again he thought it would be all too easy to become deeply involved with this woman, but, until he was completely certain of her, it was too much of a risk. 'Harriett, I'm sorry, but I must go.'

She nodded and gave him a tearful smile. 'I'll be fine now. Sorry. Oh, and by the way, my friends call me Harry.'

He gave her a look meant to convey trust, confidence and warmth. 'The sun, the moon and Harry, eh? It's very tempting.'

'Stay, James. Please.'

'Work. You need rest. Let's see what happens when we get a little further down the road, Harry, eh?'

She gave a little pout, then smiled up at him.

He arranged to pick her up in the morning, ten minutes after the time he had fixed with Pearlman. Then he took her in his arms, gave her a big, consoling squeeze, and kissed her lightly on both cheeks. 'Okay, Harry. Goodnight. Sleep well, and banish the nightmares.'

'I'll try.'

'Tomorrow, then.'

'It's another day, and the trip to Pangbourne'll be like a picnic after the past twenty-four hours. See you, James.'

Leaving the building he spotted the lone van at the end of the street, while one of the foot patrol stepped from a doorway to be seen. His security was there, in place.

As he started the car, Bond thought he trusted Ms Harriett Horner just about as much as he trusted Pearly Pearlman, which was not a lot. He also smiled at the thought that their first call tomorrow would not be at Manderson Hall, Pangbourne. He had much more devious plans, and it would be interesting to see if any news of the Pangbourne trip had leaked.

Now, as he prepared for the day, safe within the small kingdom of his own apartment, he began to sort out the whys and wherefores of the situation.

On getting in, after one in the morning, he knew it was best to put everything out of mind and allow that complex computer, the subconscious, to work away while he slept. Often he found this the ideal way of solving a problem, or putting his finger on some small inconsistency that had raised its head during the waking hours. But on this occasion, sleep had not brought any answers.

During his morning routine he began to assemble the threads logically, in the hope that they would provide truth, and possibly some clues or answers.

Emma Dupré had died by drowning. His telephone number was the only one in her Filofax. What if that had been intentional? Certainly somebody was on to him the moment M had instructed his return to London. He wondered, now, if the Dupré death had, in some way, been an elaborate set-up. She would never have known if the number had been planted on her. What if? What if? What if?

What if Trilby Shrivenham had been let loose in a dazed, drug-infested state, her mind filled with prophetic clues? Why, though? Why should a man like Father Valentine – or Vladimir Scorpius as he really was – wish to lure someone like Bond, or even his service? Could it be that he was boasting? – 'Look, I've given you fair warning. Now, see what I've been able to do. Kill when I've already told you in riddles. Listen out. Listen out for more riddles.'

It might well be like that; particularly if Scorpius was the complex intellectual villain his dossier claimed. Yet, however it was, someone had known Bond would be summoned, just as someone had known he would be at the *Avante Carte* offices.

Then, once more, they had known Harriett – Harry, he kept reminding himself – was at the Kilburn safe house. Had they come there to dispose of her, or rescue her? After all, life did not appear sacred to them. Sacrifice? He wondered, just as he wondered who had done all the tipping off. Pearlman? Harry? or someone else? Wolkovsky? Bond's mind wandered around in circles.

He pondered on the Kilburn Priory safe house situation. Todd Sweeney had been adamant that Harry had made no calls out of Kilburn, but did he really know? After all, there had been a short period of time while poor old Danny was out, and Todd had been in the control room. Bond knew there were ways of using an external line in that house without being seen on the monitors, or picked up by the sound-stealing bugs. He then began to wonder about Todd, making a mental note to pull his file. One thing was sure. He could trust nobody. Not even himself, he thought, his mind wandering back to the previous night, the smell and feel of Harry in his arms. A desirable lady. Certainly he could easily let that situation get out of control if he did not watch out.

Breakfast over, Bond went back into his bedroom, slipped out of the towelling robe he was wearing and put on comfortable slacks, shirt and light jacket – after strapping on the harness for his 9 mm ASP, and the one for the nasty little telescopic Concealable Operations Baton, a handy and secure blunt instrument which could either stop a man, reassemble his bones in an incorrect order, or kill, if used by a trained man.

Before going down into the underground car park, he made one telephone call. He spoke to Bill Tanner for three minutes. Yes, the terrorist wounded in the Kilburn raid had been moved securely down to the clinic in Surrey, where he had visited Sir James Molony and Trilby Shrivenham the previous afternoon. And, yes, Tanner assured him, there had been a team watching Manderson Hall. Yes, the code words were known and had been kept contained within a trusted Service cabal. M, as they all suspected, was still with COBRA. 'They won't reach any operational agreements until late today, you can bet on it!' Bill Tanner said, laughing as they closed the line.

Bond told May he did not know what time he would be home, if at all, and was met with a disapproving lecture on bodies needing rest and sleep as well as exercise – 'And I know well, Mr James, what kind of exercise you were up to last night. Lipstick all over your collar. Whisht, away with you, you wicked man, you.'

He picked up Pearlman right on the button, the SAS sergeant sliding into the passenger seat next to him. He was shaved and well spruced up, casually dressed in cavalry twill slacks, a light cotton rollneck and blazer. 'These threads do for the chief, then, boss?' He grinned.

'Admirable,' Bond smiled back, taking in the man's carefully groomed appearance, and trying to detect any slyness in his eyes.

The security van was still in place near the block in which Harry lived. She came out onto the pavement, looking radiant in black denim. Jeans and jacket by Calvin Klein, Bond thought, and a white shirt by heaven knew who.

She was her old self, greeting Bond with a dazzling smile and the kind of look that often passes between lovers. Harry and Pearlman were introduced, and Bond swung out into the traffic, taking the road towards the Hogarth roundabout, then heading for Guildford. As they passed through Hampton Court, with all its happy and tragic memories enshrined in the brickwork, Pearlman asked if they were on the right road.

'I usually come this way for Surrey. Bushy Park, Hampton Court, it's as good a road as any. A pretty run.'

'I thought we were going to Pangbourne?' Did he detect a hint of alarm in Harry's voice from the rear of the car?

'I thought you said Pangbourne, and all, boss.' Something there, in Pearly's voice.

'Slight change of plan.' He kept his eyes on the road. 'Not Pangbourne after all. Our lords and masters decided we'd be better off trying a little interrogation.'

'Interrogation?' A slight rise to the upper register from Harry.

'Who's being interrogated, then, boss?' Almost menacing.

'The guy who got himself wounded trying to kill or snatch Harry here at Kilburn.' His voice remained level, and, almost as he finished the sentence, the radio crackled into life.

'Harvester One. Oddball to Harvester One.'

Lazily Bond reached forward for the hand mike. 'Oddball, this is Harvester One. I hear you. Come in Oddball.'

'Oddball to Harvester One. Earthquake. Repeat, Earthquake.'

'Harvester One. Understood, Oddball. I'll be in touch. Roger over and out.'

'Thank you, Harvester One. Out.'

Bond understood all too well. 'Earthquake' was the agreed codeword if an incident had taken place that morning at Manderson Hall, Pangbourne, where a team had been watching since the early hours. Now something had happened. It meant that someone had tipped off the Meek Ones, or Scorpius, about the proposed visit by Bond and his team.

Inside the Bentley there was a new, unpleasant tension.

12

Death-Name

'This a private game, boss, or can anyone join in?' Pearlman asked some fifteen minutes after the warning call came in.

'Sorry.' Bond was relaxed at the wheel of the car, concentrating on the road, yet ready for anything which might erupt from either Pearly or Harry Horner. 'Sorry, I should have given you an extra briefing. You know we're on a covert operation and you've both been given the okay to work with me. Name of the Op is Harvester – hence Harvester One. That's me.'

'Earthquake?' Harry asked from the rear. In the driving mirror Bond saw that she had moved forward, her face framed between Pearlman's shoulders and his own.

'We were going out to the estate at Pangbourne where the Meek Ones used to have their HQ – ask Pearly about that. He did some observation down there. Literally my instructions were changed at the last minute. Earthquake sounds sinister, but it's not. It only means they're ready for us at the clinic we keep near Puttenham. Okay?' He was a master dissembler.

'The place where we're going to interrogate the guy who got shot up in Kilburn?'

Bond gave a half laugh. 'Shot himself up, really. Moral to all of us – never fire a shotgun at close range, particularly when you're shooting at a steel-plated door.'

'It didn't look like steel.' Harriett sounded rather wistful, as though she was sorry for the man.

'You'd have been happier if it'd been plain wood?' Bond actually smiled. Both Pearly and Harriett were a little on edge. He wondered if they could both be plants. Two members of the Meek Ones. Sleeper or penetration agents in place to keep tabs on what the authorities were doing about this strange quasi-religious society or was he simply imagining the tension?

They continued in silence, negotiating the outskirts of Guildford and climbing the long dual carriageway leading to the Hog's Back, Guildford Cathedral on the skyline to their left. Fifteen minutes later Bond took the turning off the Hog's Back and they were soon being checked by the security people at the gates of the clinic. As usual there were two men on duty in the little gatehouse, while – Bond knew – another pair operated the phalanx of closed-circuit cameras which kept their probing eyes on the whole clinic, both inside and out.

An ambulance and three or four cars were parked in the grid just to the right of the main, low white building, and he noted that Sir James Molony's Lancia was there, waxed, polished and gleaming in the weak sun which battled with cloud in an attempt to make a decent spring day.

The Reception desk was manned by a former member of 42 Commando, Royal Marines: a man Bond knew had been invalided from the Service after being wounded in the Falklands War. Without any prompting the ex-Marine lifted the internal telephone and spoke quietly, saying that the party from London had arrived for Sir James Molony. They waited in silence, sitting around the Reception area. Bond felt the other two looked uncomfortable, and his earlier intuition nagged and worried at his mind like a bad toothache.

It was ten minutes before Sir James appeared, spruce and smiling, doing some invisible hand-washing. By this time Bond was jumping at shadows, and the first thing to cross his mind was the meaning some psychiatrists put on that odd hand-washing motion – the Pontius Pilate syndrome, a signal of guilt pestering the subconscious.

He introduced the pair as his 'colleagues', giving no names. Molony shook hands with each in turn, calling Harriett 'my dear', and apologising for keeping them waiting. 'Been dealing with the Shrivenham girl.' He gave Bond a brisk smile.

'How's she coming along?'

'Much better than I expected. Been awake and perfectly normal for several hours this morning. Then lapsed a little. Back in dreamland again now. It'll take a few days, you know. Thank heaven her father's gone back to town. But we have two uncles and her brother visiting today.'

Bond looked up sharply. 'I didn't know she had a brother.'

'Oh my goodness, yes. Brother and a sister. Between ourselves I don't get on with the brother. Asks too many questions. A little medical knowledge is a dangerous thing, James. The fellow read medicine at Oxford. Got sent down, though, so gave it all up.'

'I wouldn't mind a word with him when we've finished.' In addition to his concern about Pearly and Harriett, something vague, but worrying, clicked into Bond's mind about the Shrivenham son – Trilby's brother. Something he'd heard or read? He tried to push it away in order to concentrate on the vital job in hand. 'And our patient?' he asked of Sir James Molony.

The consultant smiled – knowing and almost secret. 'All ready for you. I presume your colleagues have experience of these things?'

'Not sure.' Bond turned to Pearly and Harriett. 'Have either of you done any courses on drug-assisted interrogation?'

'Yes,' from Harriett.

'No,' from Pearly.

'Well,' Molony beamed at them, taking over from Bond. 'It's much more sophisticated than in the old days when we just used to pump the suspect full of Soap, and run questions past him.' Soap was the old Service jargon for Sodium Pentathol. 'We have better facilities now. Hypnotics that leave the mind and the subconscious clear, and the brain lucid.' He turned back to Bond. 'You'll be doing all the work, I presume?'

'Providing you do the medical stuff.'

'Already done, dear boy, already done. He's fast asleep. Just one quick shot of the truth serum – as the popular spy novels call it – and he's all yours.' Molony looked from Harriett to Pearly and back again. 'It's not really a truth serum, of course. But you get quite a long way down provided you ask the right questions.' He turned his twinkling eyes onto Bond. 'Presumably you've got the right questions?'

'I hope so. Did anyone get any more details when he arrived down here? Name, anything like that?'

'They tried, but he went blind, deaf and dumb. M agreed this was the only way. I was quite bucked when he told me last night that you were coming down.'

That's torn it, Bond thought. He did not even look at Pearly and Harry, but the pair could not have missed the remark. Now they would know, guilty or not, that he had lied to them about the sudden change of plans. They would be more alert, if guilty; angry if innocent. There was a brief pause then Molony said they should be going down.

They walked along the corridor, past the sliding metal door of the room that housed the security watchers who, at this moment, would be operating their cameras, sweeping the grounds, forecourt, and all the open interior areas – the corridors and exits from the clinic. They probably had Molony and his three visitors on the screens now. Indeed they would have tracked them from the Bentley, and watched them in Reception, even logged their conversation on tape.

Molony continued to talk. He had been very impressed with the security used to bring the Kilburn terrorist from the London Clinic. He described the operation as 'smooth as a kidney transplant'. Sir James was known for his use of medical terms during informal conversation. It was said that he had once scandalised a dinner party by saying the pudding looked like a gall bladder.

Most of the bandages had been removed from the patient's face, replaced by smaller adhesive dressings. The curtains were closed, and two Anglepoise lamps were adjusted to throw light on the top end of the bed. Molony gestured towards a chair set near to the man's head. 'Looks as if he's had a rotten shave, eh?' The consultant beamed again as Bond took his place on the chair.

'We seem to be superfluous.' Harriett's tone hinted at pique. She was certainly close to anger.

'Boss, we are to be trusted, I suppose?' Pearlman asked.

'Of course,' Bond said quickly, 'and no, no, you're not superfluous. Far from it. Harry, you've had dealings with these people; Pearly's been briefed. If anything comes up that strikes either of you as interesting, I want you to tell me. It might help some line of questioning.' He slewed his body so that he could look towards Harriett. 'This man, here. Have you ever seen him before?'

She came closer, peering over his shoulder. There was a long pause before she said, 'He's familiar. Two men interviewed me for the *Avante Carte* job – Hathaway, and a taller one – taller and of a much larger build. I saw no women when I went for the interview. There were other people about. I took them to be executives, and this was one of them. I remember thinking he was very smart: grey pin-striped suit; soft voice. Looked like any other businessman out after the job of managing a high-powered credit firm. Come to think of it, I saw him again. I was getting into a taxi outside the offices and I spotted him hailing a cab coming up behind mine.'

'Did you watch it? The cab, I mean. Did it follow you?'

'Maybe. It was rush hour. Difficult to see.'

Was all that true, Bond wondered. Or was it simply an attempt to reinforce her cover? 'A general hood-of-all-work, I should imagine,' he said, almost to himself. Then – 'Okay, Sir James, let's get on with it, if you're ready.'

The injection took a couple of minutes to work. The patient lay, perfectly still, his head unmoving on the pillow, then there was a flicker of the eyelids. A minute later he seemed to be wide awake – eyes staring, unblinking, at the ceiling. Bond took a deep breath and spoke. 'The meek shall inherit the earth,' he began.

> 'The blood of the fathers will fall upon the sons.
> The blood of the mothers will pass also.'

The voice was natural, quiet, and with the slight trace of an accent Bond had noted at the London Clinic.

'Tell me your name.' he asked.

'My name in the world, or my name in death?'

Bond felt a slight shiver pass through his body. The possible horror they had uncovered began to worm its way into his mind. Oh God, a voice said at the back of his brain. If this is what I think, we're in for a time of true despair. 'Both,' he said at last. 'Your name in the world, first.'

'My true name is Ahmed. Ahmed el Kadar.'

'You are from where?'

'In the world my country is called Libya. But I have, naturally, disowned my country. I am a citizen of the world of the Meek Ones, which is the world in its final confusion.'

'And your name in death?'

'My name in death is Joseph.'

'Is there significance in that name?' As no response appeared to be forthcoming, he quickly repeated, 'The meek shall inherit.'

'If you know that, you know that death-names are chosen at random. Death is the only significant thing.'

Judging this to be some form of basic catechism, Bond asked, 'Why is death the only significant thing?'

'Death in itself has no significance. Only the way a Meek One dies, the bravery he shows, is significant, because it is his way, as a true believer, to paradise. The Meek shall only inherit if we – the ones chosen to go before – change the state of the world.'

'Good.' He seemed to be praising a diligent student. 'How shall the Meek Ones change the world?'

'By death. By bringing the final revolution which will set man, woman and child free from the yokes of man-made political ideals. The world can flourish only when those who rule – justly and unjustly – are laid low. And when all embrace the true way.'

'Only then?'

'Only when the corrupt ideals, which men call politics, are smashed open, and crushed like the eggs of a deadly spider. Only then can the world flourish and the people be free. All revolutions, until now, have been false, just as power, and the ambition to gain power in the imperfect world are false. The Meek shall inherit, but only when the endless wheel of revenge has turned full circle.'

'Are all the Meek Ones ready?'

'Those who have been chosen, and seen the truth, are ready and waiting.'

'Where do they wait?'

'In their appointed places. The unmarried and childless will do the simple tasks. The married, with children to follow after them, will do the great things. All have orders, or will be given orders. They are now scattered to the four corners of the earth. They will breed and die, so that their children can breed and die for the truth, until the wheel has turned fully.'

'What are your own orders?'

'I have carried out my first task, and failed.'

'Joseph, what was your first task?'

'To destroy the female serpent who came to kill our Father. Our Father, Valentine, is often at risk from enemies. They must all be destroyed. I failed. Next time I shall not fail.'

'Have you a new task, Joseph?'

'As I have failed, a new task will come.'

'In the usual way?'

'Of course.'

'Directly from our Father, Valentine?'

'Directly, from his mouth only, or from one who can speak his death-name.'

'And his death-name is?'

There was a long silence. 'Our Father – Valentine – Joseph? His death-name, Joseph?'

'Only our Father Valentine's death-name changes with the sun and the moon. It is a word we cannot repeat, even to each other.'

'But he will come?'

The man in the bed smiled, as though in some kind of ecstasy. 'He will come, or send one to take me to him. I know he will come soon.'

'And when he comes you will be given a task which may lead to death?'

'I have fathered a child, so I am a chosen Meek One. I am allowed a death-task, and the glory it will bring to me, and to my wife and our son. Yes, the next task will be a death-task.'

'Do you know where our Father, Valentine, is now?'

'We are all scattered, but, like the God of the Christians, our Father, Valentine, knows where each of us is at any time. He can reach and pluck us out, ordering us to a new task.' The hair on Bond's neck bristled, and he again felt the cold clammy sense of horror crawling over his own flesh. If he was reasoning correctly, this was worse than he had ever imagined. 'Let our Father, Valentine, come for you, or send one to take you to him. It will be good, Joseph. Rest now.' He signalled for Sir James to do what was needed to return the patient to peaceful sleep and erase all memory of this conversation from his mind.

'What was all that about?' Harriett gasped, in the corridor outside Joseph's room.

'This guy's a loony, boss.' Pearly was laughing. 'All that old bunny about death-names, and death-tasks and our Father, Valentine, knowing where everybody is.'

'Think about it, Pearly.' Bond sounded, and looked, grim. 'Both of you, think about the implications of what that man said. Think about what happened in Glastonbury last evening, and put it in context. It should wipe any smile from your face.'

Molony joined them in the corridor. 'I've sent for a nurse, James. I suppose, after that, we double all security.' He looked as grave as Bond.

'But what . . .?' Harriett began.

'We might even have to move him again.' Bond overrode the girl, then rounded on both of them. 'Can't you begin to understand? That man, in there, really believes that Father Valentine is a kind of all-knowing god; and we know who he *really* is. Valentine is Vladimir Scorpius who was dangerous enough when he was supplier of arms to more than half the world's terrorist organisations. That man,' he jerked his thumb towards the door, 'and hundreds like him – members of the Society of Meek Ones – have swallowed a crock of mumbo-jumbo. He, and the others, *believe* it.'

'Believe what? Death-names, tasks? What do they believe, boss?'

'I don't believe you can't really see it, Pearly. Or are you just playing dumb, for my benefit?' He gave a massive shrug, and an irritated kind of sigh. 'Well, we're going to have to get back to London. I want a quick look at Sir James' other patient and her visitors. Just wait for me in the car. I'll be along in a moment.' He tossed the car keys to Pearly, knowing the chance he was taking, but willing to risk Harry or Pearly – or even the two of them – making a run for it. He still found it very hard to believe that neither of them had followed the obscene logic of the man who called himself Ahmed el Kadar – death-name, Joseph. But – in front of Harriet and Pearly – he had shown his own understanding of the terrible, and evil, basics behind the Society of Meek Ones.

Pearly caught the keys. 'Beyond me, boss.' He grinned. 'Unless you're saying that these people're motivated by some religious fervour to act as rent-a-killer.'

'That's exactly what I am saying, Pearly, and you know it. Just as you know these people are not just hired killers. The Meek Ones *expect* to die for the beliefs Scorpius has implanted in them. Heaven knows how he's done it – he can't just have chosen exceptionally gullible proselytes. Anyway, I'll be up in a minute. Go ahead.'

Harriett still looked angry, while Pearly was a picture of bland disbelief. They nodded and went along the corridor, climbing the stairs that would eventually lead them to the clinic's Reception area.

'A pretty terrifying picture.' Sir James Molony spoke in almost a whisper. 'Tell me if I have it right. This man is a typical member of the Meek Ones. He believes everything that Valentine tells him. He's convinced that the world must be changed through revolution; that those who have been chosen will gladly die for that revolution, for they will attain some kind of paradise.'

Bond nodded in assent. He suddenly felt very weary. 'Yes, that's it as I see it. They believe all that and more. The same thing is there in many religions – as you well know, Sir James. If taken to its logical conclusion, as Valentine – I should say Scorpius – has managed to do, we're now up against a small army of kamikazes. People who'll die just as Scorpius orders them. It's a self-perpetuating death-machine. Thinking of the man's previous career, I wonder if this is but a horrible extension. Lease terror. Sell a particular kind of murder, or mass murder. He provides not only the weapons, but the whole service. If you want a certain type of terrorist campaign, or just one act of violence, Scorpius will give you the entire thing – gift wrapped – for a fee.'

Molony laid a hand on Bond's shoulder. 'The whole conception is hideous. I'll get on to M. Double the security.'

'I'd better tell you now.' Bond lowered his own voice. 'There's something lurking around my brain concerning Trilby Shrivenham's brother. I'd like to see him, and the uncles.' He almost went on to share his worries over Harriett and Pearly, but there was already enough to cause anxiety to the consultant.

To give maximum security to the man who called himself Ahmed el Kadar, his room had been on the deepest level of the clinic. By-passing the lifts, they walked up two sets of stairs to get onto the second floor below ground where Trilby Shrivenham was located.

There was nobody on duty outside her door, no guards in the passageway itself. Bond's stomach turned over, and he began to walk more quickly, the walk turning into a trot, with the elderly Molony puffing to keep up with him, but obviously equally concerned.

Bond pushed the door open and stopped, for a second, standing horrified in the doorway. The nurse who had stayed on duty now lay sprawled on the floor, her head skewed at an unnatural angle. The room was in shambles, with Trilby Shrivenham half out of the bed, terribly still, her long hair hanging like a waterfall brushing the floor. The drip had been ripped from her arm, shattered.

'Damn. My fault,' Bond breathed, as Molony pushed past him. 'I shouldn't have let the others come up here alone.' He reached for the automatic inside his jacket, turning, ready to dash up the stairs.

He heard Molony – by the girl's side – say she was still alive, his hand going out to press the bell to summon assistance. 'I'll get someone.' Bond began to run towards the stairs. At the same time a uniformed nursing sister appeared at the top. 'Down there!' Bond shouted at her. 'The Shrivenham girl's room! Sir James needs you!'

But as the sister gathered momentum, coming down the stairs at a lickety-split pace, he saw her face was parchment grey, the eyes glazed as though in shock. 'Upstairs . . .!' She paused as they met, and her voice drew a photographic image of terror. 'Up there! The security people! I think they're all . . . They're all gone! Dead! Please, quickly. One of them's my husband!'

'Get down to Sir James,' Bond commanded. 'I'll handle everything else,' and he lunged upwards.

With the pistol at the ready, Bond reached the passage off which the security room lay. The sliding steel door was open. He stopped for a moment, to take in the scene. Both the guards were dead. It was a small room and his first thought was that he had never seen so much blood in such a confined space.

There was nothing he could do for the two men, so he carried on to the main level, hugged his back to the wall and peered into Reception. The carnage there appeared wanton, and he wondered how they had managed it without making a great deal of noise.

He stepped forward, the pistol still raised, and, as he did so, remembered the truth which had been niggling in his mind. Trilby Shrivenham *did* have a brother, but the accent was on *did*. The Hon Marcus Shrivenham had died five years ago in a mountaineering accident. Switzerland – Mont Blanc – he thought, as though it mattered now.

13

Scatter

The former member of 42 Commando, Royal Marines, looked as though he had caught the full blast of a heavy calibre bullet in the face. Bond could only recognise him from his build and the uniform. As in the small operations room, there appeared to be blood everywhere. It could not have come simply from the security man on Reception.

Then he saw the other horrors – the two nurses, one on her back, the other spread-eagled, as though she had been thrown against the wall, then dumped without ceremony, or thought for her dignity: for her uniform skirt had flown upwards, leaving her in an almost naked state.

Both girls had been gunned down – why no noise, he kept asking – and the bullets had severed arteries. When this occurs, blood travels, jets, sometimes over considerable distances.

All Bond could think of was finding out if Pearly and Harriett had assisted in this. Whoever had posed as Trilby's brother, and uncles, were certainly to blame. Had the SAS man and – or – the American IRS girl helped?

Then he saw the other body, outside, face-down on the clinic's steps, small rivers of blood forming a crimson tracery down the stone. A big man, dark-haired and dressed well, in a conservative black pin-striped suit. One of the 'uncles'? Or even Trilby's 'brother'? It was certainly not Pearly.

From here he could see the little security booth and its barber-pole checkpoint. The pole was up, and the glass around the booth shattered.

With automatic still at the ready, Bond ran down the steps, straight across the forecourt to the booth. There was nothing he could now do for the occupants. They were both dead, one still seated behind the smashed glass checking window, his uniform front soaked dark brown. There was a look of incredible surprise on his face.

Turning, he began to walk back to the clinic. There were things that had to be done fast. As he walked he saw, almost with incredulity, the racing green Mulsanne Turbo still in the place in which he had parked it. Only the ambulance had gone.

Inside again he wiped some of the blood away from one of the Reception telephones and dialled the usual emergency number. In all Service establishments there was a system for emergencies, like the public 999 call for ambulance, police or fire service. Dialling the number from here meant that it would ring in the nearest Secret

Intelligence Service related office. Maybe a substation of the Special Branch, or the Military Intelligence Office of some Army, Naval or Air Force base. In this case it was the latter: the Air Intelligence Office at Farnborough – that show place for the world's aircraft which doubles under many guises: accident investigation to aircraft testing. There is always a Royal Air Force presence at Farnborough, and, naturally, an Intelligence Office.

Bond identified himself under his normal contact name, Predator. He then gave the cipher for the clinic – which was Hospice – and the signal for a top-level emergency – Flash Red. This ensured that, within a short time there would be a 'Disposal Unit' plus a heavy security section at the clinic.

In effect, this lifted any burden from Bond. He did not need to stay at the site. In the time it took him to walk from the telephone to the main doors, London would be informed. He went outside again and looked down at the body on the steps. A pistol lay on the ground a few paces away, and he could see, without picking it up that the weapon was a clumsy-looking Walther P4 – a normal Walther P1 fitted with a long suppressor, or noise-reduction unit: an ungainly cylinder jutting from the barrel, making the weapon around three times its normal length.

It was efficient enough, and accounted for the silent manner in which the assault had been carried out.

Thinking it best to speak to Sir James before leaving, Bond quickly went inside again. As the car was still there he could get away – a set of spare keys always rested, in a magnetic box, welded to the rear underside of the chassis. In any case, he could always fall back on the remote control.

Molony and the nursing sister had been joined by a male nurse, and were working on Trilby. Sir James, in his shirt sleeves, glanced up as Bond appeared in the doorway.

'She's going to be alright.' He was in the act of putting the needle into the girl's arm for a new drip. 'I presume our security people did not check the visitors thoroughly enough.'

'They've paid dearly for it.' Bond looked towards the nursing sister whose husband had been one of the security personnel. A shadow crossed her face but she went on working. 'I would suggest,' he continued, 'that you have a roll-call of all your staff.'

'Being done already,' said the male nurse.

Molony added that two of their regular surgeons were on the way over.

'I fear they can be of little help now.' Bond moved forward a pace. 'You'll have new security people here any minute. I don't suppose any of you know the number of the ambulance that was outside?'

The male nurse rattled off the registration number, and Bond thanked him. 'I don't know which way they went, but I'll circulate the number. I think they used it as a fast getaway vehicle. I'm on my way now, Sir James. I'd advise you to keep that other fellow as close as you can. This could well have been an attempt to release him and do away with Trilby at the same time.'

Molony nodded. 'From the look of things, your colleagues surprised them.'

Could be, Bond thought. Could be, if they did not help the bogus relatives who had to be members of the Meek Ones.

Two lorries, three cars and an ambulance drew into the forecourt as Bond left the building. A red-faced RAF regiment officer, with drawn pistol, challenged him, only clearing him when he had both inspected his ID and made a telephone call to the priority number of the HQ in Regent's Park.

The cleaning-up went on as Bond walked to his Bentley. Already he had given the number of the ambulance to the senior plainclothes policeman who arrived, somewhat full of himself, while the RAF Regiment Squadron Leader had been finally clearing 007.

He thought of the ambulance now, and took a moment to inspect the ground around the white-marked place where it had been parked. As he approached, his foot hit something on the ground – the keys to the Bentley. There was something attached to the key ring. He picked it up to see a small stick-pin had been pushed into the ring. The pin bore a small black marker at the blunt end. On the marker, neatly engraved and almost too small for the naked eye to read, were three letters. *IRS*.

So, he considered, Harriett could well have been trying to leave some kind of message. He still took no chances, opening the doors, and starting the Bentley with the remote control unit always kept in his back pocket, and making sure nothing odd was fitted to the underside of the car.

Bond only climbed into the driving seat when he was quite satisfied that all was safe, and he did not attempt to use the radio until he had gone a good three miles. Only then did he call up the Regent's Park HQ control.

He passed on the important information first – details of the ambulance, which he was now certain had been used for the getaway; then a quick rundown on the number of casualties, and his opinion on what should be provided at the clinic in the way of a new official Service security. He asked for any information regarding the ambulance to be patched through to him, then made a final request.

'With respect, I ask permission to use *Scatter* immediately.'

There was a long silence at the distant end, and he knew the duty controller would be running a finger down the long list of special ciphers. He also knew that under the word *Scatter* the man would find eleven words – *Permission for use of Scatter to be obtained from CSS only*. Which meant nobody in the radio control room would know what *Scatter* was – even once M had given, or withheld, permission.

Only M, his Chief of Staff and half a dozen senior officers, with need-to-know, could identify *Scatter*, for it was the deepest hiding place the Service kept in London. So secret that it was used mainly for highly furtive meetings between M and officers working under cover. By requesting its use, Bond knew he would be safe from the Meek Ones – who would certainly be after him – for a breathing space. He also knew that, by nightfall, M would visit him, and he had much to talk about with his Chief.

Bond wound his way across country until he reached the M4 – which would provide him easiest access to *Scatter*. Somewhere east of the Heathrow Airport exit, the radio crackled into life again.

'Oddball to Predator. Come in Predator.'

Bond went through his normal radio routine, and back came the answer. 'Predator, ambulance about which you passed information earlier has been found abandoned near Byfleet, on a remote stretch of road. Marks indicate that car was waiting for changeover. Also there are signs of a struggle. Out.'

He acknowledged. Perhaps he had been too hard, after all, on Harriett and Pearly – or at least one of them. The rising hot blood in his body left him in no doubt that he hoped it was Harriett who could be vindicated. Then the chill thought struck him – if she was still alive. The Meek Ones, should they run true to form, were unlikely to let anyone live who had shown themselves to be active enemies.

He came in past Olympia, heading for *Scatter*.

At the Kensington High Street end of the Earls Court Road, there is a narrow cul de sac which leads into a small, beautiful square. A large laburnum bush stands in the centre, and three sides of the square are lined by rows of narrow, three-storey Georgian terraced houses. The safe house known as *Scatter* is the last house at the south-western corner. It is painted cream, with a grey door and similar coloured window frames. There are window boxes outside the two windows on the second and top floors which become a blaze of colour by mid-summer. Only when you get close do you notice the metal grilles built into the windows, but these are not out of place. It is mainly people of means who live in the square, and there are elaborate security precautions taken with all the houses – large red alarm boxes are visible on most, and burglar-proof devices litter the window frames at ground level.

He parked the car in the space provided by the Borough of Kensington and Chelsea, switched off the radio, activated the car's alarm and climbed out.

Scatter's house-minder is a Mrs Madeleine Findlay, the daughter of an old colleague of M's, and one of the few attractive women Bond found oblivious to his charm – which he had tried, to no avail, many times. She was, to use M's words, 'More silent than the grave. I doubt if she will even have a headstone carved in her own name.'

She opened up immediately and ushered him in.

'There's trouble,' she began.

'Don't I know it.' Bond sank into a chair, set so that he could view the entire little square through the thick net curtains.

'I doubt if you do, sir.' Already she had a light raincoat on and was preparing to leave. Mrs Findlay was always ready to leave when *Scatter* was in use. Only M appeared to know where she went, and how to get her back.

'Oh?'

'He says will you call him immediately. On the scrambler. The keys are on the table, as you can see, the alarms are deactivated, as are the *son et lumière* devices,' by which she meant the facilities installed to steal both conversation and video recordings. 'I'll be off now.' She gave him a tiny flash of a smile, and was gone, walking across the square with long, attractive strides – all woman.

There were two telephones on the ledge of a bookcase near the window. They looked identical, but the few people who had access to *Scatter* knew that the right-hand instrument was a direct scrambler line to M. James Bond dialled.

The distant instrument rang twice before M answered, and they both went through the routine establishing codes.

'Glad you got in.' M sounded subdued.

'The clinic's like an abattoir.'

'Not the only place, I fear.'

'Oh, no?'

'I'm afraid it's "Oh, yes".'

'Where?'

'Chichester. Near the cathedral. Local Labour Party candidate had a former Labour Prime Minister there.' M gave the name.

'Killed?' Bond felt the shock even more, coming on top of what he had seen and heard in the last hours.

'Both of them, and over thirty people in the crowd. Another forty injured.'

'Same MO?'

'We think so. Bailey's here with me now. Watch the television, get some rest. I shall be over shortly.

The line was closed abruptly, and Bond crossed to the big colour television on the far side of the room. All four channels had live broadcasts coming from the scene of this latest disaster. He could make out the cathedral, seemingly in the background amidst desolation, very similar to that in Glastonbury the evening before. The Meek Ones had struck again. If it went on, people would stay clear of the hustings. The General Election would become a farce, which was just what the Meek Ones wanted – or, perhaps, whoever had paid for their work had demanded.

The cameras roamed over the scene of destruction, only too familiar in these days when terror stalked in many guises. Then, one camera picked up the police helping to get traffic through a particularly badly congested area.

A large Audi was being held up while a truck passed through, its sides nearly scraping debris. The camera held, for a moment, on the Audi.

At first, Bond did not see it, then his eyes caught the face of the passenger in the front seat. There was no doubt as to who it was, for he had studied the photographs with care. There, smiling at his own handiwork, was Father Valentine himself, and in the back, squashed between two heavy-set men, he caught a glimpse of a chalk-white frightened face. Harriett Horner was being held in Scorpius' own car.

He was just able to catch enough of the registration number to memorise it, and even with his almost legendary ability to hold numbers in his head for years, Bond found himself repeating it over and over as he reached for the telephone and started to dial.

14

Lures and Smart Cards

M arrived after dark. Bond did not even look at the clock – time had lost its meaning with the horror played, almost constantly, on the television. He kept having to remind himself that this was real, not something imagined by a scriptwriter.

M looked old and haggard. Bond could not recall a time when his old chief moved and talked like this – a man suddenly bereft of vigour, so that he appeared to have pain in every joint, and difficulty with each word he spoke.

He said he had not come alone. 'I thought it better to be watched. There's one team in the High Street and another in the Earls Court Road, but none of them know exactly where I am. Bailey is on the corner of the square. I thought it safe to let him come.'

'Is anyone safe, now?' Bond took M's coat and poured him a stiff whisky, which he tossed back in one and then put his glass forward for another. This time, Bond made it a smaller measure.

When they were settled, Bond began to talk – setting out his theory built from the strange drug-assisted interrogation of the man who called himself Ahmed el Kadar – and Joseph in death.

M became very silent, and when the explanation was over he looked up at Bond with eyes that seemed to mirror every Arctic waste, cold sea, or ice-pack in the world. 'And you believe this?'

'It seems to be the only explanation.'

'That a man would hire out people, willing to die at his say-so, acting as human bombs?'

'I presume that's what happened in Chichester, and it certainly occurred in Glastonbury. We all saw it.'

M nodded. 'Yes. Chichester was the same. A young woman. The attacks take place in the open, so there's no way of screening the crowd. Bailey's been with the Head of Branch and the Metropolitan Commissioner. They've all agreed on an attempt at some form of crowd control during election walkabouts, but that can never be one hundred per cent safe. James, how in the name of heaven do we end it?'

'I've no idea, sir. Scorpius, or Valentine or whatever we're going to call him, appears to have set in motion a complete, self-perpetuating killing machine. Reading between the lines on the interrogation of el Kadar, the Meek Ones live in purity for Scorpius' own satisfaction. The whole basis of a pure, unsullied, moral line is to avoid any sexually transmitted diseases, and to form close unions, one man to one woman. Thinking back, that's another of the Meek One's dogmas – no divorce, and that makes admirable sense. Once a couple have produced a child, one of the parents, at least, can offer themselves to this revolutionary zeal and kill themselves for the cause, knowing they will have left behind another child who, in due course, can do the same thing.'

'Death without end, Amen.'

'Quite, sir. They believe they're dying for some great and higher purpose. They will attain paradise and in the end the world will become a paradise of its own. If Scorpius has this knack – this charisma – this fervour and ability to make people believe him, then he's home and dry. There are plenty of bidders in the world of terrorism who can raise funds, and pay huge amounts of money for one act or a whole campaign of terror.'

'Unless he's stopped now – and quickly – Lord knows what will happen.' M looked as though the load was too heavy for him to carry. He sighed, and continued. His weariness was that of a man near the end of his tether. 'For one thing, we'll be forced to take unpleasant restrictive measures to limit a campaign. No public meetings without a close inspection of every single person who attends; theatres; restaurants; football matches. A whole way of life and freedom ending.'

'Then you do believe it's a campaign, sir?'

'Oh, it's a campaign without doubt. Terror, and things you don't know about as yet. Either the Meek Ones are mounting their own campaign to demoralise the Election, or their leader is being paid handsomely to do it on behalf of others.'

'Nobody's yet put me in the picture regarding *Earthquake*.'

'*Earthquake?*' as though he did not even understand.

'It was the signal I received on the way to the Surrey clinic, sir. Remember, you put a team over at Manderson Hall, Pangbourne, to duplicate what I was supposed to do.'

'Oh, that. Yes, it is one of the facts you don't know about as yet. We've got six members of the Meek Ones. They're being held in custody on drugs charges. Gives us a chance to interrogate them.'

'Meek Ones on drugs charges?'

M gave a long series of little nods. 'I put a team of watchers, and a couple of Bill Tanner's hoods, to eyeball the place from four in the morning. Bailey lent me a pair of his plainclothes men as well. They saw this little group approach at first light. Four men and two women. They were armed, and ready to die. A couple of shots were fired when the team went in – about nine o'clock. It looked as if they were ready for somebody, though they denied it. Said they'd come back for things left behind.'

'Pearlman was supposed to have gone through the place with a fine toothcomb!'

'Well, he missed out. There are a dozen attics at the top of the house – old servants' quarters, but converted into bedrooms. Under one of the beds the team found a trapdoor. It led to a treasure trove for the drugs squad – heroin, coke, you name it, they had it.'

'Part of the Meek Ones' dogma is no alcohol and no drugs.'

'The impression we're getting is that it was not for personal consumption. One of the girls admits to having brought in loads of the muck. The theory is that it was to be used later – a back-up to be distributed free of charge to members of the Armed Services. Like the VC did to the US personnel in Nam.'

'What else don't I know about?'

M paused for a few seconds, and looked at his wristwatch. 'All in good time, James. Someone else is being brought here. We have a second – maybe a third – lead.'

'Nothing on the Audi in which I saw him? Saw Scorpius, and the IRS girl?'

'We have the police on alert. You got the number right, we ran through the tape ourselves. I should imagine every copper in the country has his eyes skinned for that vehicle. But, James,' M seemed to have become avuncular, usually he only called Bond by his first name when a deniable instruction was coming up. This time, the telltale brusqueness was not there in his voice. 'James,' he repeated, 'even if we get this man Scorpius, how can we be certain we can destroy the whole evil nest he's created?'

'We can't. Not until every last one of them – every man, woman and child – is brought to book. Death is too good for Scorpius – anyway I don't believe this eye for an eye business. *You* know that. I've been in the game too long, and there's something particularly vile about snuffing out life, if there's another way.'

'Often there *is* no other way.' M appeared more calm and in control now. 'I would say there's probably no other way as far as Scorpius is concerned. His followers? Well, they're a different matter.'

'You realise, sir, that even if we can get Scorpius – and get him alive – there might be no way to stop his present operation. By now most of the major public appearances of all target politicians during this Election are set. Every newspaper in the country'll have lists. Anyone can get their hands on the itineraries . . .'

'We've forestalled some of it,' M cut in quickly. 'The most important public functions have been shifted around. Heads of C13, C7, D11 – the whole shooting match, if you'll pardon the pun – were called in to COBRA. Alterations have been made across the board. The two major political parties have agreed. Different places on different days, and at different times. It's a start, but only a start. Anyone already rolling, on Scorpius' orders, will follow through, I should imagine. The Meek Ones aren't idiots, but they all fall into a particularly vulnerable psychological pattern.'

'Such as?' Bond had already thought about this. It fascinated him.

'Such as people with political or religious ambivalence – those not satisfied with the norm. People who want more from religion. The have-nots who believe it's either the current political ideologies – left and right – that have caused their plight, or the ones who blame it on God. A new ideal, and a new God, gives them a fresh hope. The business about actually being in at the beginning of it all. Dying for the cause that will do away with their previous predicaments – well, that's heady stuff for folk with chips on their shoulders.'

True enough, Bond thought. So that was what COBRA had been up to – reorganising the election schedule, and getting a lecture from some tame Whitehall shrink. The silence grew between them.

After some three minutes, M spoke again – 'I would presume that you consider Scorpius is a sane man?'

'Without doubt.' What was he after now, Bond wondered? 'Evil. A skilled illegal arms dealer. A man with incredible personal magnetism, and a huge financial motive, yes. Sane, yes.'

'Mmm.' M nodded agreement. 'Taking yourself as a sane man, Bond,' he had dropped the 'James' and was holding out his glass, tapping it for a refill, 'taking yourself as a sane man, put yourself in Scorpius' shoes. You've proved this great power. You've got one massive contract – to completely disrupt the British General Election, possibly even more than that – and the promise of an even larger job if this one works. Say, a similar disruption in the United States, during their next Presidential Election. What would you do? If you'd set things in motion; given all the instructions; what would you do?'

Bond had no hesitation. 'Get out,' he said, quietly. 'Get out, and as far away from the British Isles as I could. Then sit and wait.'

'Precisely. That's COBRA's reading as well. We've had alerts out at every port and airport – though I think me lad-o is too clever to go out via a normal route. He's probably got some nice safe exit already arranged.'

'Just as he's got someone in a prime position to inform him of exactly what we're up to.'

'You still believe that?'

'It's obvious, sir. More obvious than ever when you consider the sleight-of-hand we've tried to get away with. My prime suspects have always been the SAS man, Pearlman, and the American IRS girl. But there could be more than one. Somebody – whichever way you look at it – is one step in front of us.' He ticked the already well-worn items off on his fingers. 'One, somebody knew as soon as I was called down from Hereford after Emma Dupré's body was found. Two, Trilby Shrivenham turns up with all that muddled riddle, yet we still don't know what the score is. Three, they know exactly where we've put the IRS girl. Four, I tell both Pearlman and the girl that we're going off to Manderson Hall, last refuge of the Meek Ones in this country, when we were really going down to Surrey to interrogate their man caught in the Kilburn thing. I could swear that it put Pearlman and Harriett on edge, but what happens? Massacre. A foiled attempt at killing the Shrivenham girl, and pulling their own man out. Somehow they managed to cover both ends – the business at Manderson Hall, where everyone thought we were going – the *Earthquake* team – and the massacre at the Surrey Clinic. *Someone* had to know. Someone *had* to inform on us. We should be out searching for him now.'

'Witch-hunts rarely help. But, yes, I should imagine you're right – in a limited sense. Pearlman seems the most probable suspect. You say nobody followed you to the Kilburn house; you're also sure Pearlman showed surprise at the change of plans. But what if he was simply the stalking horse? The odd clandestine call from him and they get some information; a really good team working on *his* back. You would all have been followed to Surrey. Or, better still, the trio visiting the Shrivenham girl get a message. You thought of that?'

'Can we check?'

M reached for the telephone, dialled, and started a long, low conversation, during which Bond tried to readjust, to reassemble the logic of the thing.

At last M put the telephone down and stared at Bond. 'Should've thought of that sooner. The one posing as the Shrivenham girl's brother took a private call about fifteen minutes before you arrived. The poor fellow on Reception logged it, and nobody thought of filleting the record.'

Bond had just about crystallised his thoughts. He opened his mouth to speak, when the telephone rang again. Three times, then stop. Another twice, and stop. On the third set of rings, M picked up. There was another low-key conversation. When he put the instrument down this time, M glared at Bond. 'They've found the Audi,' he said without either exuberance or enthusiasm. 'In a ditch, covered with bits of tree and leaves. Just off a B road in Kent. Really out of the way. Only it's five miles from an old landing field.'

'When?' Bond asked, meaning when had the car been found.

'Accidentally, about an hour ago. Shouldn't really have been discovered for a day or two. Road's not much used, but some farmer with too much drink in him was on auto-pilot, sneaking home. Went a shade too far to the left and dented his nice Range Rover. Not badly, but enough to get the local garage out to pull him from the ditch. Pure good luck. The local bobby was filling up his Panda when the call came in. He went along.'

'And the airfield?'

M nodded sadly. 'You've got it, 007. A plane in the night. Unusual around there. Place is just a single airstrip. No buildings. No control. No night flying, though the runway's in reasonable condition. Wartime, of course. Used to be a satellite field for Manston. Still is, in a way. Some local flying school uses it for their pupils to practise rollers.' He meant roller landings, what in wartime the Royal Air Force referred to as 'circuits and bumps'.

'And something went out of there tonight?'

M nodded. 'Again convenient. Member of the local club lives just the other side of the place. Late afternoon a nice little Piper Comanche – twin engined . . .'

'Seats six at a pinch.'

'This one did. Anyway, getting dusk and it comes in with one engine out. Our flying club man trots out to see if he can give a hand. Says the pilot's a nice guy. Off to France. Engine problem. Needs some spare. Borrows the club man's phone. Calls somebody to bring over a spare first thing, and refuses food and shelter. "Have to stay with the aircraft," all that kind of thing. Then, tonight, off she goes. Flying club fellow almost has a heart attack. Must have taken off blind.'

'So he's gone.'

'That's what I'd say. You?'

'Quite likely.' Bond continued. He had thought the whole thing through, and his conclusions were worrying. 'What if Emma Dupré was allowed to get away?' he asked. 'And what if my telephone number was planted?'

M cocked an eyebrow, as though he had already made up his mind that Bond's theory – whatever it was – consisted of garbage. 'Go on,' he said, though behind the instruction you could hear that he was dubious.

To start with, the thing Bond could not get into his head was the 'why me?' factor. 'I've puzzled for a long time about why I was picked up by a belligerent surveillance team on the way down to London. It's really only just struck me.'

He said that, if Emma had been intentionally allowed loose, with the telephone number in her Filofax, it could only be for one reason. 'If Scorpius and those working with his Meek Ones were about to start this horrifying campaign, they needed to be sure of information reaching them from the inside. They needed to be one step ahead of any action that was taken. Therefore, sir, Emma's Filofax, with its one telephone number, was a personal lure – that's been clear all along. She might not even have been meant to die. But she did. To Scorpius it didn't matter either way. Once my number was identified I would become involved. If I am lured to be involved, then our Service would be involved. Add those together and the algebra's easy. It all equals a penetration agent – one who can report straight back to Scorpius, or his nominee – who is close to our Service, or can become close to it and me – or whoever's on the operation. QED. As m'tutor used to say, "Quite Easily Done."'

'There's sense in it, I'll admit,' M scowled. He had been glancing constantly at his watch as Bond spoke. 'Scorpius had to lure us in, because he had someone close. Someone with your ear or, come to that, my ear.'

'Either, or someone who could easily gain access to us.'

'Mmm,' M grunted. He was becoming agitated about the time. He rose and went to the window, cautioning Bond to switch off the two small 'student' lamps, throwing their soft greenish light over the room.

M twitched carefully at the curtain, taking a peek outside, standing very still for a moment. Then – 'Ah, at last.'

There was the sound of a car parking outside. M told him to hold the lights until their visitor was inside, then he went to the door. There were quiet voices, and the shuffling of feet. 'Right, let there be light.' M was being melodramatic about the whole thing.

There, just inside the doorway, was Bill Tanner. By the arm he held the delicious Ann Reilly, known throughout the Service as Q'ute. Her eyes were covered by a tight black bandage.

'You can take it off now, my dear,' M purred. 'Ms Reilly isn't in the magic circle which has need-to-know of this place. Hence the cloak and dagger stuff.'

Q'ute blinked, allowing her eyes to become accustomed to the subdued light. 'Hallo, James,' she said brightly. 'I should have known it was you I had to brief. Who else would be so hidden away where no passionate young girl can find him?'

'Just take a seat, and get on with the explanation,' M told her.

They sat close, on two high-backed leather chairs and a small settee. From her bag, Q'ute drew one of the *Avante Carte* pieces of plastic. 'We haven't completed testing it yet,' she began, 'but, so far, this innocent-looking thing appears to have the powers of a sorcerer.'

She then launched into a long lecture about 'Smart Cards' and the way they worked – magnetic strips built into the cards that would pour information into a particular type of computer workstation and so glean more information – shown up on the workstation screen – from larger databanks.

A lot of what she said was highly technical, and dealt mainly with the type of credit card that allowed you to draw fixed amounts of money from a bank dispensing machine – spitting your card out if you did not have the funds to meet the amount.

'You know, of course,' she went on, 'that certain cards will do more than just get you a few pounds when the bank's closed. They will give you an update on the status of your account, and, in certain cases, you can also put money into your account by using the card.'

She paused, holding the *Avante Carte* between thumb and index finger. 'This little beauty is different. This one here belonged to Trilby Shrivenham, and we'll be taking it apart tomorrow. We've dismantled the Emma Dupré card, and that's already given up a lot of secrets. The so-called *Avante Carte* is probably the most sophisticated smart card I've ever come across.

'You see, not only does it contain magnetic strips, but also tiny slivers of memory – what the computer people call ROM – Read Only Memory, and also RAM – Random Access Memory. This means that the card will act as a small computer. It can be especially programmed to do a specific job, and its most sinister feature is an input-output chip.'

She could see M's eyes starting to glaze – and he had already heard it all – so she quickly came to the point. 'I'll just tell you the tasks that this card *can* do. Whether it is designed to do them we have yet to discover. First, simply by inserting it into an electronic cash dispensing machine, and keying in a sequence of numbers you can make it gain the attention of the mainframe computers of all known British clearing banks. Think what that means. You can talk to the records of all the major British banks.

'In turn, it means that you can by-pass those records, and manipulate them. The most obvious criminal aspect is that, in theory, if your card is correctly programmed by a master computer, and if you know a wealthy institution's account numbers, it is possible to remove money, electronically – through a cash dispenser – from the wealthy account to your own, or another designated account. The rest is obvious.'

'You mean you can bankrupt someone, or make yourself a millionaire for a day.'

'Probably for long enough to get your hands on the cash.' She flicked the card with a manicured fingernail. 'This is a very dirty piece of electronics, James. Its criminal and intelligence potential is enormous.'

'So, what's it been used for to date?' Bond asked, and Q'ute gave M an 'am I allowed to tell him?' look. M nodded.

'The interesting thing is that Trilby Shrivenham's card has never been used. But we think *she* has been used – to glean the numbers of her father's main accounts.'

'They've been pinching Lord Shrivenham's cash?'

'Not quite, James.' Bill Tanner spoke for the first time. 'Quite the opposite. By one of those odd coincidences that rarely happen in fiction but often do in real life, old Basil Shrivenham took a look at a deposit account that's been sitting idle for a couple of years. Just sitting there collecting interest. Not huge, but not to be sneezed at. In fact it's an account earmarked in his will for Trilby herself. This morning he asked for the balance – which should have been around £200,000. When he heard what was there he asked them to recheck it. They did, and it was accurate. An account which should show a couple of hundred grand, now contains nearly three million, sterling.'

'And it's all been put in within the last week, electronically,' M added. 'You see the point, Bond?'

He nodded. 'Yes, someone, if it becomes necessary, will move that money into an even more sensitive account. It will become some sort of well-hidden slush fund for Shrivenham's political party.'

'That's it, 007. On the button. And at the right moment, the press – at least the gutter press – will get true copies of bank statements, and copies of various electronic transactions. The present government, trying to gain yet another term of power, will be involved in a British version of Watergate.'

'But with everything else going for them . . .' Bond blurted, then caught M's eye and closed his mouth.

They continued to talk for another hour or so, after which M said it was time to go. Q'ute was blindfolded again, and led out to the car by Bill Tanner, while M loitered in the house. 'What I want you to do, is to lie low, here, tonight. At least you'll be safe.' He lowered his voice again, as though there was still a chance of their being overheard. 'Tomorrow's another day. I have most of the European services – those I can trust anyway – on the *qui vive* for friend Scorpius. I would hope to have more information by the afternoon. Call me at two minutes past the hour, every hour after midday. I hope to be able to point you towards Scorpius by then.' He gave Bond a sidelong look. 'Of course, if you get any new leads yourself, don't hesitate. Follow up. Try to let us know. But remember, James, I want this business settled no matter what it costs, and it's up to you. Keep it in mind. The rule of law, and every Englishman's way of life rests on our success, as, I suspect, do a very large number of innocent lives.'

When Bond was left alone, he went into the long narrow kitchen, cooked himself an *omelette aux fines herbes*, which he washed down with a reasonable bottle of Chablis – though, with some amusement, he realised that the good Mrs Findlay probably got her wine, for the house, in bulk from a supermarket. Nothing wrong with that, he said to himself, though it would have been nice if someone had warned him. Constant exposure to that kind of bottle could damage the palate.

Finally he checked all the locks and alarms, took a shower and climbed into the large double bed which was the centrepiece of the main bedroom. Desperately tired though he was, Bond lay on his back for a while, turning the day's events over in his mind before sliding into a deep and easy sleep.

Bond did not know what woke him, but his eyes snapped open, and he moved, as though in sleep, to slip his hand under the pillow for the pistol he had placed there on going to bed. He could see the red glow of the clock alarm reading out the time – 05.11.

Then he froze. The pistol was not there and he knew that, against all possibilities, there was someone else in the room.

Slowly he moved his legs, positioning himself to spring once his eyes had adjusted to the darkness. But he was too late. With no warning, a rough hand clamped itself over his mouth, the fingers splayed to hold his head down, and a body stretched hard over his thighs, making any further movement impossible. The assailant was immensely strong.

He felt warm breath near to his ear, then the whisper – 'Sorry about this, boss, but it's the only way. I can save you a lot of distress.' There was no need for any further explanation. Bond's intuition had been right. The cold muzzle of his own automatic pistol was pressed hard against his temple. For a second, he thought Pearlman was going to finish it all there and then.

Pearly Pearlman reached over and snapped on the light, still holding Bond down on the bed. 'Good morning, boss,' he said. 'We're going for a little journey, but you won't need much in the way of clothes. Also I have to tell you a story. For the good of your soul.'

15

Being Young and Foolish

Under the wicked eye of the ASP automatic, Bond dressed, angry that he could not even shower or shave. Pearlman – clad in night gear: black jeans, rollneck, hood, trainers – said time was short. 'I've got to get you out of here before any of your own blokes latch on. Anyway, you're as slippery as an eel, Mr Bond – if you'll forgive the simile. I don't intend to offer you any chances. Lord knows what you'd do if I let you take a shower. I know a lot about this place, but maybe not everything. It could be booby-trapped. I'm sure you appreciate that I can't take the risk. More 'n my job's worth, so to speak.'

As he put on the clothes, neatly folded, or hung in the fitted closet before he had gone to bed, Bond's mind began to search for a way out. All over the house there were alarm buttons which, if touched, would alert the Regent's Park Duty Officer. Even if he got to one of these, he knew there would be an unavoidable time-lag before anyone arrived. At HQ, the signal would come up on a VDU, flashing the word *Scatter*. The DO would then have to contact one of the very few people who knew the location of this most highly classified safe house.

Pearlman was handling the situation with the natural caution of a very well-trained man. At the order for Bond to get dressed, he leaped back, putting distance between them. *Never stand close to a person you control with a gun*, they taught. Rightly so, for there are a dozen ways to disarm someone with a hand gun should they be foolish enough to stay close to you.

'Fingers laced and hands on the head.' Pearlman did not miss a trick. 'Now, press down, elbows tucked in. You know the drill, boss. You go downstairs, real quietly. If you fall, or pretend to fall, you're dead and I'm not kidding. I wouldn't like it, either, because you're the best bit of collateral that's come my way in a long time. Okay, let's go.'

There were no alternatives. You could hear the genuine menace in Pearlman's words. Bond had no doubt that a slip – accidental or calculated – would mean a shroud and, if he was lucky, a few lines in the obit columns of *The Times*.

He went along the passage and down the narrow stairs as though walking on eggs. At the foot of the staircase, Pearlman spoke again, 'Stand still, boss. Good. Now, when I say "go" you walk very slowly into that nice sitting room.' He was making certain his quarry could

not stray from his line of vision. A couple of seconds later Bond heard
him say, 'Go.'

'Keep the hands on your head, fingers laced . . . Now walk slowly
to the chair by the bookcase . . . Good . . . Now, turn around and sit
down. And please don't do anything stupid. It wouldn't help anyhow,
because all the alarms are deactivated.'

They now sat at opposite ends of the room. Bond still with hands
on head and fingers laced; Pearlman with the pistol very steady, his
finger tight on the trigger.

'How did you get in, Pearly, let alone dismantle the alarm system?'

'Questions, questions. No, boss, you don't get me to boast to you.
How would you have done it?'

'I still don't know how you *found* me, and how you got in is a miracle.
This house is kept as close as skin to flesh.'

'All in good time. First, *I've* a story to tell. I read a book once, where
someone in the intelligence game said just that, and when he'd finished
the telling of it, the lives of those who listened changed dramatically.
I think you'll find the same'll happen with this story.'

'Tell me, then.'

'We've both seen a lot of life and a lot of death, right?'

Bond nodded as Pearlman continued – 'Violent, horrible deaths.
This is a bloody time for the world. Like the Bible says, there's a time
for living and a time for dying. We live in an age when it's a time for
dying – suddenly, most often by war, or the hands of terrorists striking
in the streets. It's like people such as us were born to die that way.'

Bond nodded agreement.

'I find it obscene. Horrible. Just like you, right?'

Once more Bond nodded.

'Okay. There's a song my Mum used to sing. She died when I was
twelve, and the Old Man never got over it. Cashed in his own ticket
on the train of life a couple of years later. Taught it by my Grandma
she was – the song, I mean. Later I got to know it was a poem really
– "Down by the Salley Gardens". Part of it suits me and my story. It
goes –

> "She bid me take love easy, as the leaves grow on the tree;
> But I, being young and foolish, with her would not agree.
> In a field by the river my love and I did stand,
> And on my leaning shoulder she laid her snow-white hand.
> She bid me take life easy, as the grass grows on the weirs;
> But I was young and foolish, and now am full of tears."'

He hesitated, as though Yeats' poem genuinely moved him. 'Senti-
mental, is it, boss? Maybe. But I *was* young and foolish, and there *was*
a girl. All my life, I've had discipline, boss. Became a boy soldier at

fifteen, and spent my leaves with my grandparents, though the Army was father, mother, brothers and sisters to me. But there was this girl. Nearly twenty years ago now. We was going to be married. But I got posted abroad – one of those sudden things, you know. Telegram recalling you off leave. Radio silence, so to speak. We was still giving away bits of the empire in those days, and there was a lot of policing to do, if you know what I mean.' He gave a wry smile and winked at Bond. 'Any old how, I didn't hear from my girl. I wrote. Wrote to her parents. Nothing, not till I got home and found she'd had my baby, and died of it. Maudlin stuff, eh, Mr Bond? Kind of woman's love story stuff. But I can tell you that hurt more 'n any bullet.'

'I know.' Bond meant it. He knew as well as anyone.

'One thing I swore: I'd always look after the child. And I did. She was mine. I never married, but she was looked after. I paid up and spent all my leave with her – she lived with her grandparents, my poor dead girl's Mum and Dad. Then I did the selection course and got into the SAS. After that, every time I risked my life it was for her. For Ruth. Took my name and all. Ruth Pearlman. Good Jewish girl, boss, and so she was until just over a year ago. I got home on leave and she was gone. Her grandparents were in pieces over it – but what mattered to them was that Ruth had turned her back on her faith, and found a new one. It was even worse than if she'd become a *goyim* – a Christian – a *shiksa*.

'Anyhow, I found out where she'd got to, and went down to see her in that damned great mausoleum, Manderson Hall. Tried to reason with her, naturally, like any father would. But all she could talk about was her new religion – that Valentine, or Scorpius, or whatever you want to call him, really does hold them. Gives them a kind of madness, a fervour. "Got a lot of your faith in it, Dad," she said. "We say *Kaddish* for the dead even." Hu! As if *Kaddish* was all that mattered. I tell you, Mr Bond, I know a fair bit about comparative religions. Read a lot. She thought it was good because in this airy-fairy mishmash of religions they still said *Kaddish*.' He was silent for a moment, eyes ablaze. Bond could not have moved to take action against him even if it were possible.

'*Yisgaddal,*
Veyiskaddash,
Shemay rabbah . . .

She thought that was enough. She was a Meek One. You think they said *Kaddish* for those poor buggers in Glastonbury? Or the ones in Chichester? Or the thing that'll happen, God knows where, today? Will they hell?'

'You know where it's going to be, today, Pearly?'

Pearlman laughed. 'You always had me for one of them, boss, didn't you? I could sense it, from the moment we got involved in the car business – coming down from Hereford – you had me marked. Well, you were right, I suppose. In one way you were right. But, more important, you were wrong. So wrong that I held back from saying anything.'

'That's why you come to me in the night, with my own gun?'

'The only way you'll listen, boss. The only way any of your people'll listen. Yes, I became involved with the Meek Ones, and that murdering Father Valentine who acts as their Son of God made man – that's what he is to them, you know. He's the Messiah to the Meek Ones. What he says goes. Go forth and kill thyselves in a crowd near this politician, or that VIP. They go. Don't look back or you'll be turned into a pillar of salt. And my little Ruth, not quite twenty yet, is the light of this bastard's life. Because she's had a baby – oh, married of course. Their ceremony followed by a trip down the Register Office to make it fully legal. So she's all set to go to the Meek Ones' paradise in a hundred fragments. And, for all my cleverness, there's sod all I can do. If you can't beat 'em, join 'em, eh, boss?'

'That's what they say.'

'When I went down to see her the first time, I got introduced to their God, to our Father, Valentine. He saw me as a likely lad, and I played along. Went down to Pangbourne a couple of times. Then went to the wedding. I couldn't stop it, even though the bloke's a dyed-in-the-wool Marxist at heart. He believes all the Meek Ones stuff because, subconsciously, he sees it as part of the great revolution. That was eleven months ago now, and she's had the baby – I'm a grandfather at thirty-seven, boss. Little boy. Joshua. At least she had the decency to give him a good name. And it was after the wedding that Valentine put the bite on me. "I don't want you to live with us, John," he said. "I know you draw strength from your daughter being one of us, and I see you also believe." I'd played the cards right, see. I'd let them all think I was sold. "I need you in the world," Valentine tells me. "I need you to watch, listen, and report for me. You shall be like the spies the blessed Moses sent to spy out the land of Canaan." Very good, he is. Quotes the Bible, the Koran and a hundred books that might not exist for all I know.'

'Yes?' Bond's arms were tiring, but he did not dare move. He found Pearlman's narrative more interesting than he had expected. There were chinks here that Bond could exploit, lever open and use to advantage.

Pearlman still talked. 'Valentine – Scorpius if you like – told me that when the moment came he would have specific things for me to do. He'd want information. Then, a month or so ago, he gave me a list of people. Just names. Never heard of any of them. I was to let

him know if one of the names became a face up in Bradbury Lines.
Yours did. So I informed on you, and nearly got us both killed. Any
old how, he was well pleased, and I strung along as best I could.
Stupidly I wanted to trap him. I kept him well informed. Right up to
the Glastonbury business, and after. It was only then that I saw what
he was really at, and it worried me sick, boss, because the last time I
was with him – just after little Joshua was born – he told me that a
great opportunity had come up. When it was over, Britain would be
a place fit for heroes. The world would follow in the wake of what was
to happen. He also told me that my little Ruth had probably the most
important part to play in this great thing – this dawning of a new age.
He said I should be proud of what she would do.'

Bond believed every word. Nobody could tell this story without its
being true. 'What happened at the clinic, Pearly?'

'Yesterday? What didn't bloody happen? That American bird –
Harriett – stumbled on the three guys in Trilby's room. There was a
lot of noise coming from in there – not surprising, they were about to
kill her. Harriett opened the door, and they stood like statues. I
knew them all. The whole trio, they're part of Valentine's personal
bodyguard, personal hoodlums if you ask me. Anyhow, they recognised
me, and one of them shouted, "What's going on?" I pretended they'd
been rumbled and they started to get out. Suddenly I saw young
Harriett lift her skirt. She'd only got a damned great snub-nosed Colt
in a thigh holster. Then the shooting began. They were like maniacs
– killed anything that moved, including one of their own. He got in
crossfire on the steps. I had to box clever. Too bloody clever, though.
I caught Harriett, and told her to stay still, but the others thought I'd
given them a little present – which in a way I had, 'cos they'd already
tried to snatch her in Kilburn. They told me to duck out and they
took her with them. I think their car was down the road 'cos they
pinched the ambulance. I'm sorry, boss. She's a good kid, they got
away with her, and that was my fault.'

'So what happened then? And why are you here, Pearly?'

'I had this emergency number, from Valentine. To use if there was
trouble. I legged it out of the clinic, then hid up and telephoned the
number. I was told where you were – this was ten o'clock last night.
They knew exactly where you were. Just like they knew about the
alarm system and the security system. They said it would be easy,
because you would not be watched. The place was so secure, your
Service didn't need to watch you. They've got it all sewn up. But you
figured that, didn't you? They have someone right there, in the heart
of your Service, who might have been working for them a long time.
Whoever it is, he's trusted, and he – or she – gives them each move.'

'Yes, I had thought that. And it's worrying, because it has to be someone I've cared for over a long time. But, Pearly, what are *you* going to do?'

'My orders are to bring you in. Take you to our Father, Valentine.'

'So you're going to do it? I'm to be your hostage for your daughter, Ruth.'

'No. No, I didn't see it like that. I thought that, maybe, the two of us stand more chance of really getting this madman. I want a partnership, boss. Let them think I've brought you along. Mind you, I suspect the great Father Valentine has some plans for you. You and the girl Harriett. They still have her.'

'Maybe it's human sacrifice time.'

'Nothing would surprise me. Will you come – I mean quietly – as my partner not as a hostage?' He paused letting the pistol drop into his lap. 'If I can't get my daughter out of it and make her sane again, I might as well not be around. It's really up to you, boss. I leave it all up to you. See?' He took hold of the ASP by the barrel and offered it, across the room.

Bond let his hands drop from his head, reached forward and took the pistol by the butt. 'So, where do we have to go, Pearly? Where's he hiding?' He checked the gun, and noted the safety was off. Pearlman had meant it. He would have killed if necessary, though he had come for another purpose, to plead for Bond's help – not to save his country, but his daughter.

'A long way from here. He's set all the fuses. Organised his bit of terror, guaranteed to leave England in tatters, with no General Election and Government. It's set, like the fuse on a time bomb – several time bombs. He's not going to be around while it happens. He's long gone, together with those of the faithful that are left. Those who aren't earmarked to die as yet, for his paradise and his bank accounts.'

'Where?' As he asked, so the telephone started to ring. 'I thought you'd fixed the electrics?' He looked from the phone to Pearlman.

'Everything but the telephone. If you don't answer, your people will be here like ferrets down a rabbit hole. Answer it.'

M was at the other end. 'The clinic again,' he said, almost cryptically.

'What about it?'

'Nobody dead as far as we know. But they lifted Trilby, and their man got away.'

'El Kadar? Also known in death as Joseph?'

'The same. No trace of Scorpius, though.'

'I might have.'

'Oh?'

In the background Pearly whispered that they should get going.

'Don't worry if you find me missing.'

'We need you here.' M had caught the clue. Now he gave Bond a chance to offer information.

'A possibility's come up. It's okay. Something that can help in a really big way. Ultra-sensitive.'

'Got you.' M had caught the 'Ultra' which was a plea for a team to watch wherever he went.

'Far?' M asked.

'Wait and see. I'll get back to you.' In plain language, 'Probably. Make sure the team's prepared.'

'What identities?' M referred to the cover documents Bond would still have stashed somewhere safely.

'One and Six.'

'Use One.'

'Right, I'll be in touch,' Bond said closing the line, reasonably secure in the fact that even a small team would be on their tail if he could stall Pearlman for a short time.

He looked back at Pearlman. 'Come and help me pack – only the bare necessities.'

'It really will have to be bare. I was supposed to pick you up and have you running in what you stand up in.'

'Where is Valentine?' Bond asked as they moved up the stairs.

'With around sixty of his flock.'

'Where, Pearly? Or I don't leave here – with you or without you.'

'Okay. We take a Piedmont Airlines flight to Charlotte, North Carolina. Then we go down to a real millionaires' paradise off the coast of South Carolina. It's a perfect hide-away in spite of the well-heeled tourists. Place called Hilton Head Island – hotels, private homes, great beaches, sea birds, golf courses by the dozen, rattlesnakes, alligators and water moccasins. A good mixture.'

'Just the place for friend Valentine/Scorpius. He should be at home with the water moccasins. They're almost as deadly as he is.' The water moccasin, Bond knew, was a highly belligerent snake with a deadly bite. It is also one of the few snakes that will readily eat carrion.

'Perhaps he thinks you'll make a nice meal for them.'

Bond would somehow have to find time to get his hands on the emergency identity. M's instructions were for him to use Number One. That was his standard cover, in the name of Boldman. When the time came to meet Scorpius, he hoped he could live up to the alias.

16

Welcome Night Music

At eleven o'clock that same evening a colourful, though highly controversial trade union leader was leaving a plush working men's club situated in one of the safe Labour Party boroughs of Newcastle-upon-Tyne. The trade union leader had been speaking for – and with – the local Labour Party candidate. They were both happy men. The meeting had gone well. Both the Labour candidate and the trade union leader had successfully put down the very few hecklers in the hall, and, at the end, there was a standing ovation.

Because of the recent emergency orders, the police had thought it a wise precaution to bring both men to their waiting cars at the rear of the building. Fifteen burly constables blocked off the small crowd, forming a human aisle to the first car, though the two men came out together, shaking hands and full of mutual self-congratulations.

They had just got to the union leader's car when a press photographer whispered to one of the policemen – 'Give us a chance, mate. Let's get a picture?' The policeman nodded, and broke ranks for a second. It was his last second on earth.

The photographer, once through the cordon, hurled himself at the two men by the car. There was a sound like a clap of thunder and a massive flash as the photographer exploded himself. All fifteen policemen, the drivers of the two official cars, the union leader and his secretary, the candidate and his agent, plus twelve people nearby were killed instantly. Sixteen others were seriously injured. One died in hospital the following day.

It was six o'clock in the evening for James Bond, who was aboard a Piedmont Airlines Dash 7 STOL aircraft, ex-Charlotte, North Carolina, just coming in on finals at the small airstrip of Hilton Head Island.

Hilton Head is the southernmost point of South Carolina, and the largest of the Sea Islands which stretch along 250 miles of coastline from the Carolinas to Florida. Shaped like a trainer shoe, you can reach it by land, sea and air. By land across the Byrnes Bridge, on Route 278, and by air from Savannah – only forty miles west – Atlanta, Georgia, or Charlotte, North Carolina.

The view from the aircraft reminded Bond of happy days in the Caribbean. Lush grassland; tropical trees and beaches that dazzled, like long stretches of gold; sprawling luxury hotels, and private houses set in wonderful locations. On the way in they passed over three golf courses. The island has a total of fourteen.

At *Scatter*, they had quickly made the decision that Bond was to act the role of Pearlman's prisoner in order to carry out what the SAS man called 'A Wooden Horse Op on Scorpius'. Yet there had been still a great deal of talking to do. Bond was not prepared to go blind into the devil's mouth. So, there followed a long question and answer session, during which Pearlman passed on a great deal of information regarding the Meek Ones in general, and his daughter, Ruth, in particular. He even showed Bond a passport-type photograph of the girl, red-headed, freckled and laughing into the camera. 'She was always laughing,' the SAS man said, with a hint of self-pity. 'Ruth's much more serious now.'

They made coffee and toast, sitting in the main room of the narrow little house talking, with Bond discussing strategy. Outside, the dawn came up, not with the bang of thunder, but with a whimper of cloud and a chilly breeze. Dawn slowly broke into day.

'We'll have to get a shift on.' Pearlman began to get agitated as the time wore on. They went upstairs, and the conversation turned to specifics.

'No way can we go in armed,' Pearlman said, as Bond searched the main bedroom cupboards – finding one of Q'ute's neat overnight-briefcases. There were usually at least two kept in readiness at *Scatter* – large black briefcases to which an extra section could be added, clipped on to the side and fitted with a third combination lock.

'That's the truth.' Bond gave the SAS man a blank look. Q'ute's briefcases were really very special. Not only did they have a foolproof method of screening, for the airport security 'Friskem' machines, but also they contained an undetectable false section large enough to take several of Q Branch's more ingenious items, plus a weapon.

'Must pack my shaving gear.' Bond headed into the bathroom, leaving Pearlman sitting in the bedroom leafing through the latest edition of *Intelligence Quarterly*. Once out of sight, Bond activated the locks to reveal the safe compartment, which had once been checked by no fewer than twenty security officers, none of whom detected the foam-rubber lined secret area. Working quickly, he checked that the weapon was in place – a neat Browning Compact, developed from the FN High-Power to provide a genuine pocket pistol capable of firing full-power 9mm rounds. The other specialist equipment was there also.

He closed the compartment and carefully packed a razor and travel set of *Dunhill Edition* cream shave and cologne – another standard, provided by Mrs Findlay who, as housekeeper, felt her gentlemen should have the best. Unhappily, Bond considered, she was not so meticulous with regard to clothes.

The house had seen many comings and goings, and its walls held the secrets of years. Men and women had been lodged here for varying periods of time and the bedroom wardrobes were divided up for them – skirts and dresses in various sizes; suits and jeans, straight from the peg in Large, Medium or Small.

As for accessories, they appeared to have come from Marks & Spencer, in standard sizes also. In the bedroom, Bond rummaged through the various drawers, providing himself with a couple of changes of underwear, socks, shirts and, with certain reservations, pyjamas. He was unhappy with the texture and lurid colours of the underwear, and almost angry when it came to the socks. He had always sworn he would never wear nylon; now there was no alternative. At least a couple of the shirts would fit. He fussed and grumbled over the lack of sartorial taste shown by the housekeeper.

With some flamboyance, he locked the ASP and his Baton, together with spare ammunition, in a steel-lined box-safe, hidden and bolted to the floor at the rear of the fitted wardrobe.

'Best that way, boss.' Pearlman looked up from his reading. 'Don't want to be nobbled by our own security people on the way out.'

Bond agreed with him, safe in the knowledge that he at least had some hardware at his disposal. In the bathroom he had also taken an extra precaution. Among the items left in the case by Q Branch were several innocent-looking pens. He had taken one of them which he immediately activated as a homing device. Its range was only fifteen miles and he could turn it off when going through airport security, but it would give him an edge during the first phase of the operation.

They left the house together – Pearlman with a blue roll bag; 007 with Q Branch's speciality overnight-briefcase.

Upstairs, Bond had partially drawn one curtain in the main bedroom, leaving what he thought was a rather ugly china vase on the ledge. Later that morning it would be spotted by Mrs Findlay, making her rounds, and she would know it was safe to go back in and file her own report by telephone.

In Kensington High Street, Bond searched for a taxi while Pearlman used a public telephone box – one out of the available three happily remained unvandalised.

'We're all set,' he said once they were settled in the back of the cab. Bond had given the cabbie instructions to go to a branch of Barclays Bank in Oxford Street.

'Later,' he cautioned Pearlman. 'If you could pay off this cab and wait for me, I'll only be a few minutes.'

Pearlman lowered his voice. 'You won't do a runner on me, boss?'

'Don't worry. Just pay off the cab, keep out of sight and wait.'

In Oxford Street, Bond was happy to see a Service watcher show himself in a car that overtook the cab when it stopped. Leaving Pearlman to settle up, he went into the bank, passing a card over the counter to the nearest available teller, who looked at it, and said, 'If you'd like to come to the end of the counter, I'll let you in, sir.'

She unlocked the door which gave entrance to a passage running alongside the manager's office, and led him down a flight of stairs to the vault and deposit boxes. Checking the number on his card she brightly produced a key. Together they went to Box 700. Bond took out his key ring, selected the correct one and inserted it into the right-hand lock, while the bank teller put her master key into the left-hand hole. They turned the keys and the twelve-by-seven-inch door swung back.

'I'll only be a minute.' He slid out the box and carried it into the little, bare private room provided in the deposit-box area. Taking great care he placed everything from his pockets – except money – into an empty thick manila envelope from a pile at the bottom of the metal box. He then slit open one of the bulky envelopes which filled the box. From it he extracted the Boldman passport, cheque-book, a wallet containing credit cards, a small leather notepad with the words James Boldman printed at the bottom of each page, and two crumpled envelopes, open and with letters enclosed. The envelopes were addressed to James Boldman Esq and carried an address which could be proved if anyone went to the trouble of checking. 'Mr Boldman's away at the moment,' they would tell any caller who asked for him.

He distributed the items in various pockets, and added a couple of other things – a Visa slip from HMV Records in the sum of £24.70, and the return half of a first-class ticket for Wembley: part of the address on the envelopes.

The box was returned and locked. All field operatives keep other 'lives' in most major cities within their territory. Bond had similar boxes in Paris, Rome, Vienna, Madrid, Berlin and Copenhagen. He also knew how to get hold of material like this at an hour's notice, in Washington, New York, Miami and Los Angeles.

He was now, to all intents and purposes, Mr James Boldman. Outside, Pearlman loitered, blending into the background. The newly created Boldman glimpsed a cab driver talking to his fare across the road. He knew both faces and stayed happy in the knowledge that there was a team close by.

'Up to you, now, Pearly,' he said.

'Right. Heathrow, I think. We've plenty of time so there's no rush.' Together they hailed another passing cab.

At Heathrow Airport, Pearlman led them to the helicopter shuttle desk – Heathrow-Gatwick. 'We go on the noon flight to Charlotte, North Carolina.' He smiled, a shade too self-satisfied for Bond. Pearlman had already produced their flight tickets for Piedmont Airlines PI161. 'We have seats on the shuttle and can check in here. Should make it in time.' It was eleven o'clock exactly. If Pearlman was anxious to dodge surveillance he was going the right way about it, though Bond knew the team would quickly make their enquiries. Time would be tight, but a second unit might just catch them. After that, he would be off limits and only *sanctioned* Secret Intelligence Service personnel, combined with the CIA, would be able to take over.

They made Gatwick with time to spare, and, as they boarded PI161, Bond was not a little alarmed to see none other than David Wolkovsky himself – the Agency's London resident – with another watcher, behind them in the line-up for boarding. If the Meek Ones knew what he thought they did, Wolkovsky was completely unprotected. Unless, the thought struck home like a poisoned dart, Wolkovsky was the Meek Ones' penetration agent passing on everyone's moves to Scorpius or his lieutenants.

The more Bond thought about it, the less he liked the fact of Wolkovsky being on his back. The Agency's top man in London would have access to most moves – from his own people, the Branch, MI5 and Bond's own Service. He had not thought of the possibility before. Now that particular profile made a great deal of sense.

In the first-class cabin, after take-off, he leaned over and warned Pearlman, 'We might just have a porpoise treading on our tails.'

'Then we move bloody fast at Charlotte. There'll be no hanging around in any case. Give me his number when you can.'

'I'm glad to say that he seems to be travelling steerage, but we'll see.'

Pearlman gave a quick smile. 'There are things you have to know. First, we can relax until we get to Charlotte.' He went on to explain the rest of it. At Charlotte they would take the connecting flight to Hilton Head, and that was where the fun would begin. 'Scorpius'll have someone watching every arrival through today. He'll mark us and call ahead to the island. Your freedom will end there. They'll meet us with a limo. I haven't been there, of course, but I gather he has quite a spread on the north-west side of the island. Used to be a plantation, and it's screened by trees on three sides, the Atlantic Ocean on the fourth. The whole island has security checkpoints and the residents with spreads like Ten Pines Plantation – that's his – have their own security: electronic and live. The checkpoints are manned twenty-four hours, because of the many tourists who go down there. I'm told it's breathtaking, fabulous weather, and hell's own expensive. But plenty of people live on the island as well as those who go vacationing, for the golf tournaments, and conventions. Island paradise they all say.'

The limousine would take them directly to Ten Pines, and their story would be that Bond had come along quietly once Pearly had told him they held Harriett captive.

'I suppose she is there?'

'It's what I've been told. Your reputation is that of a knight in shining armour.' Pearlman gave him a sidelong glance. 'My instructions were to tell you it was not just for your own good, but for Harriett's as well. No harm would come to her. They said you wouldn't resist it. Would you have?'

'Depends. I'm doing it for you and your daughter, Pearly. I'm also coming along because it seems to be the only way of getting close to the devil, and I always reckon if you can get close to the devil you stand a chance of beating him – which is my job. I'm still interested to know why they chose me in particular.'

'It's been you all along. Ever since you were flushed out of Hereford, anyway.' He frowned as though trying to work out by pure logic why indeed it should be Bond. A little later, after they had eaten, he said it was all too possible that Bond would be held prisoner. 'You're not to worry, though. Once I've found out where Ruth is, I'll find a way of springing you – and the Horner bit as well.'

'I would appreciate that, Pearly. Don't fancy being incarcerated by Scorpius for any length of time. One could have a nasty accident as Scorpius' house guest.' Then, as though to himself, 'I wonder if they've taken the Shrivenham girl there as well.'

'Shouldn't be surprised.' Pearlman settled back to watch the in-flight movie. Though he had already seen it, Bond sat through it again. *The Untouchables*. A favourite actor of his played a Chicago cop.

They landed at Charlotte a little after four fifteen, local time. Pearly stayed very close to Bond, usually behind him, his left shoulder close to the right-hand side of Bond's back. They only had time to check in for the flight to Hilton Head, and a short wait in the departure lounge, before being taken out to the comfortable, and quiet, Dash 7 which seemed to get them airborne almost before it started its take-off run. Of Wolkovsky there was no sign.

And now here they were, on finals into the little airport, with the sun slowly turning into a ball of red which would settle into dusk within an hour. Below, the airfield looked ordered and tidy with its neat rows of light private aircraft tethered and chocked, tucked away for the night.

Passengers, waiting to board for the trip to Charlotte, sat in garden chairs outside the little hut that served for the airport Arrivals and Departures lounge, and, as they descended the short steps from the aircraft, Bond easily picked out the reception committee. A uniformed driver standing by a stretch limo that looked as though it could house a football team. Nearer the aircraft were three young men in grey lightweight suits, white shirts and identical ties. As they grew closer, Bond saw that the ties were of navy-blue silk, each bearing an identical logo pattern – the intertwined Greek A and Ω – that was on the *Avante Carte* credit cards.

'Hi, John,' one of the young men greeted Pearlman. He was what Bond had heard a certain class of young, and not-so-young American ladies refer to as a 'hunk' – good looks, good height, muscular, light of hair, and with teeth which seemed to have been polished especially for flashing semaphore, or bending iron bars. The other two men were cast from similar moulds.

'Bob,' Pearlman responded.

'Greetings from the beginning to the end,' all three men chorused, and Pearlman responded with the same words. This was obviously the salutation of the Meek Ones.

'And this,' – the one called Bob, looked hard at Bond – 'this must be the famous Mr Bond.'

'Boldman, if you don't mind.' He gave the young man a hard, icy look as if to say that he was not going to stand for any fooling around. 'James Boldman.'

'Please yourself.' Bob could give back in kind, for his stance now suggested that instead of flesh and bone under the suit, he was made of steel plating. 'Whatever you wish to call yourself, I'm positive our leader, our Father, Valentine, will be delighted to see you.' He turned back to Pearlman. 'He give you any bother?'

'Came like a lamb. Did just as our Father, Valentine, prophesied.'

'Well, he'll be waiting.'

The three men closed around them and Bond felt the overnight briefcase taken skilfully from his hand. Whichever one of them had done it, knew a lot about the persuasive arts for, though it caused no pain, Bond felt him use a particular control pressure on the back of his hand.

They were quickly inside the car. The engine purred into life, and very gently the limo glided forward.

Bond remained silent. Around him, outside the car, you could sense the exclusiveness of this place, with its controlled and ordered wide roads, the wonderful stretches of green which showed between palm, pine and a host of other trees, Spanish moss dripping down towards the verges at one moment, then a small mall of shops giving way to side roads with security barriers. Hotels peeped out at intervals; there were golfers, completing a day's play on some of the distant greens, and the feel of the island was one of rich reward. A place for the lotus eater and the money-maker. As they progressed towards Ten Pines, he realised there was another facet. The island was unreal. Once there, the resident or vacationer might lose all track of time and all sense of the real world. An ideal place for Father Valentine to further corrupt his Meek Ones.

They turned left, went through something that resembled a very large storm drain, and came out of the other side, hemmed in by grassy, manicured banks which gave way to trees. For a second, though there was absolutely no similarity, it reminded Bond of those belts of nurtured forest which flank the roadside after you pass through the Helmstedt checkpoint to drive on the Autobahn through East Germany to the divided, land-locked island that is Berlin. Within those belts of trees soldiers lurked, camouflaged, in hide-outs or watchtowers. He felt now that there was a different breed of soldier within these thick strips of trees which obviously ringed Ten Pines.

They broke from the trees to drive through perfect lawns towards a massive, two-storey structure which looked more like an hotel than a house. It appeared to be circular, built of stone, intermingled with great wooden beams, and topped by an octagonal tower. The whole place was bathed in light, for the day was on the edge of death and night began to close in.

The limo pulled up in front of a great porchway surrounding a pair of high, weathered doors, and the three-man reception party was out of the car and in position, covering it from every possible angle, almost before it stopped.

'Do the honours please, John,' Bob said, and Pearlman quickly frisked Bond.

'He's clean.'

Bob nodded. 'I'm sorry about that, Mr Bond. We couldn't really do it in public at the airport, and you were safe enough in the car. Now we can go in.'

The doors opened onto a semi-circular hall, high-roofed but with no sign of a staircase. A series of doors led from the hall, and two large chandeliers hung, one higher than the other, from the wooden vaulted ceiling. To left and right of the chandeliers, big fans turned lazily to stir cool air. There were no pictures, just plain wood, with varnished and highly polished blocks underfoot.

Pearlman closed in to his now familiar position, just behind Bond's right shoulder. For a second they all just stood, as though waiting for some event. Static seemed to crackle between the trio of bodyguards.

Then, to their left one of the doors opened and a small, slim, bronzed figure walked with two long strides which appeared to bring him into their midst. From the photographs, Bond had thought he was a tall man, but he barely touched five six. The eyes, however, and the voice had a power of their own. The voice was pitched low, gentle, almost a whisper.

'Mr Bond, how nice of you to make such a long trip.' He flicked a look at Pearlman. 'Well done, John. I was sure you wouldn't let me down.' Then to Bond again, 'Welcome to Ten Pines, Mr Bond. As you know, my name is Valentine. The faithful call me their Father, Valentine. Welcome, and greetings from the beginning to the end.'

As he said the last words, so a terrible noise filled the hallway, coming from somewhere deep within this strange building – the sound of a human being in great pain. Bond shuddered, recognising the scream which seemed to rise and fall in appalling intensity.

It could have come only from Harriett Horner.

Valentine cocked his head. 'Ah,' he said, his voice still soft, almost caressing. 'Ah, a little night music to welcome you.'

17

The Prayer Hall

James Bond took one pace forward. The screaming had reached a new pitch, echoing sheer, brutal terror. He tried to take another step and, while nobody attempted to restrain him, he stopped, unable to move, as though paralysed.

He saw Valentine, now leaning against the door, a slight smile on his lips. For a second, as he looked at Valentine's slim face, radiating good health, Bond saw it, again, overlapped by the photograph of Vladimir Scorpius, just as he had seen it in the dossier.

He looked at the ears – Scorpius' ears; then the hair, thinning, yet immaculate – Scorpius' hair; the jawline, once pudgy, now tight skin stretched over minimal flesh – Scorpius' jawline; the cheekbones – Scorpius' cheekbones; and last of all the eyes, *black as night*, old Basil Shrivenham had said. Scorpius' eyes, black as night, and holding Bond immobile.

The eyes glittered, as though fires lay deep within them; behind the irises a worm seemed to move in the fires. The pupils began to enlarge, as though swallowing him. Bond dragged his own eyes away, thrusting into his head a different image of Scorpius – one he pulled from somewhere way down in the darkness of his own subconscious: Scorpius impaled on a dagger, with his own hand, James Bond's hand on the haft which was fashioned like a serpent. *He* held the dagger, and, in the second before plunging it into Scorpius' throat, he was able to look again, and step forward, close to the man.

'Ah.' The smile remained on Scorpius' face, but the eyes had lost their brightness, and it seemed that a twinge of fear showed – there for a tiny moment, then gone. 'Come, Mr James Bond.' The voice remained steady, soft, soothing, 'Let's go and see what that noise was really about. I think you might be quite impressed.'

'I doubt it.'

'Is that the way you repay my hospitality? Doubts? Mr Bond, I really think you have much to learn. Come.' He lifted one hand, fingers splayed – the gesture of a mediaeval prince? Possibly. Then the fingers gave a small beckoning movement. 'Come. All of you come to the Prayer Hall.'

So, Bond thought, this is the true evil. Undeniably Scorpius had a power, held by many great public figures, and often unrecognised by them. Scorpius had been cursed with a strong will, combined with an overdeveloped hypnotic strength. This he probably wielded almost as a reflex by now. The power by itself would only be limited, but invaluable, say, for addressing those who wished to believe in him. With a man or woman of sufficient intelligence, Scorpius would be forced to fall back on other methods – the use of hypnotic drugs, and the like. But his will and mental strength combined to make him a dangerous adversary.

If Scorpius had operated solely on the unsubtle pressures of physical force, or a will to cause panic and fear in those near to him, he would be easier meat. Bond now recognised that the task was greater than he had imagined. He had to pit not only muscle, cunning, and skill against the man, but also mental power.

For a second, as they all stood, poised to follow the beckoning man, he saw complete evil, the ultimate enemy; one who could, by word, deed and warped reason, convince other mortals that obscene and horrific deeds were, in every way, works of goodness, charity and right. In Scorpius' world all morality was turned topsy-turvy. Evil became good. Wrong became right. While that which was good and right became evil and wrong.

It was plain enough in the simple action of following the man to what he called the Prayer Hall. Bond's intuition told him the Prayer Hall was a place to which no right-minded person should go. Yet, in spite of this, he followed.

Through the door, where Scorpius had first appeared as Father Valentine, was a large room, lined with books. A simple desk stood under a window at the far end, but, in spite of the rows of leather-bound spines in the tall bookcases, the whole chamber had about it the feel of austerity. Again, there were no pictures, and no rugs or carpets on the floor.

'Come,' Scorpius repeated, and they passed through the room via a door set between the bookcases to the right. Down an equally bare corridor to a pair of double doors which made Bond think of the interior entrances to stalls or circle in a theatre or cinema.

He was not far wrong; the doors led into a vast amphitheatre, a great crescent-shaped room where tier upon tier of seats rose up from a dais below. There were no windows, only dim lighting hidden in the roof, and like a theatre or cinema the rows of seating were divided by three aisles of steps which ran down to the dais – a platform on which rested a plain wooden table.

There appeared to be about sixty or seventy men and women in the place. Their attention was riveted upon the dais, lit dramatically by two spotlights which accented the inherent bareness of the place. In front of the table was a large, high-backed wooden chair. Two young men, robed like acolytes – their scarlet cassocks providing the only colour to the scene – flanked the chair, facing towards its occupant:

Harriett Horner, who, as Scorpius and his party entered the chamber, let out another piercing series of screams.

She was anchored to the chair by restraining straps of leather around her arms, legs and waist, and, as she screamed, so she struggled against the straps like someone undergoing terrible torture, trapped and unable to escape.

Bond muttered an oath and Scorpius turned on him. 'Have care, Bond. You will see things now that even you might not believe possible. Ms Horner is only going through what most neophytes face when they come here to join this holy society.'

'Unholy society!' Bond spat back. 'She did not come here of her own accord.'

'No? And what of you, James Bond? I suppose you did not make the journey to visit us of *your* own will?'

Bond avoided the man's eyes. 'I came to see you, talk to you and stop the terror you're hell bent on inflicting.'

'Really? How interesting. We shall see why you've really come to the Meek Ones.' He made another gesture, and one of the young men – who were undoubtedly his bodyguards – came forward holding a long white cassock – similar to the soutane worn by the Pope himself. Once he had completed buttoning the garment, Scorpius pulled a wide silk sash into place around his waist, took a white skull-cap from one of the other bodyguards, and began to make his way down the centre aisle of steps leading to the platform below.

A low murmur came from the assembly as he made his progress. They all knelt in front of their seats and the murmur assumed the proportions of a chant – 'Our Father, Valentine. Greetings from the beginning to the end. Our Father, Valentine. Greetings, greetings, greetings. From the beginning to the end we praise our Father, Valentine, giver of paradise, power of good, creator of the new world without end,' and so on, and so on, and so on, until Scorpius reached the dais.

The two acolytes were now kneeling, their faces radiant with some inner ecstasy they appeared to share from the very presence of Scorpius. It sickened Bond even to watch this profane and horribly real manifestation of iniquity.

But Harriett had ceased to scream, and he saw that Scorpius had placed his hands on her head. He raised his own head and began to speak to the girl –

'You have looked into the dark pit, sister?' Scorpius asked.

'I have looked into the dark pit.' Harriett's voice was strong, but unnatural. This, Bond thought, was no simple manifestation of hypnosis. Certainly Scorpius was responsible, but his own, extraordinary power alone had not rendered Harriett into this speaking clock

of a puppet she appeared to have become. A kind of revolting litany
continued between the two.

'You looked into the dark pit which is the world as we now know
it, sister. What did you see?'

'Horrors of corruption. Men, women and children debased by their
own folly and beliefs in material wealth.'

'Was it terrifying to see these people destroying themselves, living
in a false and disgusting world which they fondly imagine to be
paradise?'

'I saw those I knew, labouring under these terrible beliefs. They
cannot be forgiven. They frighten and terrify me.'

'So much so that you screamed in anguish for them?'

'The screams are my prayers that they will see the truth.'

'Will they see the truth and embrace it?'

'Not until a new order is brought by fire and death. Only then will
they understand.' The voice, though that of a robot, became agitated,
rising unnaturally.

'Peace, sister Harriett. Be at peace. You have seen truth. You will
see, and understand more. But now, be at peace.' He turned to face
the entire assembly. 'I have news, my brothers and sisters. Our brother
whose death-name is Philip has earned eternal peace and the reward
of paradise. He has destroyed two important men who walked in the
darkness of their own tainted beliefs. He has brought paradise closer
to us. This act was done in England only an hour or so ago. Yet it has
brought us many years nearer to our own paradise when all men will
walk equal on this earth, when all the earth's bounty will be equally
shared, when we shall all find peace of mind and breathe pure air
without threat of darkness. Praise be to Philip, our brother and a
Meek One who has already found this paradise. Greetings, Philip,
from the beginning to the end.'

Like a great rising moan the assembly joined in, chanting, 'Greetings, Philip, from the beginning to the end,' and as a hush fell over
the chamber, there was the lone, drugged voice of Harriett, rising and
falling, out of control, crying out her greetings to this unknown Philip,
from the beginning to the end.

Scorpius said something quietly to one of the acolytes and they
moved to either side of the chair. Harriett appeared to have slumped
forward, collapsed against the straps, which the young men in red
cassocks unbuckled, helping the girl to her feet and guiding her behind
the table. Scorpius turned to the assembly again, raising his right
hand, the index and middle fingers extended in an obscene imitation
of the Papal blessing.

'I commend you all to whatever pleasures your bodies and souls
have need of this night,' he intoned. 'Soon there will be news of other

victories, and the final work will be started. We expect many new believers to come to this place and join our blessed society. There will be more weddings and many births to set free those of you who cannot yet go forth and give yourselves to paradise. Have patience, your hour will come. Go forth in peace.'

From hidden loudspeakers came the distant sound of music, throbbing, ethereal, electronic music of the kind these young people would find most appealing, yet there was also an hypnotic quality about it.

As the music rose, so a thin mist began to curl from vents in the platform. A dry ice machine, Bond thought. Friend Scorpius has some very good FX people working for him. As he thought it, Scorpius appeared to be enveloped by the mist. The illusion was of a man transported, slowly melting before the eyes of all who watched.

The assembly began to file out. Most were in their early twenties, one or two older – maybe thirty or more – but they took little notice of the three bodyguards, Pearlman and Bond, who suddenly spotted a recognisable face in the crowd. The face in the photograph he had seen in the early hours of that morning, in England. The face of Ruth Pearlman.

Her eyes stared straight ahead, yet, as she approached the group, her pace slowed, as though she had been sleepwalking and was at the moment of waking. Her eyes moved and she looked straight at her father.

She stood stock still, then her freckled face glowed into a delighted smile of recognition. 'Daddy!' She ran towards Pearlman, throwing her arms around his neck. 'Oh, what a lovely surprise. Our Father, Valentine, told me only yesterday that he might have a wonderful gift for me before I went . . .' She stopped, glancing at the other faces, knowing she was on the verge of saying something forbidden. 'Oh, but how lovely.' She hugged her father again and again, until one of the bodyguards gently eased her away.

'It has been arranged that you will have time enough with your parent.' The smooth young thug took her by the shoulders. 'For now, sister, you must go to your quarters. You must meditate, tend to your child. Your hour of glory will come soon enough.'

'What hour . . .?' Pearlman began, then changed his mind, glancing towards Bond who saw, in the other man's eyes, a plea for help.

As Ruth was led away, so the bodyguard called Bob came up behind Bond. 'Father Valentine hopes you will do him the honour of dining with him, in his private suite, this evening. What luggage you have has been taken to the guest suite. One of my men will show you the way. I shall call for you in, shall we say, half an hour. Give you a chance to freshen up and have a word with your fellow guest.'

'Fellow guest?' Bond queried, but Bob had already signalled to one of the other young giants, whom he referred to as Jack.

Jack placed a hand firmly on Bond's forearm. 'This way, Mr Bond. I wouldn't like you to be late for dinner with Father Valentine.' He started to guide his charge from the amphitheatre, but Bond shook himself free.

'Get your hands off me!'

'Gently, Mr Bond, we don't want to cause a scene in this holy place, do we?'

'Just keep your hands to yourself then.'

Jack gave a little mocking bow, and gestured for Bond to go ahead of them. 'I'll tell you when to go left and right, and up stairs. Carry on, Mr Bond.' They began to make a long journey, up stairs and down corridors, with Bond trying to keep a check on the direction they were going. They did not pass through Scorpius' study again, nor go near to the main hall and it took just around eight minutes for them to reach an area which, Bond deduced, was on the ground level, towards the rear of the building.

They passed though a fire door, and suddenly the austere bareness, which seemed to be the hallmark of the interior decor, gave way to unusual magnificence – a long and ornate corridor, lit with intricate, garishly coloured chandeliers which looked Mexican in origin. There was a heavy pile carpet underfoot, and, though the corridor must have stretched for a good forty yards, there were only four doors – two in the left-hand wall, and two to the right – each decorated with false columns and a gilded carved cornice incorporating love knots and cherubs. It all seemed a little much, and quite out of place, Bond thought, then he realised that the decor was as vulgar and repulsive as the real Scorpius. He should not be surprised by anything.

Jack stopped at the second door, tapped on it and opened up. 'The sitting room, sir. There are bedrooms to the left and right. Bathrooms and dressing rooms in the interconnecting passages. I think you'll find everything in order, but should we have forgotten anything, please use the telephone.' He gave a little sneer. 'It's only internal, I'm afraid. You will not be able to get an outside line. Oh, I'm afraid your razor had to be removed. Delicate weapon, a razor. You'll find a simple electric shaver in the bathroom. Bob will be here for you in twenty minutes or so. Enjoy yourself.' With another of his mock bows, Jack withdrew and, as the door closed, Bond heard the ominous thump of security locks sliding into place. He had already noticed a small, numeric key pad recessed into the pillar outside. Never mind, he thought, if they haven't discovered the secrets of my luggage, an electronic lock should not cause much of a problem.

He turned to look at the room, ornate and overdone, with repro-

duction Louis XV furnishings, modern pictures, and fabrics of loud –
almost hysterical – colours. The curtains were not yet pulled for the
night and they disclosed that the entire length of one wall was a huge
window through which the exterior floodlighting revealed a stretch of
sand beyond which marshy land, replete with reeds, ran to another
rich golden beach and the pounding sea.

He explored the passage running off to the left of this main room
with a hideously modern bathroom in two shades of green on the left,
and a dressing room which looked more like a big department store
fitting room, to the right. The door ahead took him into a bedroom of
equal size and bad taste as the sitting room. The bed was huge – a
reproduction four-poster at the foot of which stood his briefcase. The
right-hand wall, like the one in the sitting room, was another giant
window.

It could be the bedroom of an hotel with more investment than
taste, but, Bond thought, this could be used as a lever. It was quite
possible that Scorpius, the old arms dealer, had developed this ornate
and terrible style as he became the wealthy recluse. They had never
managed to sneak any pictures of *Vladem 1* – the yacht. It was most
probably very similar to this. Vladimir Scorpius, the flim-flam holy
man, the evil designing spirit behind his rent-a-terrorist business,
preying on the emotional gullibility of the young, had an Achilles' heel
– vulgarity and pretensions. Well, Vladimir, Bond thought, I can
exploit this in ways you will never have dreamed of, because you
probably believe all this – your outward show of power.

He stepped towards his briefcase, hesitating for a moment before
lifting it on to the bed. Take care, he thought. With a set-up like this,
Scorpius would almost certainly have his guest rooms wired for *son et
lumière*. He placed the briefcase on the bed. The locks had been
tampered with, the combinations found – it was easy enough even
with a sophisticated system – but he could tell by the weight, and feel
of the case, that the secret compartment had remained untouched.
Certainly no X-ray machine would show it; nor would measurements.
Q'ute had used exceptionally clever methods in the installation.

Noting the razor and spare blades were the only things to have been
removed, he took out a clean shirt, socks and underwear, then closed
and locked the case again, leaving it on the bed, as though it was
unimportant. Later there would be a way of getting to the weapons
and other devices he might need.

Stripping off his clothes, Bond showered quickly, rubbed himself
down with one of the big rough towels which were piled neatly in a
chrome container above the bath, then, naked, went through into the
bedroom. He had just tossed the towel back into the bathroom when
there was a little amused cough from the bedroom door. He looked

up. Harriett Horner stood there in a towelling robe, her face pale and stress marks showing around the eyes, but her mouth in an amused smile at finding Bond naked.

'They told me you had arrived, James. Thank God you've come. Oh, thank God!' She ran to him, unabashed by his nakedness, twisting her arms around his neck, kissing his face, then putting her lips close to his ear and whispering, 'They're wired for sound, but no pictures as far as I can see.' Loudly again. 'I really couldn't believe it when our Father, Valentine, told me about you.'

Her lips close to his ear again, and another fast whisper. 'It's been grim. He's using drugs and powerful hypnotism on me. Trying to make me believe, and become a Meek One. He's getting through, but I've been able to remember it all.'

Loudly again, 'Is it tonight he's going to ask you?'

'Ask me what?' Bond watched as she gave him a wicked little wink.

'Oh, James.' She kissed him again, as though she meant it. Not an unpleasant experience. Again her lips came close to his ear for the whispering routine, 'Prepare yourself, this is going to come as a shock.'

'Ask me what?' Bond repeated.

'If you'll marry me.' She was excited, but did not smile. 'He says that if you'll agree to marry me, and live here under the Meek Ones' discipline, he'll do us no harm. Please, James. Please say yes.'

'To save our lives, of course. But I can't see the sinister Scorpius letting any of us off the leash that easily.' He looked at Harriett, and her eyes seemed already dead. Then came the soft tapping on the main sitting-room door. It would be Bob to take Bond to Scorpius.

'So you'll marry me, James?' Harry Horner pressed close to him.

Well, he thought, it would not be a fate worse than death, that was for sure. Though the threat of death could not be far away. A smile flicked across his mouth – a gesture of comfort. 'I'll think about it, Harry. I'll give it some really serious thought.'

18

Meet Mrs Scorpius

'How nice of you to join me for dinner, Mr Bond.' Even Scorpius' voice seemed to take on sinister undertones – a voice of honey and milk, mixed with strychnine. He was now dressed casually, yet managed to give the impression of being formal – dark slacks and a white silk shirt, open at the neck. Under the shirt, Bond could see the outline of a medallion – gold, naturally – hanging from a heavy chain around his neck. On his left wrist there was the famed Scorpius Chronometer with its twelve diamonds for the normal display and tiny windows for the digital functions.

'Did I have any alternative but to dine with you?' As he looked him in the eye, Bond consciously summoned a vivid picture into his head – this time Scorpius was at his mercy, strapped to a table. Bond held a huge branding iron just above the flesh of his chest. If he brought images such as this to file in and out of his mind, he had little to fear from the man. It was when you allowed your eyes to meet his that you became vulnerable.

He sensed Scorpius wince inwardly. 'You are a very clever man, Mr Bond.' It was as near as he would allow himself to reveal weakness. 'I was warned of that, but I imagined you were merely a strong physical man, used to violence, and an able fighting opponent. I had no idea you had willpower as well. Nor that you were intelligent. Someone once called you a blunt instrument. I find you are more than a bludgeon.'

When 'Bodyguard Bob' arrived in the guest quarters, Harriett had quickly disentangled herself, and with great poise walked to the door, asking him to wait. 'Mr Bond will be with you momentarily,' she said, lapsing into the incorrect American use of the final word. Bond was dressed in minutes, and she whispered goodnight, kissing him lightly on the cheek, and telling him to 'Watch out for the food. That's how they started on me.'

He was taken along the corridors again, through to Scorpius' bare, austere study, where Bob went straight to the fitted bookcase nearest the window, and pulled out a book on the third shelf. There was a click, and that part of the bookcase swung open to reveal a door. Bond was quick to notice that the spine of the false book showed it to be a fat imitation copy of Tolstoy's *War and Peace*. Somewhere within Vladimir Scorpius there was a spark of humour.

He did not know what to expect, but the dining room into which he was shown – to be greeted by Scorpius – was a disaster area of styles. Here, it became obvious that the master of this strange house had been thoroughly influenced by a number of restaurants, favourite eating places of his past life. Bond imagined that he detected some panelling copied from the Connaught in London, a zinc bar from Fouquet's in Paris, and at least two reproductions of original book-jacket artwork he had seen in the vulgar décor of Langan's Brasserie. The man appeared obsessed by reproductions. An odd attitude from one who could have had the originals twice over.

'I've planned only a simple meal for us.' Scorpius smiled, and Bond thought he could detect the leer of one of the Borgias. 'Very simple. Especially for you, Mr Bond. Airline food is not substantial, but I always find myself unable to eat a great deal for the first twenty-four hours after flying the Atlantic.'

Bond held up a hand. 'Just one thing, er . . . *Father* Valentine . . .'

'Yes, my son?'

Off guard for a second, Bond looked up, into the full power of the man's eyes. From a long way off he heard Scorpius repeat, 'Yes, my son?' Then he tore his own eyes away, concentrating on a Scorpius whose body was being riddled with bullets.

'When you sup with the devil, they say you should use a long spoon. I'm sorry if I seem to abuse what you call your hospitality, but I shall require you to taste every course set in front of me.'

Scorpius laughed. 'I can do better than that. My wife will taste it for you. I shall see to it. You have no need to fear me, Mr Bond.'

'I don't fear you.'

'Funny, I had the impression you did. Why else would you have need of a food taster at my table?'

'Because you are an expert in the use of certain kinds of drug; an expert in manipulating people, so that they believe the religious hodgepodge you throw at them. You are – let's cut the formalities – you are expert in sending young and impressionable people to their deaths, along with innocent victims; and you do it for money, right, Vladimir Scorpius?'

There was silence for a second, no more. 'So.' Scorpius did not sound in any way shaken. His voice did not waver. 'So. I did not believe it. I was told, but thought it an exaggeration. I should have known my informant wouldn't feed me with dreams. I should have realised that someone would identify me sooner or later in spite of the careful precautions.' He took a deep breath. 'Who else knows, Mr Bond? Who knows, apart from you, your Chief of Service, MI5, and the Special Branch? Do they know, here, in America?'

'By now.' Bond looked him full in the eyes this time, and as he spoke kept a supremely vivid fantasy in the front of his mind. 'By now,

a very large number of people know. I would guess the American
Service is familiar with your dossier as well – unless you have some
control over that . . .'

'Maybe I have. We shall see. Well, it is good that I shall be able to
retire quite happily when this job is done.'

'I wouldn't be so certain of that. The people I'm speaking about
know exactly what you are doing, and how you're doing it.'

Scorpius spread his hands. 'Yet they cannot stop it. There is no way
– except by draconian security, the banning of all public meetings,
the closing of cinemas, opera houses, concert halls, theatres and
restaurants. Where my dear Meek Ones go, there can never be
complete safety.'

'Your Meek Ones will soon be brought to book.'

'How? Tell me how. There is no way, Bond. They are above law
and order; they can walk anywhere undetected. And they can operate
without me. That is the beauty. Only married couples, who have
produced at least one child, can undertake the death-tasks. In turn,
when the child is old enough, he or she will marry, and the process
regenerate itself. I can go, disappear for ever – once the present
operation is complete. The faithful will mourn, but the work will go
on.' He stopped for a short breath. 'You see, Mr Bond, these young
people, the Society of Meek Ones, cannot give up, even if I die or
disappear, tomorrow. The current campaign will be over in a very few
days, and I cannot stop it now. Once it's running, those chosen for
death-tasks will perform them. I have no more contact with them.
They are like well-programmed robots. They have the plastique. They
have their orders. They will die and take the leaders of Britain, together
with the potential leaders of Britain, and the leader of . . .' He smiled.
'No, I'll let you find out for yourself. But they will do it, and, if the
game's up for me, I have plenty on which to fall back. A fortune from
this job alone, and a myriad hiding places.

'The Meek Ones will go on, simply because they believe. They
really *do* believe. Nobody will have to pay for their services any more,
for they'll do it for their faith. Ha!' He finished with a short laugh.
'To think that a brilliant idea like that will never be used again to
feather a nest.' His voice dropped to almost a whisper, which was
totally commanding.

'You can be as cold-blooded as that?' Bond could hardly credit that
one human being was capable of such depravity. 'A true holy war, I
can understand. But a holy war based on lies and disbelief . . .'

'Please don't be a hypocrite, Bond. All holy wars have been fought
for the motive of profit. That's how I came up with my own idea. For
years I had been getting rich on holy wars. Then I thought, why do
I not get richer? Why don't I provide the manpower as well as the

weapons. Where's the wrong in that? In a way I am saving lives, by sacrificing young, emotional, ingenuous people who wish to die for an ideal.'

Bond was so repulsed by this last outburst that he stepped back towards the door.

'Don't leave, Mr Bond. Don't even think of it. Because I can furnish you with the means to stop the Meek Ones if I so desire.'

Bond shook his head. 'You wouldn't though, Scorpius. You wouldn't give up. I thought, until now, that I had already met the most evil people alive in the world today. And I imagined I knew of all those before this, but you leave me in no doubt that I was wrong. You are evil personified. A death-bringer, a dreamer of nightmares. The worst since . . .'

'Hitler? Stalin? Oh, I think not. If, once this business is concluded, I gave you a full list of the faithful, together with their locations, what would you say? I might do that you know. Or can't you believe me?'

'I believe you'd do it for a price, and I haven't enough to pay you.'

'You might have. No man knows what he has to give. My friend, I have walked the wicked paths of this earth for many more years than you. I might give you details for the future, if you do something in return.' His eyes were clear of menace now. It was as though he really had an offer to make, though Bond was in no doubt that the man's words were cheap, worthless, and any promises made would be counterfeit.

'Why do you think I had John Pearlman bring you here?' Scorpius asked, in almost a whisper. The low, controlled voice became even more sinister once you were in his company for any length of time.

'I don't know. Why me in the first place? Why was I involved? Why me?'

'There is a simple answer. Why not? It is the answer that Fate gives to all who ask that question, when disaster, death, tragedy, hardship overtakes them. "Why me? Why me? Why me?"' He beat his breast with a clenched fist at each question. 'And Fate answers these fools – "Why not?" In your case, Mr Bond, it was because you were there. You happened to be in the right place at the right time. I had an informer who could be put close to you. You were not the only one I could have used, but, as I'm sure you've already deduced, you were set up, just so that my particular informer could give me better intelligence. If that person was near to you, I would be able to stay one jump ahead. And I did, even though I didn't believe your people had discovered my true identity. So, Mr Bond, you are in the right place, at the right time, now.'

'How so?'

'I ask only a very small favour. In return I'll give you every name, every known address of every Meek One – including those left here.'

'But only after the terrible damage is done.' Pretend; act as though you really believe him, Bond told himself. Yes, there probably *was* 'a small favour', but one that would suit Scorpius and nobody else.

'Naturally, after this particular campaign is over, yes.'

'So what's the favour?' As he asked, Bond knew that it could only be some form of death warrant for himself.

'In a moment. Let me provide some collateral.' He moved towards the longest wall in the room. The zinc bar stood in front of it, while two fairly awful reproduction pictures, mounted together in a large frame, hung above it. Scorpius felt under the bar and, a second later, the pictures slid upwards and a large-scale map of England seemed to float down to replace them. Scorpius pulled out a drawer under the bar and flicked a switch. A winking light came on, and Bond could see it was at the true position of Glastonbury.

'You see?' Scorpius appeared to have quite abandoned the power he could wield from his personality and those devastating eyes. 'I can afford to let you see this. You will be here until it is all complete, make no mistake about that. There is no escape from the Ten Pines Plantation. Only death waits for you outside these walls – quite unpleasant some of the deaths that squirm, or scurry out there. So, this I can afford. First, the nice little town of Glastonbury – but you know what happened there. And Chichester.' Another light winked from the map. 'You know that also. I wonder if you know what occurred only a few hours ago near Newcastle-upon-Tyne?' The pin of light began to pulse as he carefully named the trade union leader and the Labour candidate. 'Where else? What else will happen? What else is there that I cannot stop happening? Let us see.' His hand touched something else on the panel jutting from the zinc bar. Manchester lit up, and he named a former Cabinet Minister from the Government that had 'gone to the country'. 'That is tomorrow.' He sounded like someone who planned a holiday, not a man passing sentence of death upon several innocent people in order to dispose of one. Another button – Birmingham, a Member of Parliament who had a reputation as a firebrand; Oxford – two candidates, Labour and Conservative. 'Two in a day; should hit the headlines.'

It went on and on. The campaign seemed without pattern, candidates from all parties: former Ministers; two ex-Chief Whips; the Lord Chancellor. London, Ealing, Edinburgh, Glasgow, London again – Kensington, not far from where Bond had hidden the previous night – Cambridge, Canterbury, Leeds, York. Practically every major town in England, Scotland and Wales, plus Belfast. The dates were there, positive. The targets had been selected. Next to each winking light, Bond could see the names of the victims, etched in scarlet, and below them, another name – too small to read from this distance, but almost certainly the human death-bringer.

'What if they change days and times?' he asked, his stomach turning with horror at the carnage.

'They have.' Scorpius smiled directly at Bond. The eyes began to dig into 007's mind again. Bond had dropped his guard, so he pulled his head to one side and replaced his thoughts with those of Scorpius as a victim of one of his own terrible human bombs. 'They *have* changed times and venues. I am in possession of the whole new list.'

'How d'you know it's correct – your list?' The answer did not really matter. The man was simply putting on a terrible display of power. He was like a child showing-off – a mad, bad, death-master child.

'I know it is correct,' Scorpius gave a smile that was more wicked and evil for its seeming openness, 'because I trust the one who's informing me.'

'You didn't trust the intelligence about yourself.'

'No! And obviously I'm very foolish. It's one of the first rules, isn't it? You as an operative with many years' experience should know. One of the first rules is do not rule out intelligence that does not fit what you want to believe. Do not only believe that which you want to believe. True?'

'True.' Bond nodded. 'I notice, though, that one obvious victim is missing.'

'Oh? Who could that be?'

'The Prime Minister. Unless you have some reason for keeping the PM alive.'

Scorpius laughed, a low, deep chuckle. 'Oh, no, James Bond. The Prime Minister is *not* forgotten. Certainly not. But I have a very special fate for the Prime Minister that does not show on this map.'

Bond's mind was working hard, probing, taking in every target, every place, noting them in his memory, holding them there in the hope that he might get out and give some kind of warning. 'You said you could not stop the running of the operation.'

'Correct.'

'Yet you are able to let those who have death-tasks know that dates and times have been changed. How?'

'That is relatively easy. I know where they are. I can contact them. I can change time and location. The one thing I cannot alter is their individual targets.' He explained how the men and women were drawn into the net of the Meek Ones. How they were chosen and manipulated so that there was no fear of death, for in their deaths they would attain paradise. 'All that is relatively easy.' He sounded like some dusty university don lecturing on a piece of dull history. 'However, the final motivation, the method used for defining the target must be exact. It must also be buried so deeply into the subconscious of my human missiles, that they consciously forget it. If, by chance, a weak link is arrested, hours of interrogation will not reveal the target. Interrogators might well be able to guess in some cases, but not with certainty.'

'And you cannot, or will not put an end to this . . . this . . . battlefield?'

'Cannot, and will not. No, I cannot do it except by handing over all those times, places and names to you, or someone like you, and then adding the names of those who will do the final job.'

'And if the target does not show himself – or herself – what then?'

'The missile I have sent will search out that target. No other. Every specific target is already dead, because there is one person out there and running with one mission in life – to dispose of a target. A specific target. Leave it a week, a month, a year even. Eventually, without my help, the one with the death-task will find the target, and – boom!' he quietly snapped his fingers, making the very idea even more horrific.

In his head, James Bond gathered together the whole collection of information so far. His memory would hold it – times, places, and most especially targets. His concentration was such that, for a second, he did not realise Scorpius was still speaking. 'There!' He pointed to the twelfth target on the map – the whole of which now winked like a Christmas tree. 'When we get *there*, I think something quite different will blow up. Another fly in the ointment.'

'What sort of fly?'

'Oh, a little financial problem.'

'If you mean *Avante Carte* and the supposed slush fund built up in Lord Shrivenham's account . . .?' Bond stopped in mid-sentence, for the door had opened and a third person came gently into the room.

'Shrivenham? Ah-ha! There is something much better than that in store. Lord Shrivenham was a neat little – what do those women detective writers call it? A little red herring. *Avante Carte*, of which you have seen two, has a much more subtle financial bomb built into it. We can forget about dear old Basil Shrivenham, can't we, my darling?' He was looking past Bond to the door. 'You have, I think, met my wife, Mr Bond. If not, meet Mrs Scorpius now.'

'Yes, we have met, under most amusing circumstances. And Vladi is right, we can forget about poor old Daddy,' said Trilby Shrivenham, looking in perfect health. 'Now, shall we have dinner? I think Vladi has a proposition to put to you.'

19

Why Not Tonight?

'So, it *was* all play-acting in London – the coma, the riddles, "the blood of the fathers will fall upon the sons," all that stuff, and the demonic voice?' Bond looked first at Vladimir Scorpius, and then at the Hon Trilby Shrivenham, revealed now as his self-styled wife.

'Not exactly.' Trilby stretched out a hand and squeezed Scorpius' arm. 'I'm not that good at acting.'

Bond noticed her hand shook slightly as she touched her husband. If indeed he was her husband.

Trilby, as he had guessed when seeing her unconscious at home – and again at the Puttenham Clinic with Molony – was a tall, slender girl of proportions that would do credit to any model featured in the pages of glossy magazines. She wore a dramatic dress in equally dramatic red silk. If put to it, he would have guessed that it was probably by Azzedine Alaia. Her long hair had been cut recently, and restyled, but there was one off-key note. She had been too liberal and heavy-handed with the make-up.

Somehow it was all wrong. Trilby Shrivenham's face – with its high cheekbones, well-proportioned mouth and deep hazel eyes – was not in need of what appeared to be almost a full stage make-up. Also, it would take an insensitive dolt not to notice that she was strung out with tension. Every time she spoke, Trilby either touched, or looked at Scorpius, as though seeking reassurance.

'It really *wasn't* play-acting, was it, dear heart?' Her fingers bit into Scorpius' arm, so that he tore it away from her, brushing her hand off him as though it was an irritating insect.

'She was a volunteer.' Scorpius' voice maintained the cold, calm, frighteningly low pitch, but he rendered the line very quickly. With Trilby's sudden appearance, Bond became even more alert than before. Scorpius continued to talk: 'We needed some kind of back-up to poor little Emma Dupré – she was not supposed to die, you know. That was a terrible shock to all of us.'

'Oh, yes, I'll bet it was. You're most sensitive where death is concerned, aren't you?'

Scorpius ignored Bond's bitter remark. 'Yes, we *are* all sensitive. You should believe that, Mr Bond. Emma really thought we'd allowed her to escape. She had some scruples about what we were doing, I admit. But I thought I might turn this to our advantage – that I could use her in various ways. You see, I made certain that, when she left,

Emma carried clues – particularly your telephone number. When I first heard, through our contact, that she had been drowned I became alarmed. It was possible the clues she had been given had gone with her.'

'My telephone number?'

'That, and what you call the riddle, about the blood of the fathers falling upon the sons. I had implanted *that* in poor Emma's subconscious. At that time, Mr Bond, it was my desire to put the British authorities on the alert. Once the first death-task was done, I hoped they would realise that they were up against an unbeatable force. It was meant to cause panic, possibly even more – a huge security clamp-down that would render the General Election hopeless, for instance. In any case, it is bound to do that eventually.' He raised a hand, the same princely gesture Bond had noticed after first arriving – the hand lifted imperiously, index finger jutting upwards, while the other fingers remained curled, the whole hand moving at a flick of the wrist.

Bond could not buy the story. For the first time he detected a note of uncertainty, a concocted tale, embedded in Scorpius' explanations. It would be folly to challenge the man at this stage. Scorpius had already shown he had great power at his fingertips; he had proved it in the diabolical human-bomb outrages, and the outline of his future plans. Pretend, Bond told himself again. Make him think you are lapping it all up without a second thought.

'At the time, I was lining up further contracts so that the Meek Ones would spread their word, and terror, throughout the world.' Scorpius seemed to be speaking to the air, with a note of great regret.

Bond could not let *that* pass. 'Contracts that would wreak more havoc, and cause the deaths of many innocent people. Contracts that would line your pockets.'

'Unhappily, that is now unrealistic.' Scorpius' eyes had gone dead, and he spoke very slowly.

'I would have said, *happily* it is unrealistic.' Keep shaking him, Bond thought. Who knows, even with such a devious and cruel mind, Scorpius might just be thrown off balance.

'What's unrealistic, darling?' There was an almost frightened look about Trilby, a terror behind the over made-up face and the outward elegance.

'Nothing for you to worry about, my dear.' He patted her hand, which still shook slightly.

'I only worry for *you*, angel.' She looked at him, then away, sharply.

Not only did Bond feel nauseated by the endearments that passed between Scorpius and the girl, but he was also alarmed by the surface quality of the conversation. It reeked of manipulation and a

Never-Never Land of unreality. 'So, you *allowed* Trilby to act as . . .?'

'He told you, I volunteered.' Trilby answered, a shade too brightly. 'You must understand, Mr Bond, that I owe my life to Vladi. He brought me into the light; got me right off heroin, when I was a bad case. When I first told him that I loved him he was concerned; he thought it was a case of what the psychiatrists call transference. A patient falling in love with her doctor, as a substitute for the illness. In my case the addiction.' It was the longest speech Scorpius had allowed her to make, and she reeled it off as though the main points had been learned by heart.

'Yes, I *do* know what it means. You've had remarkable success with drug addiction, Scorpius. How d'you account for that?'

'In the same way many clinics manage it. There's nothing magical about getting people off drugs if they truly want to live.' He began to become pompous, as though getting onto a hobby horse. 'Vitamin injections, discipline, abstinence syndrome suppressants – methadone in the case of heroin – and very deep hypnosis to help the most unpleasant side effects.' He paused, as though expecting Bond to applaud. The silence lasted for twenty seconds or so, before he spoke again.

'I think that's where I score – if you'll excuse the expression. Through my own particular use of very deep hypnosis. In the clinics, people do go through hell coming off. With me, it's easier. But there are cases even I cannot help – those who have reached the stage of not caring whether they live or die. The death-wish addict. Sometimes they can recover for a time. A large number of my death-*task* people are like that. But enough, let us eat.'

The map had been electronically returned to its hiding place, and the big framed prints now occupied the space over the zinc bar. Bond had been careful to note exactly where the operating switches were hidden. He was determined to return alone and make a list of the death-task names. Just as he was determined to get out of the Ten Pines Plantation alive, and as soon as possible.

Now, Scorpius pressed a bell at the corner of the bar.

The grey-suited bodyguards acted as waiters. There were six of them in all, and even the stylish cut of their clothes could not hide the tiny bulges which indicated that the whole half dozen were armed.

The only items of genuine taste in the room consisted of a beautiful Caroline dining table, kept in exquisite condition, and with the original chairs. There was space enough to sit twelve people. Tonight they set it for three only; the place settings looked like real Georgian silverware and the glasses were Waterford crystal. 'Bodyguard Bob' announced that dinner was served, leaving a large silver bowl in the centre of the table. From this, Trilby served the best of summer soups – gazpacho, ice-cold and with the correct side dishes of croûtons, chopped onion, tomato and peppers.

'I hope you like this, Mr Bond, or may I call you James?'

'By all means, Trilby. Why not? Soon you'll be in need of first-name friends.'

She looked up at him, alarmed, almost spilling a ladle of soup. 'What do you mean?' The panic was clear in her eyes, and the voice rose onto a higher register. Suddenly she became clumsy in ladling out the thick gazpacho.

'Nothing, my dear,' Scorpius soothed. 'He does not approve of me, or the Meek Ones. So he does not approve of you either. It is of no matter. You cannot be loved by every man, you know.'

The spicy soup was placed before Bond, but he turned to Scorpius. 'Will you be my taster?'

'You need a taster for something that comes from the same tureen as our portions?'

Bond reminded him of supping with the devil. Scorpius gave a small shrug, dipped his spoon into Bond's bowl and drank. 'That satisfy you?'

'Just.'

'I don't think that's very nice,' said Trilby. It was meant to sound cross, but came out too glibly. 'You're Vladi's guest. It's no way for a guest to behave.' Her voice remained close to the edge of hysteria.

'My dear Trilby, if Vladi would stop this bloody terrorist campaign now, and hand over *all* the Meek Ones, then, possibly I would find better manners – particularly if I came to visit you both in jail.'

'Jail is somewhere neither of us will see,' Scorpius said very quickly, his eyes turning towards Trilby. At the end of the rapid sentence he laughed, and, somehow, Bond believed him. The man was so warped in his attitude to death and terror – a psychotic who would possibly take his own life, and Trilby's also, rather than be caught: but only as a final resort.

They made small talk until the main dish arrived, succulent and lean lamb chops, cooked with rosemary and other herbs, served on a huge salver, surrounded with small roast potatoes and beans.

'There.' Scorpius smiled. 'You could well be in one of your English gentlemen's clubs. I asked for the main course to be very English tonight, especially for you, James Bond. Help yourself. We shall also eat from this same dish, and I shall taste the wine for you, in case that is laced with some deadly poison.' He gave another laugh, more unpleasant this time, and went to the zinc bar where two bottles of Chablis Grand Cru had been left to breathe. They were from Les Preuses, one of the best of those seven small vineyards that dot the southern-facing slopes from Chablis itself. Scorpius tasted from both bottles, making it an extravagant production number.

In the end, Bond had to admit that it was many years since he had tasted lamb as tender and sweet as this, or drunk such an excellent classic Chablis.

As they ate and drank he continued to press Scorpius regarding Trilby's return to her home. 'When I saw her, she appeared to be in a particularly vulnerable and collapsed state.'

'It was a small risk,' Scorpius replied. 'One we were both willing to take. The point was that she knew the meaning of the words I placed in her mind. Trilby has always been a true follower of the Meek Ones. She is bound to the faith, just as she is dedicated to our aims. I travelled to London with her – from Pangbourne – and gave her the final doses of LSD in the car as we approached her father's house. She had seven, *seven*, mind you, days of intensive hypnosis.' He smiled, and there was a wickedness in the smile that would have pleased the Marquis de Sade. Bond could almost feel the shade of the Marquis in the room with them.

Scorpius still smiled as he said, with a certain relish, 'It was good to pay back her father for some of the indignity he put me through. It would have suited our purpose better if his bank, the truly terrible Gomme-Keogh, had backed the *Avante Carte* venture.'

'So your people were trying to get Trilby out of our clinic when they were surprised. We all imagined they were bent on killing her.'

'Indeed, yes, of course they were rescuing her. Why would my people attempt to kill her? That whole business was bad luck. Pearlman was there, but the foolish Horner girl started the trouble. Which brings me, Mr Bond, to my previous offer.'

'Which was?' Bond asked, as though he had forgotten about Scorpius' vague promise – that, in return for a small favour, he would hand over what was left of the Meek Ones, once the current campaign was over. Bond had no reason to think Scorpius would ever honour a promise, or indeed demand a *small* favour. His was a world of exceptionally large favours, littered with broken promises and devious intentions.

Scorpius repeated the words he had used earlier – 'I ask only one very small favour. In return I'll give you every name, every known address of every Meek One – including those left here – after this particular campaign is completed.'

Bond smiled, his eyes on the now empty plate in front of him. 'Oh, let's not discuss business over such a pleasant meal. I can wait to hear of the favour you ask. Let it rest, Scorpius.'

'As you wish. The pudding has been left on the bar. Again, we all eat from the same dish.'

'A peach cobbler,' Trilby said. 'I trust you like peach cobbler?' Her speech was still brittle, nervous, too fast.

'Simple, delightful fare.' In fact the dish – peaches skinned and simmered for five minutes in a syrup of sugar and water, sometimes with a bag of rose petals – was an old favourite. As a general rule, Bond eschewed puddings, but this, or a really good Meringue Chantilly, seldom failed to tempt him. 'Tell me,' he began, making it sound as though he was starting to adjust to the infernal company, 'you said I could never escape from this place.'

'Mr Bond, you must not even think of it.'

'Why?'

'Even if I told you it would not matter. There is no way out of Ten Pines Plantation, except with permission from myself.'

'The glass windows of the guest rooms look out onto beaches and the sea. There are sliding doors with no locking devices. Why couldn't I simply walk down to the sea and swim away? Have you armed guards on watch, twenty-four hours a day?'

'The armed guards are for the *front* of this property.' Scorpius sounded as though he was trying to humour Bond. 'There is a great half-circle of trees which swarm, and I use the word advisedly, with guards and dogs. The way to the sea needs no dogs or armed sharpshooters. The way to the sea has very unpleasant natural hazards – to which I have added a few embellishments of my own.'

'Such as?'

'The alligators do not come into this area. They don't really like the sea. But there is a small stretch of reedy, soggy marshland between the rear of the house and the main beach which leads to the sea. We have large warnings posted at the extremities to keep tourists at bay. Even so, I admit there have been unfortunate accidents. Nobody – and I mean nobody – has ever walked from the plantation to the sea and lived to tell the story. You've heard of the water moccasin?'

Bond nodded. 'Usually known as the cottonmouth. Yes.'

'Then you would agree they are dangerous snakes?'

'Very, unless you get treatment pretty fast.'

'Quite so. The water moccasin's venom is used in medicine, for the treatment of haemorrhagic conditions, and the like. It destroys red blood cells; coagulates the blood. One bite is exceptionally serious if not treated quickly. Several bites are certain death.'

'Several?'

Scorpius nodded. 'The marshes, near our beaches – those that back upon Ten Pines – are sealed off with ten-foot metal plates at the extremities. You see, we have a colony of water moccasins in the marsh. They have been there for years and the locals know all about them.'

'Don't they get out to sea?'

'No, they're generally nocturnal creatures, and don't thrive in the sea. But, in the marshes it's a different story. When you consider that the female produces around fifteen young every two years, you will understand why we have no need for armed guards.'

Trilby shuddered, and Scorpius put out a hand to soothe her. 'My young wife is especially nervous of them. We had an incident on her first visit here. The man, who did not matter to us, was bitten forty times. So, you understand, Mr Bond. Water moccasins bear a government health warning – that is not to mention the rattlers, black widows, scorpions and similar dangerous life that abounds here.' He gave a smile which could only be described as terrible. 'The pelicans, cormorants and sandpipers are nice to watch, and the average tourist rarely comes within spitting distance of the dangerous creatures. The hotels here take many precautions, though golfers sometimes meet alligators. Never run straight away from those things. But you know that.'

'I know they can run fast if they're roused, but only in straight lines. If you zig-zag you should be safe.'

'You've enjoyed the meal?' Trilby asked, as though she wanted to change the subject.

Bond said, yes, very much. He turned down the coffee and liqueurs.

'So, I've warned you,' Scorpius continued, 'and, lest you think you're immortal, know that I have also added some refinements between the house and the sea. So put any thought of beach parties out of your head. It's not worth it.'

No, Bond thought, but perhaps, because of its danger, there *was* a way to the sea and safety. Possibly he had it back in the guest room, in Q'ute's handy emergency pack, hidden within the overnight briefcase.

'The meal is over,' Scorpius said, pointedly.

'So?'

'So, shouldn't we discuss my offer?'

'I don't really know.' In the back of his mind, Bond had gone through the moral implications of doing any kind of deal with this mad and dreadful, warped impersonation of a man – true man he could never call him. Scorpius was a representative of all the double standards, double, even triple thought, bigotry, hatred, self-serving, and plain evil which lies within the worst part of man. To him, Scorpius was the devil's emissary on earth, the bringer of corruption, dispenser of death. He would have made an admirable member of the Spanish Inquisition; a leader of the unthinkable Children's Crusade; a Commissar of Stalin's death camps; a deceiver and pervert in the mould of Lavrenti Beria, that most monstrous leader of the Soviet secret police; or, perhaps best of all, the SS Commandant of a Nazi camp, revelling in the gassing and cremation of millions of Jews. To Bond, Scorpius was all that had ever been cruel, uncaring, revolting and unjust through history, from Genghis Khan and Attila the Hun, to Himmler and Klaus Barbie.

'Come,' Scorpius nudged him, 'the favour has its compensations. With my true identity revealed, I realise the Meek Ones must go. Let me perform one act that might seem worthy to you, by delivering their future into your hands. Why not? At least hear me out?'

It just did not ring true. This was the dark angel, Bond thought, the fallen angel, Satan himself speaking, pouring honey into his ear – honey laced with poison. The temptation was too great. Maybe he could stop the horror before it went any further. But, if that proved impossible, perhaps this walking demon might just keep the one promise. No, he told himself, that is what Scorpius would have him believe. Do it again – pretend. Act. It was the only way.

'Alright. Tell me. What is this favour?'

'I won't bore you with a long, tortuous story, but this concerns the Horner girl.'

Bond had not believed Harriett when she had clung to him and said that, if he agreed to marry her, Scorpius would allow them to live in peace within the Society of the Meek Ones. Now, he thought that he knew what was to come.

'It goes back a long way,' Scorpius continued, his voice like rough sandpaper, low, harsh and strangely uncertain. 'Enough to say that I was once indebted to Harriett Horner's father. Coincidence is an impossible thing.' He sounded as though his thoughts were far away. 'It might be difficult for you to believe, but believe it you must. The Horner girl is my godchild. I owe her father my freedom and life. Once, when she was a tiny child he asked me to make sure she was well cared for and looked after. Coincidence placed us in an odd juxtaposition. How could I ever know that she would grow to be an IRS agent? That the United States IRS are out to get me is no secret. But they can never win, and I have Harriett, my godchild, here as my prisoner. What am I to do with her? Well, I have you here, also, Mr Bond. My senses say I should have you shot, out of hand, for you are a *very* dangerous man. However, I can keep you confined here for as long as I like.

'When I leave, which will have to be soon, I would like to leave with one tiny corner of my conscience clear. In return for the information I shall give you – once the present series of tasks are completed – I ask you, James Bond, to marry Harriett Horner.'

It was unthinkable, but Bond needed time. 'Does Harriett know all this?'

'All what?' Scorpius shrugged, spreading his hands.

'About her being your godchild? About her father and you?'

'No! No, and she must never be told.' A shade too fast, and tinged with anxiety. A raw nerve perhaps? Certainly it was out of character for Scorpius.

'Why not?'

Scorpius hesitated. 'Because of how I must appear to the world.'

'When would you want the ceremony to take place?' Bond asked.

'As soon as possible. I can preside over the ceremony, naturally.'

That brought some hope. A marriage performed by Scorpius would be invalid anywhere outside the Society. He needed time. Maybe Wolkovsky's people were already alerted. Time. But why should Scorpius give him time as he appeared to be doing? The whole idea was crazy.

'When you say as soon as possible, how soon?'

'Why not tonight?'

Bond did not believe a word of it; the story of Harriett being Scorpius' godchild; of promises to her father; of coincidence; of Scorpius showing concern for her future. He guessed the real answer might be to keep both Harriett and himself happy and out of the way, while the last stages of terror were played out. He did not even know if Harriett was Scorpius' spy or not, though he suspected she had always told him the truth. He certainly did not believe in the tale about Trilby, and the state in which she had arrived at her parents' home. He did not know what to believe about her being the wife of Vladimir Scorpius. Plainly, Bond now considered, he knew very little of the truth – who to trust; who to doubt; who to destroy, as he planned to destroy Scorpius himself.

Vladimir Scorpius spoke again, the voice even lower than before. 'Why not tonight?'

Without looking at him, Bond replied, 'Why not?' Play for time. Maybe he would still find a way. Though, as he accepted Scorpius' proposal, once more James Bond knew, deeply within him, that he was simply accepting his own death-warrant. Nothing else made sense in Scorpius' nightmare world.

20

The Past is a Bucket of Ashes

Everything seemed completely unreal. In many ways life had taken on a dream-like quality. There they were in the Prayer Hall, now decorated with flowers – Aretha Franklin, with Detroit's New Bethel Baptist Church Choir, belting out 'Walk In The Light' through the hidden speakers, while Bond, with Pearly Pearlman as his best man, stood waiting near the steps to the platform where Vladimir Scorpius, gloriously arrayed in his 'Papal' robes, smiled unctuously.

The moment Bond had agreed to the wedding that night, Scorpius' hand had reached out for the telephone.

'Wait!' sharply from Bond. 'What're you doing?'

'If the ceremony's to be tonight there's a great deal to be done.'

'Well,' Bond spoke quietly, 'the arrangements will have to wait.'

'You can't back out now.' There was alarm in Scorpius' voice.

'I'm not backing out. If I am to marry Harriett, I shall have to ask her first.'

'There's no need. She'll marry you. I know she'll marry you.'

'I want to hear *that* from her.'

'Trilby.' Scorpius' voice rose for the first time that evening. 'Get the Horner girl and bring her here, this instant.'

'No!' Bond held up a hand. 'I wish to see her in private. Back in the guest rooms. If not, the deal's off, Scorpius. If you want me to go through with this, I have to see her alone. I *must* ask her, like any man would ask any woman. Also, she must understand what she is getting into.'

Scorpius hesitated for a moment, then put the telephone down and nodded. 'Very well. But she'll marry you alright.'

Bond thought he heard Trilby stifle some kind of choke in her throat. He looked towards her, and she had turned pale, you could see it even under the thick make-up. Again he thought, why? Why marriage? A whim of the mad Scorpius? Some subtle torture? Why, in heaven's name was Scorpius so anxious to go through with such a farce?

A knock on the door heralded the arrival of 'Bodyguard Bob', who was told to lead Bond back to the guest rooms and wait for him there.

'You shouldn't . . .' Trilby's voice trembled. 'Really, you shouldn't . . .'

'I shouldn't what?' Bond asked.

'Yes,' Scorpius, harsh and menacing, 'Yes, Trilby, *what* shouldn't Mr James Bond do?'

'You shouldn't see her,' Trilby almost sobbed. 'It's such bad luck to see the bride on her wedding day. The groom should never be allowed to see the bride on the day!'

'I don't think we need bother with superstition.' Scorpius now sounded almost intolerably patronising.

'I have to see her, Trilby. It would not be right if I did not propose to her.'

Trilby gave a little nod, her eyes brimming with tears.

'You okay?'

'Yes,' she said in a small voice. 'Yes . . . It's just . . . Well, I get so emotional about weddings.'

Bond touched her shoulder in a gesture of comfort, and to his surprise she shrank away from him, as though he were a leper.

Harriett was lying on her bed, wrapped in a towelling robe when Bond arrived back in the guest apartments. A logo on the pocket of the robe said *Hilton Hotel Disney Village*. It seemed appropriate to Bond.

'James! You've been away for ever.' She swung her legs over the side of the bed and dropped the book. He saw that she had been reading McCarry's *Tears of Autumn*.

Bond nodded towards the book. 'You like him as well. Good. We have one thing in common.' As he spoke he cupped a hand to his ear, looked up at the ceiling and made a circling motion with his index finger signifying that ceilings, walls, telephones, lamps and anything else in the room almost certainly had ears.

She nodded, understanding him: she had already said they were stealing sound, though not, as far as she knew, secretly looking at them through one of the many devices that were available on the sophisticated market of electronics. In cases like this there was one way, and only one way, of dealing with matters. Bond – and many like him – had used it before.

'Harriett, my dear,' he began, taking her hand and leading her into the furthest corner of the room, where there was a large, comfortable-looking armchair. 'This is damnably difficult, Harry. I've only done it once before.' Under cover of speech, he had taken a silver Tiffany pencil and small leather note pad from his pocket. Now, he seated himself in the armchair, pulling Harriett onto his knees.

'Only once, James?' She gave him a sly smile. 'A good-looking, well-made man like you?' One arm snaked around his neck and she nuzzled her head close to him as he placed the note pad on her towelling-covered thigh and began to write.

'I have talked for a long time with our host,' he said aloud. 'For reasons I won't go into now, it would seem that our immediate futures are only secure if . . .'

'Go on, James.' She looked down at what he had written on the pad –

When did Trilby Shrivenham marry Scorpius?

She took the pencil from him as he continued to speak,'. . . if we get married.'

I did not know they were married! she had written, but as he glanced at her, Bond saw fear in her face which had suddenly paled.

Then she said aloud, 'Married? I told you, James. I told you that was what he wanted. You believe me now?' She shook her head, frowning, concerned, trying to tell him something else.

'Yes . . .' He took the pencil from her. 'Yes, but I'm rather old-fashioned about these things. I am, naturally, fond of you. Very fond of you.' Her close proximity, with only the towelling robe between him and her naked flesh began to make him uncomfortable.

'So I see.' She allowed a hand to trail into his lap. Leaning forward she read what he had written –

You realise that, if we marry I shall do my best to escape, and take you with me as soon as possible.

'What I'm trying to say, Harry, is that if I did ask you, and if you accepted, it would be a marriage for our mutual salvation. Our mutual well-being.' He wrote on the pad –

For the present at least.

She took the pencil again. 'Of course, James.' A long pause as she wrote –

If you are going to escape you'd bloody well better take me with you.

'James, what you're saying is that you're not in love with me, right?'

'Right.' On the pad he wrote –

Scorpius is going to perform the ceremony tonight. You realise that it will be in no way legal or binding to either of us?

'And?' she queried, snatching the pencil from him and writing.

'And, in spite of that, I'm asking you to go through with it. I'm asking you to marry me.'

She had written –

I do know that, but it is the only way. You should know that HE wanted to marry me!

'Then I accept,' she smiled at him, a brilliant illumination of her whole face – sun peeping for a second from behind dark clouds.

'Thank you. Might I . . .?'

He had written –

And you turned him down?

'Can't you wait until the ceremony is over?' She looked down at his query and nodded violently – her face grave again behind the lightness

of her words and voice. She took the pencil from him and scribbled –
Yes, and landed us both in trouble. Tell all later. Let's get on with it.

'I was going to say, might I kiss you?'

She plunged her lips down on his. Either Harriett Horner was an expert who had majored in kissing, or she had not kissed, or been kissed, in a long time.

As he came up for air, Bond realised there could be two other explanations. Scorpius had detailed her to go through this whole business to keep him occupied – which had been a thought earlier – or she genuinely wanted him with an explosive passion.

'Oh, James,' she whispered. 'I'm so glad it's tonight. I really hadn't anything better to do.'

He gave her a withering, slightly cruel, smile and wrote on the pad –
Tonight we plan our escape.

Breathing heavily, to give any listeners the idea that they were once more clasped in an embrace, she wrote –
Okay, but only after the consummation. We might as well get something out of this.

'James, you don't know how much I've wanted this since we first met.' She was almost convincing. Perhaps she means it, he considered. Then he wrote quickly –
Yes. You are a splendid girl.

Well, Bond thought, they would go through with it. Maybe this was a chance he had been waiting for; maybe Harriett's turning down Scorpius was some kind of key to the constant question banging away in his mind – why a wedding? Why did this seem to matter so much to Scorpius? He still did not know a great deal about Harriett. Now that he had revealed an immediate plan to escape, her true intentions would be made clear very quickly. If she was in some way a double – part of Scorpius' team – she would let their captors know, and certainly take steps to prevent herself becoming involved in any dangerous attempt to escape. On the other hand, if she was on the level and working for the US Government, he could rely on her sticking close to him, so that *her* assignment could be completed. One way or the other he would soon find out if she could be trusted.

'Oh, damn,' she said, getting up and creasing her brow. He had to admit that she was very desirable, the dark hair falling down over her eyes, so that she had to sweep it away with her hand.

'What's wrong?'

'I've absolutely nothing to wear.' She looked up and grinned again, though her eyes were deeply troubled behind the light-hearted front. 'That doesn't matter for later, but what can I wear for the ceremony?'

'I'm certain Scorpius will think of something,' Bond said.

'Yes.' She frowned. 'Yes, I would say you're right – every damned thing, from the ceremony to the way we're to die. There's no way he'll let us go on living, James. You do know that, don't you?'

Bond turned away, not wanting her to see the look in his eyes. 'Then we'll have to do something to prevent it,' he said.

Vladimir indeed appeared to have thought of everything. There was full grey morning dress for Bond and his best man, complete with silk cravats and buttonholes.

And now, as they stood in the Prayer Hall, Bond saw that he had been conservative in his estimate of what Scorpius could provide.

The tape of Aretha Franklin faded, and an organ blared out the bridal march. The lights dimmed, and spots slowly came up on the centre aisle.

Bond had an odd sense of *déjà vu* as he saw his bride and her retinue. There had been a little over an hour to arrange matters, so reason told him that Scorpius must have already been well prepared – not a good omen.

The smooth hoodlum, whom Bond had dubbed 'Bodyguard Bob', came down the aisle with Harriett on his arm – she in a gown of pure white silk, a wide skirt nipped in at the waist where it turned into a low-cut bodice decorated with embroidery and pearls. On her head was a full bridal veil which covered her face and fell around her shoulders, flowing down her back to half the length of the long train which she managed with splendid elegance. She shone and glimmered in the lights, a radiant white goddess slowly descending to be joined to her waiting groom.

For a second, Bond could not stop the rise of emotion as his mind went back to the last time he stood waiting for a bride – his beloved Tracy, the wife who had so tragically been murdered while they travelled to their honeymoon. At this moment, her memory, like a wraith, seemed to cloud over Harriett so that she dissolved, her place taken by his dead wife. For a few seconds, Tracy was there again, coming towards him, her face serene. Then the reality snapped back, and he took a deep breath, clearing his head and remembering a cynical line he had once read: *The past is a bucket of ashes*.

The trick of mental and emotional confusion gave Bond an odd feeling that Harriett and he were possibly committing some kind of blasphemy. Her procession was a stunning sight, as though lit and directed by some great theatrical talent – Harriett holding a demure bouquet of pink and white flowers; Trilby in cream silk, with a wreath of flowers on her head, as matron of honour; and three of the young female Meek Ones, including Pearlman's daughter, Ruth, dressed in the same cream silk.

The spell was broken by the thought that, as long as Harriett was what she claimed to be, there was no blasphemy, for they were both going through this mock ceremony to save lives – not just their own, but others who would have died in the future.

By his side, Pearly Pearlman muttered, 'Look at my Ruth. What would her grandmother say? A good Jewish girl like Ruth taking part in all this. It's not right, and there's that wimp of a husband of hers, look at him.' He nodded towards a young man, pale, thin and bearded, sitting a couple of rows up the aisle. As Ruth passed him, the young man gazed at her with moist eyes. 'She should have married someone with a proper profession. With a future.'

Bond whispered back, 'Your son-in-law, the astronaut? Or the sky-diver?'

'Shut up,' Pearly said, a shade loudly.

Harriett arrived beside Bond, handing her bouquet to Trilby and smiling through the veil as though he was the only man she could ever love or marry. Perhaps he was. The thought did not worry him, though their combined future did. From that moment onwards, he had to keep one thought in the forefront of his mind – This is not real, he told himself. Not legal, not anything.

The odious Scorpius stepped forward and began to intone his own version of the marriage service –

'Dearly beloved, those who are meek in mind, heart and body, we have assembled here to join these two persons – Harriett and James – in marriage, according to our faith, and our belief that only those who have embraced the Society of Meek Ones, shall attain true paradise . . .'

It went on for about half an hour, a whole commixture of Christian, Jewish and other religions. Their hands were bound together by a silk scarf, similar to a stole; Bob, the bodyguard, acting as Harriett's father, passed over a velvet purse containing fifty Kruger rands; they exchanged rings; each drank three times from the same silver cup; and Bond smashed a wineglass, placed under a cloth, with his foot. This last, Scorpius explained, was the shattering of all persons who stood between the true meek and the way to paradise. Bond knew well enough that this was plagiarised from the Jewish ceremony, which is symbolic of the destruction of the Temple, and reminds the couple that marriages must be well guarded or they also can be broken.

At last, Scorpius pronounced them man and wife. Harriett's veil was thrown back, and Bond was allowed to kiss the bride.

A small party took place in a large anteroom, where they were joined by all the Meek Ones present. There were toasts in champagne – a Pol Roger '71, one of the great vintages – and good wishes, followed by short speeches. Harriett looked at Bond with admiration in her eyes, and he realised that, while he could never truly fall in love with this girl, he did care greatly for her. Certainly his sense of chivalry told him he must do everything in his power to see that she did not suffer.

By now it was very late, almost two in the morning. Already, Bond had made up his mind that, though it could well cause more deaths in England, they would have to wait until the early hours of the following day before chancing the escape plan, now well formed in his mind. At least that would give him some daylight in which to look at the terrain outside the huge windows which made up almost the entire exterior walls of the guest rooms facing the sea.

With much cheering, and many tasteless jokes, the couple were led to the guest chambers which they found almost too adequately prepared for them. The room Bond had already been allotted as his bedroom was sealed off, and the overnight-briefcase had been brought into the main sitting room. There were flowers, more champagne and chocolates. One of the bodyguards had said they would not wake them early, while Scorpius made it plain that he did not expect to see them for two or three days at least.

Bond was feeling the onset of fatigue, after the long day, coupled with time-change. He excused himself and went into the bathroom to wash and begin his nightly routine. His toilet bag had been unpacked, and its items placed on the glass shelf above double hand-basins. When he emerged, Harriett stood by the bed in her skimpy underwear. 'Look, James,' she gave him her most wicked grin, 'I've got it all.' She pointed to each item of clothing in turn. 'Something old, something new, something borrowed and they're all blue.' She came towards him, wrapping her half-clad body around him, pulling him back to the bed. It would have taken a saint to resist her, and Bond would be the first to admit that sanctity was not his strong point.

In the early hours of the morning, well down under the sheets where his words would not be picked up by the microphones, he began to question her – 'You said Scorpius proposed marriage to you?'

'He offered marriage, and a life of luxury, in return for my life, yes. He knows that I really do have the goods on him, yet when he proposed I had a feeling he was trying to prove something to himself. Trying to show that his power could deal with any problem that got in his way. I couldn't understand why he didn't just kill me straight away.'

'And you turned him down.'

She gave a small laugh. 'I told him to go . . . Well, I was very vulgar.'

'But he didn't kill you. How did it end up?'

'He flew into a mad rage, cursed and swore that he would see me suffer like the damned. Then he went quiet and said that if I wouldn't

marry him, then he would see to it that I would marry somebody else
– I guess I knew, at that moment, he meant you, James.'

'So?'

'He said he was determined to have a wedding. It was as though
he had become obsessed by it. He's completely crazy, you realise that?'

'Oh, indeed I do – now.'

'It seemed as if a marriage was essential to his plans. He has some
really horrific operation running, and . . .'

'I know.'

'. . . and, in his madness, it seems as if the idea of a wedding was
some form of superstition; as though, in his paranoia, he believed the
plan – whatever it is – would only work if he married someone.
Performed the ceremony, I mean.'

'Yes,' Bond whispered. It made some kind of sense – Scorpius, the
death-bringer, had come to believe the mumbo-jumbo he preached,
and now – on the verge of something internationally dreadful – there
had to be a sacrifice to his idea of God.

As though picking up on his thoughts, Harriett said, 'He seemed to
see a wedding as a sacrifice. He said he would give me a couple of
days' pleasure. He'd see me married, then, when his great task was
complete, he would see both bride and groom suffer the pains of the
damned. We would see what power he held in the world – that's very
important to him in his madness – then we would die, slowly . . .' She
swallowed, gulping back the tears, 'I'm frightened, James. Very
frightened. He's got something truly horrific in mind for us. The man's
the devil incarnate.' She clung to him, as though trying to find some
peace of mind in his body.

Holding her close, Bond tried to talk of his plan of escape from the
dangers ahead. He was sure of the girl now, and knew he had to do
all that was possible to save her – and, maybe hundreds of other
lives.

'Listen, Harry,' he began, 'I've got a few interesting items in my
briefcase.'

'Oh, my God,' she said, drawing him to her. 'You've enough
interesting things here.'

It would be the following afternoon before he could begin explaining
what he intended.

At this moment, though, exhausted by love-making, the couple
talked – of their lives, their childhoods, their likes and dislikes. Harriett,
Bond discovered, was an essentially serious young woman, but with
wit and strength. In many ways their sense of humour was identical,
while they discovered there was more than mere sex in their mutual
attraction. They could be both lovers and friends.

Towards the first pearly light of dawn Harriett fell into a quiet sleep. Climbing out of bed, he went, softly, over to the window. Dawn would break within the hour, and he noticed that the floodlighting had already been turned off.

Harriett stirred, and called him back to bed, her voice husky.

The next afternoon was brilliant and clear, the sun high and the sky that deep blue which is one of the wonders of life. Above the beach and sea, pelicans swept in formation, like clumsy aircraft, diving to scoop food from the ocean. Far away, down by the water's edge, Bond could see the tiny black spots that were sandpipers, foraging for tasty morsels as the tide came in.

A red biplane, used for tourist flights over the island, banked steeply, put its nose down and seemed to be set on a bombing run over Ten Pines. At the last minute, the pilot pulled out and the little stunt airplane seemed to stand on its tail, grasping at the hot air, climbing and then going into a couple of flick rolls. He wondered how the fare-paying passenger felt.

It returned three times, and Bond felt a nudge of intuition. Was it usual for tourists to get three or four close views of Scorpius' hide-away? Would it, perhaps, be better to wait another day, or even a couple of days before making his move? No, it was too much of a risk to leave it any longer. So, again he went over the very serious business of the proposed escape – first gauging the distance from the window to the reed-strewn marshy strip that held the true danger from the vast nest of water moccasins. Earlier in the day he had reckoned it at twenty paces; then ten paces through the marsh to the relative safety of the beach.

In bed, once more under the sheets, with whispers he explained his strategy to Harriett. Scorpius and his people had searched the brief-case, there was no doubt about that, for Bond had set up old and tried methods to detect any tampering – a hair here, a sliver of matchstick there. But Q'ute's technology had triumphed. No secrets had been given up.

The shielded compartment in the overnight briefcase contained the Compact 9mm Browning fully loaded, and with two spare magazines. There was a small medical kit, which would not help them one iota against the venom of the water moccasin; a set of lock-picking equipment, some assorted lengths of wire which could be used for several purposes, a vicious tool which could be used as a nine-inch lethal knife, or be transformed into a hacksaw, file or jemmy. This was the ultimate answer to its smaller, versatile brother, the Swiss Army knife.

Last of all, neatly packed in waxpaper, were a dozen strips of plastique explosive, each the size of a stick of chewing gum. Well away from these were detonators and fuses. He told Harriett about the explosives, keeping the gun, and other items to himself.

He also stressed the danger of the marshland, and rated their chances as less than fifty-fifty, particularly when she admitted that she was only a moderate swimmer, a fact which meant he would have to slow to her swimming pace, should they actually make it to the sea.

'I'm going to set up three pretty large charges from the plastique. Two sticks to each charge can produce quite an unpleasant bang,' he murmured, between kisses. He told her there were three electronic fuses which he could set to delays of between two and ten seconds. 'The first one will be two seconds, the second four and the last one eight.'

The operation would be simple and straightforward, but required meticulous timing and a cool concentration. 'Once we're out, on the other side of the window, we stand still until our eyes have adjusted to the night. I'll nudge you, and we run straight towards the marshes.' He said she must keep in step with him, counting the number of paces. 'Leave the plastique bombs to me,' he said. 'I'll have to throw them on the run – the longest fuse first, then the middle one, and the shortest last. That way we should – if I can throw accurately – get a simultaneous explosion. If I've judged it properly, the explosives should cut a path through the marsh. Nothing will live in the blast area, and any snakes within a few feet on either side should be stunned. They will certainly be frightened, but remember they are very belligerent.

'We go like bats out of hell straight through the swath I hope to cut in the marsh. With good aim, and better luck, we'll get to the other side, down the beach and into the sea. But we do have to go straight and fast. I give us less than thirty seconds to go through the blast path. If I'm wrong, and if one snake on that path, or even near it, doesn't get blown away, then we're for it.

'One of us could get bitten. If that happens, whichever one is left has to press on. If we make the water we swim to the right – I reckon we're placed nearer to the right-hand extremity of the plantation than the left. We'll have to keep going out a long way, because I suspect that, should we make it that far, Scorpius will have a lot of firepower laid down to left and right of his property.'

'You really mean that if you get badly bitten, James, I have to leave you?' she asked in a very small, uncertain voice.

'To stay means death.'

After a long pause, she held him very close. 'I don't know if I'd want to live without you now, darling James.'

'Come on, Harry, nobody's *that* important, and there're more people than the two of us to consider. Scorpius must be stopped. Stopped now, so if I go down, you go on. Understand?'

It was then that she asked him again what he really thought of their chances. There was little point in lying. Bond could only be honest with her. 'Tell me if you want to back out, Harry,' he said. 'I give us less than fifty-fifty on getting through the marshes. About fifty-fifty if we make the water.'

He told her that if she survived, and he did not, she must get to the nearest telephone and call the police. 'If I buy the farm in the marsh, you've got to make it.' He did not add that if he was lucky or, better still, if they both made it, he would take a very different course. It would not be the local police he called, but a number he knew would react at great speed. His thoughts went back to the aircraft that afternoon. It still preyed on his mind. Were they, even at this minute, preparing to knock on Scorpius' door – with shotguns and tear gas? Well, if he could get them in quickly, the Meek Ones would be contained. In many ways he wished it were possible for him to go, a thief in the night, to the dining room and look at the map, taking down all the details from the little winking lights. That would have to be left until later.

Harriett made him go over the moves several times, and at dusk they both stood by the window, looking at the ground they would traverse.

During the day, smirking bodyguards had brought food and taken away the dirty dishes. So, before dinner Bond locked himself in the bathroom, ran a bath – not that it made any difference these days, for sound-stealing equipment will filter out all extraneous noise – opened the undetectable section of the case, and began to make up the three plastique bombs. He took his time, checked and rechecked the electronic fuses, then put each of them in a separate place – one in the secret compartment; one in the briefcase itself and one in the bathroom cabinet. He knew exactly which fuse was set to each deadly and pliable little ball of plastique. He left the other items locked away, and made the only other preparation, that of adapting a shower cap – the bathroom was well-stocked with items that bore the labels of some of the best hotels in the world. Scorpius was obviously a thrifty villain. When Bond had finished with the cap, using a length of wire, he had a perfectly good waterproof holster into which he could slip the Browning pistol before going into the sea.

Over dinner – a chicken gumbo, beef Wellington and raspberry Torte – he could see that Harriett was becoming tense. Fear of the unknown, which could be death, began to show in her eyes, and the way in which she paced the room.

The food was cleared away, and they each bathed before going to bed. He had chosen four thirty in the morning as the jump-off time, and, once in bed, he felt Harriett shivering with the fear and anticipation.

'You can still call it off,' Bond whispered. 'I can always try and blast us out through the house itself, but they're both dangerous ways, and I *truly* believe that we're going by the less deadly route. The snakes'll be dazed and we can get through the marsh in seconds. I don't believe they'll follow us, either. But, if we try to go through the house, Scorpius' men'll just gun us down. They have mobility and they know the interior better than we do.'

'Don't worry, James.' She snuggled close to him. 'I'm coming, and I won't let you down. Just love me now, my dear. That's the best tonic.'

Before midnight, Bond went to the bathroom and brought out the three bombs. He would carry all of them, stacked in throwing order, in his left hand. The Browning would be in his waistband – to be transferred to the converted showercap already attached to his belt – the knife and other odds and ends were distributed around his pockets.

He went back to bed, but could not sleep. Neither could Harriett, so they made love once more, then rested in each other's arms until it was time to get ready.

Because of the microphones, they had worked out a routine for dressing in almost total silence, and by four twenty-five they stood near the window, Bond going through the moves one by one in his head. Outside, the floodlights had been turned off, and at exactly four thirty, he nodded. Harriett reached up, giving him one last kiss and hug. He held her close for a second, then slid back the door.

Harriett grabbed hold of his belt in the half light. They took about two paces forward, then Bond felt himself collide painfully with something that felt like a brick wall.

Everything around them went black, then they were flooded with light and surrounded by images of themselves.

In the fraction of a second during which it happened, Bond realised how the trap worked. Looking from the window was only an illusion. If you stepped outside you were caught in a large box – as big as a normal-sized bathroom – made entirely of glass, the edges curved so that, from the inside of the room the illusion was complete. Once you passed into the box, so the sliding door automatically closed behind you and a powerful light came on from above. The disorientating images of themselves were caused by the glass being treated so that, once the huge light above them came on, the walls turned into near perfect mirrors.

So this was what Scorpius had meant by adding some refinements of his own.

Harriett began to scream hysterically, pointing and trying to scrabble her way through the glass itself.

At ground level, hard against what they had imagined was the exterior of the guest rooms, long grilles had opened up. From the grilles, pushed forward by some unseen device, came large crawling scorpions – big insects, angry and frightened by the harsh light.

They came in droves, not tens or twenties, but, it seemed, in hundreds, until their progress appeared infinite. Some seemed to be dropping from the top of this glass prison, while others tried to climb up the glass. Some killed one another, or themselves, but the march was relentless and Bond stood frozen in horror, with Harriett screaming and clinging to him, as though rooted to the spot, hypnotised by these horrible insects. His flesh began to crawl like the insects themselves, and all he could register was the vast army marching from the bowels of the earth, and the fact that they all had their long tails back, the stings visible and ready to strike.

Harriett's screaming was in his head also, conjoining her real terror with a silent agony, the cry that would not travel from his brain to his lips. It was the screaming in every sweating nightmare, every skin-burrowing dream, and all the worst horrors of fantasy when alien things came at you silently, deadly in shuffling droves, with pointed death and poison aimed at your heart.

21

Deadly Legacy

Bond reached for the Browning, yelled 'Cover your face!', prayed that the glass was not shatterproof, and pulled the trigger three times – top, middle and bottom. This was something you did not stop to think about – locked into a glass box, in brilliant, mirrored light, with a hundred or so scorpions doubling and trebling with every second that passed. He shouted, 'Come on! Pull yourself together! Stick to the plan! Count the paces, and move!'

The glass had blown away, letting in the chill of dawn and fresh air – leaving a jagged opening through which they could pass. Bond felt a slight pain as the end of a shard ripped at his shoulder, tearing through jacket and shirt. Harriett was beside him, taking a deep breath and still clinging to his belt.

'Now, go!' They started to trot gently towards the marshes, eighteen, nineteen, twenty paces. Bond's right hand reached for the first bomb, his arm came up and he pushed on the detonator, activating the fuse, then hurling it straight ahead. They covered another two paces before the second bomb went; and two more for the third which had hardly landed before the first – furthest – plastique exploded with a heavy crack and a bloom of fire.

The other pair went off almost simultaneously, and they quickened pace. The little bombs had been well placed, ripping a trench through the marsh. In the half light they could see the way through the charred and burning reeds.

'Faster, Harry! Faster!' and they were skittering through the trench, running hard for their lives, feet splashing and sinking, slipping in the sandy water.

As they came to the beach beyond, Bond heard Harriett cry out and saw something moving fast through the reeds to their left.

He reached for the Browning, which had gone back into the waistband of his slacks as they ran from the scorpion trap. The gun came up and he put two rounds in the direction of the movement.

Then Harriett cried out again – 'James! Oh, my God, James!' He felt her tug heavily at his belt, but they were on the beach now and there was no stopping. He thrust the pistol into its waterproof bag which hung, sporran-like, from his belt, and used both hands to pull Harriett along. Her legs still moved but became more sluggish at each step.

Almost at the water's edge now, and tiny pebbles suddenly seemed to hit the sand and surf in front of them; then, from what seemed a long way behind, there came the thump – a shotgun trying to put down a cone of fire around them, but too far away to be effective.

Surf washed around Bond's ankles, and he was quickly knee-deep in the anxiously moving ocean. He plunged, and found that he had to drag Harriett with him.

'Swim, Harriett. Damn you, woman, swim!'

She was a dead weight, making little moaning noises that he put down to the considerable exertion they had both made in getting to the sea.

Bond heaved her, getting hold of a handful of the dark rollneck she had put on with her jeans. Like Bond, she wore no shoes. Together they had decided going barefoot would give them more chance during the long run to the sea.

He turned on his back, pulled the limp girl face-up, holding her under the armpits, so that the back of her head lay on his chest. Bond then started to kick with every ounce of his strength, ploughing through the water, sending up a plume of spray like a skiff being sculled fast. All the way, he talked, telling Harry they would make it together, unaware of the fact that she was becoming heavier in his arms.

The sea now started to move, the water taking on a light chop which, as he kicked, occasionally took his head under water. Once, as he came through a small wave, spluttering and spitting the salty foam from his mouth, Bond was conscious of gunfire, far off from the area of the beach and house.

Five minutes later there was the sound of a whirring motor and he thought, Hell, Scorpius has a boat coming after us. He kicked harder, going under again, tilting his body to the right. In a minute he would have to stop and get his bearings.

He went under again, came up and shouted at Harriett, 'Keep going! They won't get us! Just keep going!'

This time there was a reply, but shouted from behind his head. 'James, we're here, you're okay. Just tread water.' It was a voice he dimly recognised, and he swivelled in the water, treading hard and holding Harriett's head well clear.

A large, motorised inflatable was bobbing close to them. In the bow he could see a figure squatting, a light machine-gun balanced on the prow. There was another figure crouched behind him, and at the stern, the man shouting – 'James, stay there. We'll pick you up.'

The inflatable manoeuvred closer, and David Wolkovsky held out a hand. 'Jesus, James, what were you trying to do? Get us all killed?'

'What . . . Wha . . .?' Bond spat out more water. His limbs sagged and he heard himself tell them to take Harriett first. Then, for a while, the fatigue closed in, and he knew nothing but a cold darkness.

It could only have lasted for a few seconds. When the lights came on again he was lying in the bottom of the inflatable, shivering, wrapped in a blanket. Wolkovsky leaned over and he felt the burning of raw spirits as the CIA man dribbled brandy into his mouth.

'What happened?' Bond tried to raise himself up, but David Wolkovsky gently pushed him back. For a second all his fears returned. He had not trusted Wolkovsky, especially when he had spotted the man on the Piedmont flight.

'Shush, James. Keep warm and calm. If you'd stayed put in the house we'd have gotten to you.'

'You'd have what?'

'We mounted an op against Scorpius yesterday.' The sea, wind, and outboard motor were noisy, and Bond strained upwards, trying to lift himself in order to hear what Wolkovsky was saying.

'You did what?' he asked, coughing, clearing his throat and taking in gulps of air.

'When you disappeared into Ten Pines, with the SAS guy, we did a reconnaissance, and asked a few questions. Then we talked to M, and some of his people – three of them are with our boys here.'

Oh, God, Bond thought. He remembered questioning the wisdom of waiting, possibly for just one more day.

There had been two further atrocities in England, Wolkovsky told him. 'It was decided we couldn't wait any longer. So we laid on a joint operation. Us, FBI, and your guys. Dawn. We went in at just about the time you crashed out of that glass contraption. It's quiet in the house now, so I guess we can move back in. We were standing off in this thing, in case any of them made a run for it to the sea. They've got a damned great wooden pier for use when the tide's in. Juts out from the far end of the house. That's where we're heading now.'

Bond began to laugh. 'David. Jee-ru-sa-lem, David. We risked our lives to get out.' He raised his voice, 'Harry, we risked our lives for nothing. They were coming in to get us. Harry?' There was no reply. Bond struggled up onto one elbow. 'Harry?'

Wolkovsky put a hand on his shoulder. 'Sorry, James.' He moved, and Bond could see the contours of Harriett lying in the bottom of the inflatable, a blanket thrown over her. 'Harry?' he said again, his voice unsteady.

'James, it's no good.' Wolkovsky leaned back and pulled the blanket away from Harriett's feet. One leg of her jeans was rucked up to display four horrific marks; a quartet of deep bites where water moccasins had sunk their fangs into the soft flesh of her calf. The blood around the bites was black and congealed, while the leg itself was misshapen, massively swollen. The flesh had turned to a dark blue, the edges black, like the blood around the wounds.

'No!' Bond shouted. 'For Christ's sake, no! She can't . . .!'

'James, she was already dead when we got her into the boat.'

He lay back against the bouncing rubber, looking up at the sky. It's your own fault, he thought. One day more and you'd both be alive. The horrible irony circled around his head, then seemed to come together in a lump, which stuck deep within him as his subconscious pushed truth to the back of his mind. He struggled up, and reached inside the makeshift waterproof holster for the Browning Compact. 'Let me get Scorpius.' His eyes seemed dead as he looked into Wolkovsky's face. 'Let me be the one.'

'We've got to try and take him alive, James. We're coming into the pier now.'

Bond pulled himself into a kneeling position, and crawled forward, dragging the blanket from Harriett's face. Her hair was plastered against her scalp, but her face was in repose. He might have imagined it, but she seemed to turn her head for a second and, on the sea breeze, he heard her say, 'Goodbye, darling James. I loved you.'

Leaning forward, James Bond kissed her cheek and said aloud, 'Damn it, Harry! Why?'

He covered her face, and looked up, his eyes raging fire. 'See that she's taken care of,' he ordered. 'Don't mess her about. When we've tied all this up, I want to see she gets a proper funeral. But I'm now going to give friend Vladimir Scorpius an improper funeral.'

The inflatable bumped against the pier that he had never seen, and did not know existed. Would things have been different if he had known? Would they have waited? Gone a different way? Who could tell now?

He jogged up the pier with David Wolkovsky at his side. Pearly Pearlman stood in the doorway at the far end. 'They've got everyone contained, boss.' He looked at Bond. 'You okay, boss?'

'I'm fine, where's Scorpius? And that turncoat wife of his?'

Pearlman shook his head. 'She was never his wife. She's giving the full strength to a couple of FBI fellas at this moment. Trilby was for the chop from the start, it appears.'

'Scorpius?' Bond shouted.

'Still trying to track him down, boss. He hasn't got out, that's for sure. We've got his sidekicks, the bloody bodyguards; and the Meek Ones are all locked in what they called the Prayer Hall. There're people taking statements from them now.'

They followed Pearlman along a corridor and into the main hallway, then through to Scorpius' study. Several armed men were in the hall, and Bond spotted a colleague from London, going through the books on the shelves.

'James, nice to see you.' He grinned. 'You don't happen to know where Father Valentine kept his records, do you?'

'You not found them yet?' His voice rose angrily. 'Good grief, man. The whole terrorist plot's laid out for you in detail. Look.' He took a pace forward, located the imitation copy of *War and Peace*, and pulled. The section of bookcase came away, leaving the door to the dining room in full view.

Bond gave the door a push, and walked past his colleague who was looking up at the bookcase, muttering, 'Well, good old Wagger-Pagger.'

Bond's third step took him into the room, and face to face with Vladimir Scorpius who was in the process of pulling down the big map of the British Isles. In the second before either man took action, Bond saw that Scorpius had a large book open on the zinc bar.

'I hope you haven't done anything to harm that nice map, Vladi,' he said. His mouth hardly moved, and his eyes took in the map, still intact and only just beginning to slide down to replace the appalling prints. 'Good. We need that. Now, Scorpius, if you'd put both hands on your head . . .'

His thought processes seemed to slow and warp what next occurred. He was hardly aware of what happened, yet saw it all with the strange clarity of a camera lens. Scorpius began to move, then turned. The gun in his hand looked like a toy, and seemed to come up very slowly.

The shot was like a missile going off in the room, and Scorpius appeared to be enveloped in smoke. There was a thud as the first bullet hit the panelling – copied from London's Connaught Hotel – to Bond's right. Scorpius has fired and missed, he reasoned. Then Bond, suddenly freed from this strange sense of torpor, fired from the hip. He saw Scorpius' pistol leap from his hand as Bond's bullet grazed the man's wrist.

'Leave him! He's mine!' he shouted, and heard Wolkovsky call – 'James! Alive, James! Get him alive!'

By this time, Scorpius had leaped for the door – the same door through which Trilby, posing as Scorpius' wife, had come only such a short time ago.

Bond lunged and smashed the half-closed door open, so hard that its hinges were strained and there was an ominous cracking noise from the wood. He was in a long passage, and Scorpius ran fast, far away now, almost at the end where the passage turned.

Bond took aim, low, and fired twice, but Scorpius kept going without even looking back. Taking a deep breath, Bond followed, his feet thumping on the bare wood. He turned the corner and Scorpius was still in sight, well ahead.

Down one passage. Up steps. Into another uncarpeted corridor,

Bond gaining slightly. He skidded around the next turning and, with almost a thrill of pleasure, realised where Scorpius was heading. He fired low again, meaning to miss, for there was a more fitting reward waiting for the Guru of the Meek Ones, the one-time arms dealer who had become contractor for terror in any shape or form. It was best this way. Scorpius would die, and die in the prescribed manner of James Bond's personal law.

He was gaining on the man now, and saw the fire doors ahead. In a moment, they would be in the wing that housed the guest apartments. He caught up with Scorpius just inside the fire doors, where the bare wood changed to deep pile carpet.

Scorpius was struggling with the door that had once led into Bond's bedroom, now closed off from the suite he had shared with Harriett. He brought the man down with a flying tackle that jarred his own body and set his shoulder throbbing. For a moment he remembered having cut it on the spikes of glass surrounding the scorpion trap. If Scorpius was heading for his old room it probably meant there was no trap on the other side of *that* window. Father Valentine Vladimir Scorpius had some wild plan of escape.

Bond was on top of him now, with the Browning almost screwed into his ear. His hand wrenched at Scorpius' left wrist, heaving the man's arm up behind him, holding it high against his shoulder-blades.

'Up!' Bond commanded, stepping back and pulling Scorpius to his feet, dropping the gun from his captive's ear and holding it down, well behind his own thigh, remembering all he had ever learned about the proximity of captive and gun.

'Now, get that door open!'

Scorpius began to whimper, the fight ebbing from him, hope drifting away like a rescue raft just out of reach.

'Open the damned door, or I'll blow you away, piece by piece.'

The hand trembled with the key. You could smell the fear coming from Scorpius' sweat.

'Right, now open it.'

Slowly Scorpius obeyed, and Bond pushed him into the room. It was then he began to blubber out his last chance. 'Money, James Bond. I can make you a rich man. Let me get away! Come with me! I'll give you half of what I have. Half, Bond. Millions. Just let's get away.'

'And how do you propose to do that?'

'Please. If we're going it must be fast. The others'll be close behind.'

'Tell me, first.'

Scorpius dripped with the sweat of fear, his body trembling, the words falling over each other as he tried to speak. 'This window . . .

there's no trap here . . . If you get outside, there's a metal cover . . . like a manhole cover . . . it leads to the basement and a set of tunnels . . . you can get right out of the plantation from there . . . goes under . . .'

'So you don't have to risk life in the marsh?'

Scorpius nodded, violently, shaking with the terror that had come upon him.

'Right.' Bond dropped his voice. 'We'll go out of the window. Now.'

Scorpius gave a massive sigh of relief. 'Come with me. I'll see you get the money. You'll live a life of luxury, Bond. I promise you'll never regret it.'

'I'm sure I won't.'

Still holding Scorpius by the arm, rammed high up between the shoulder-blades, he forced the man towards the window, which slid back easily.

Seconds later they were outside, the sun already rising and warm.

'There . . .! There, there . . .! There!' Scorpius pointed, his hand shaking, down towards the square metal manhole cover.

'Good.' Bond put all his strength into the push, hurling Scorpius away from him, out towards the sand.

He scrabbled in the dirt, on all fours, trying to crawl back, so Bond put a shot directly in front of him, the round kicking up a long spurt of dust.

'But! . . . But!' Scorpius blurted.

'But me no buts,' Bond snarled. 'The next one'll go through your hand.'

'But you said . . . You said . . .'

'I said, "Good". "Good" was all I said. Move! Stand up!'

Scorpius hesitated a shade too long, so he got the promised bullet, which smashed into his hand. He looked shocked, holding the broken, bloodied paw lamely up in front of his face not believing either what he saw or felt.

'Turn and start walking!'

'Where? What? No!'

The next bullet clipped his arm, creasing it, stinging and burning into the flesh.

'Move, Scorpius! Move! Straight for the sea.'

'No! . . . No! . . . No!'

'Yes,' said Bond, clipped and commanding. 'Yes! Yes! And Yes! Move!' He fired again, aware that he had only a couple of rounds left in the clip. The last bullet nicked Scorpius' foot.

He began to scream as Bond took careful aim again, speaking softly now. 'Run! Run for the sea! Run like I ran! Like Harry ran! Go!'

Blubbering with terror, Scorpius loped away, halting and looking back, one hand dripping blood as he went. Stopping again, to turn and whimper like a dog.

Bond put one last bullet past his head, and, at last, seeing all hope was gone, Vladimir Scorpius plunged into the marsh.

He staggered two steps before the first moccasin hit him. Bond saw the creature rise at great speed out of the water and latch on to Scorpius' leg. Then another and another.

Across the sand came Scorpius' final sound, a great screeching, 'NOOOooooo!' Then he threw up his hands and fell forward. There was a sudden, horrible movement around the hump that was his body. A dozen or so fully grown water moccasins writhed and struck at the man who had been a hidden terror to so many.

Behind Bond, the door of the room was forced open. Pearlman and Wolkovsky came blundering in. 'James, for God's sake man . . .' Wolkovsky joined him and saw the moving, wriggling and squirming mass out in the marsh.

Bond shrugged. 'I couldn't do anything. I tried to wing him. Got him in the hand, arm and foot, but he wouldn't stop. I suspect he wanted it that way.' He smiled. At least Harry was avenged.

He turned to the two men. 'Hadn't we better get moving? There's a lot to do. Still a lot to find out. The credit card scam. Contact London about picking up all those human bombs, now we know where they are, and, not least, who in hell's name was Scorpius' man in London. You, Pearly?'

Pearlman shook his head, slowly. 'Don't be silly. No, not me, boss. But I think we'll figure it before the day's out. Personally I thought the bugger'd have me blown away after I brought you here.'

'You then, David? I always rated you, but I suppose if you were involved with the final taking of Ten Pines . . .'

Wolkovsky shook his head. 'Just take my word for it, James. No. There's something more immediate,' he said. 'They're sending signals back to London about the Meek Ones with death-tasks. But there's something else. Something that requires speed and tact. Come and see for yourself. We think friend Scorpius has left us a legacy. A deadly legacy, and time's running out.'

The Last Enemy

They led James Bond back along the corridors, pausing by an open door to what had obviously been Scorpius' master bedroom, which – Bond commented – appeared to have been decorated in what he called '*The Prisoner of Zenda* period'. There they searched among cupboards full of clothes, certainly not all of which had been acquired for Scorpius, and at last found a shirt, underwear, socks, tie and conservative grey suit that fitted Bond reasonably well. Pearlman had gone back to the guest rooms to collect his soft shoes.

He was allowed time to take a quick shower and change before they moved on. Back in Scorpius' amazingly bad-taste dining room they had plugged in scramblers – similar to the C500s used by Bond's service.

One of Wolkovsky's people was having an agitated conversation with someone in Washington – he heard the President mentioned several times. At the other scrambler, one of Bond's colleagues was steadily talking, reading from a long list and the book he had seen earlier lying on the zinc bar.

Peering over his shoulder, Bond saw that the officer was quietly giving London dates, times, targets, names and – where possible – last known addresses of Meek Ones involved in the death-tasks. There was a separate list containing around a hundred names. This last was headed *Avante Carte*.

'We'll have to give it a minute until Charlie's finished talking to Washington,' Wolkovsky told him.

'The *Avante Carte* business?' Bond asked. 'I gathered from Scorpius that it was more than just a phoney slush fund threat.'

'Happily, your own people in Q Branch had already got their eyes on that one.' Wolkovsky knew Q'ute on a professional basis. Now he said that she had revealed the more sinister secrets of the card. 'It seems they could do more with it than just push money around different accounts. There was a microchip in that thing which gave them access to the Stock Market. Would've thrown everyone into a panic. The world's markets would have reacted. The *Avante Carte* could actually buy and sell stock. Your people reckon the idea was to cause a massive run on sterling in the middle of the election campaign.' Now they had the names and addresses of card holders the police would be hard at it tracking down every card in Britain. 'I think they'll contain that one.' Wolkovsky shrugged. 'I have a more immediate worry on my hands. Just hang on until Charlie gets Washington's reaction.'

Bond nodded, wandering through into the bare, book-lined study. Pearly went with him. 'Why d'you think Scorpius really put my life at risk earlier on, Pearly? The car business? Hereford?'

'I really think that was an accident, boss. Thought they were being bloody clever by keeping you under surveillance. Making certain *you* were the one assigned to the job. Didn't imagine they'd get rumbled.' He looked a little shame-faced. 'I'm sorry. I should've known better than to get involved. It really was only because of Ruth, and I had no idea . . .' he floundered for words, 'no idea it'd end up like this. People getting blown away by human bombs. The whole business stinks. It was bad enough a couple of years ago, when that guy put his girlfriend on a commercial jet loaded to the gills with explosive, but these people were really made to believe they were serving future generations by decimating themselves together with innocent folk.'

'Not your fault, Pearly. Any man would have done the same if his son or daughter was mixed up in it.'

Pearlman was silent for a minute, shuffling his feet. 'Really should've reported it to someone, though. Think I'll go down to the Prayer Hall. Find Ruth and have a word.'

'You do that.' He was aware of two other people seated at Scorpius' desk. One was another colleague – John Parkinson, short, ebullient and a good 'creative' interrogator. Parkinson sat opposite a red-eyed, nervous Trilby Shrivenham.

'He said he'd have me thrown into the swamp alive if I didn't go along with him,' Trilby was saying. 'Truly, when I realised what was happening – the death-task business and all that – I got out, or tried to, just like poor Emma Dupré. Only I can't remember much about it. Scorpius had already filled me with dope. I'd an idea that he was planning to use me on a particularly sensitive target – even though I was not married, and hadn't given birth. That was the only true way of getting a death-name and a death-task.' She looked up, saw Bond and said, 'You believe me, Mr Bond, don't you? I could never have married that . . . that . . . living Satan.'

'I believe you, Trilby.' He gave her a steady, warning look. 'I didn't really fall for it when Vladi brought you in to that odd little dinner party. Nothing rang true. But you have to convince this gentleman.' He turned to Parkinson. 'Sorry, John. Your job. I shouldn't stick my oar in.'

'Right,' the interrogator agreed, icing Bond out.

'James?' Wolkovsky was beckoning from the dining-room door. The CIA man called Charlie stood behind him. They both looked as though they had received bad news.

'Proof that the world is to end today?' Bond asked, trying to lighten the atmosphere.

'Just about.' Wolkovsky sounded as though his nerves were stretched like piano wire. 'Here's your first clue.' He threw down a copy of the *New York Times*, front page upwards. The headline was in bold type and shouted – BRITISH PREMIER PLAYS HOOKY FROM ELECTION CAMPAIGN. ONE-DAY VISIT FOR TALKS WITH THE PRESIDENT.

'Oh, sweet Jesus,' Bond muttered under his breath. Then he told them what Scorpius had said when he had commented on the Prime Minister not being on the death-list. 'He told me he had special plans for the PM.' His stomach turned over as he realised what Scorpius had *actually* said. 'The words he used were, "Oh, no, James Bond. The Prime Minister is *not* forgotten. Certainly not. But I have a very special role for the Prime Minister that does not show on this map."' Bond inclined his head towards the map of the British Isles, which was twinkling away with all its lights winking on the wall. One of his colleagues was rechecking the targets shown by the pinpoints of light, making sure nothing had been left to chance. 'Later,' Bond continued, 'Scorpius stopped himself from elaborating. I would say you're right. The Prime Minister and the President, both!'

'Bet your ass we're right,' Wolkovsky said through his teeth. 'There are indications here, in this place, that a similar campaign – against this country – was in the early stages of planning.'

'Then there are no doubts. There's a death-task running against the PM during this visit. What's the schedule?'

'At the moment, the schedule doesn't matter much.' Charlie, Wolkovsky's man, sounded as disenchanted as a priest who has lost his faith.

'Why? Of course the schedule matters. This could be set for the Prime Minister and your President – both of them. Two great world leaders in one blow!'

'Exactly how we see it.' Wolkovsky looked ready to spit violently. 'Unhappily, it's not the way our Secret Service – who, as you know, are the VIP bodyguard service – sees it. Nor is it the way your Prime Minister looks at it either.'

'What?' Genuine disbelief from Bond.

Wolkovsky gave one of his characteristic shrugs. 'The Secret Service say they are the best bodyguard unit in the world.' He raised his eyes towards the ceiling. 'Even though you can pick them out a mile away by their little unobtrusive lapel pins, the dark shades, walkie-talkies that crackle from hidden holsters, or the fact that some of them wear long raincoats when it's a hundred and ten in the shade.' He put on a mock-tough face. '"It's okay, Mr President, by the time we go out that door we'll *own* the goddamned street." I actually heard one of them say that.'

'You *have* pointed out the real danger, I presume?' Bond's voice remained full of shock and disbelief. 'If there's a death-task out on the PM and possibly the President as well, then there's little they can do about it.'

'I've told them all ways.' Charlie imitated Wolkovsky's shrug. 'It appears that your Prime Minister's also oblivious to the true danger. Apparently the PM's got extra Special Branch people in tow, and the Secret Service say nobody's going to get within fifteen or twenty yards of either of them.'

'Twenty yards!' Bond gave a gesture of despair, clenching his fists and shaking them at shoulder level. 'Twenty yards could just as well be twenty inches.'

'We know that, James. So I've got a call in to Chief of Security at the White House. He's an old buddy and I might at least get him to listen. Maybe he'll even let us go up there and lend a hand.'

Behind them the telephone buzzed, and one of the spare FBI men answered, then called to Wolkovsky. 'That'll be him, now.'

Almost at the moment the CIA man turned to walk to the telephone, Pearlman reappeared through the door to Scorpius' office. His face was the shade of old parchment, his eyes wide with concern.

'Pearly . . .?' Bond began.

'She's gone,' Pearlman said, stopping and looking around him as though in a daze. 'Gone. Not here, and that wimp of a husband's just kneeling there in a kind of trance.'

Bond shook him gently by the shoulder. 'Do we know when she left?'

'I talked to the people going through the records and information being offered by Scorpius' disciples down there. Boss? Boss, I don't like it.' He sounded like a child frightened by some TV fairytale. 'They say she went yesterday and that Rudolf – that's my bloody son-in-law's name. Rudolf, like the reindeer. Rudolf, I ask you boss, who gives a boy the name Rudolf?'

'You were going to tell us what they're saying about Rudolf.'

'Yes. Well, they say he's behaving like the husband of someone who's left to carry out a death-task. Scorpius apparently taught them this way of self-hypnosis. They kneel perfectly still until the business is over. It's like willing their partner to succeed.'

Bond stayed as calm as possible. 'Pearly, it might be too late for Ruth. But would you do us one favour . . .?'

'Anything.'

'Get back down there. Try to talk with their experts. Their explosives people – or the kids who've been trained in the business. I want details of how they make the bombs, what detonates them, what safety factors they have. The lot, okay?'

'Done, boss. They're weeding the wheat from the chaff in the Prayer Hall. Those who have death-names for the future. Everything.'

'Get the full SP on it, Pearl.' Bond had no idea that he had even abbreviated Pearlman's obvious nickname. He went over to where Wolkovsky was still talking, took out his notepad and scribbled – *We know who the bomb is. It's a girl. Tell him we have a man who can finger her.*

Wolkovsky went on talking, picked up the paper while he spoke, read it, nodded to Bond and said into the telephone, 'Walter, listen, we've got some positive proof here. It's going to happen. This Meek Ones' business in England, right? You're definitely going to get it in Washington today. We now know who it is, and there's a fella here who can make the ID.' He listened, the silence punctuated with, 'Yes . . . Okay, Walter, I know . . . Yes, of course it's for real. Waddayou think it is, a video game? . . . Yes, Walter . . . Good . . . Good. Okay, you call me back when it's fixed.' He put down the telephone and turned to Bond. 'Well?' he asked.

Bond gave him a very brief résumé of the part Pearlman had played in the whole business, ending with the latest information about his daughter, Ruth. 'I've got him working on how they operate the bombs now.'

'Well, my friend seems to have bought the idea. You sure about this girl?'

'About a hundred and fifty per cent sure.'

'They're going to do what they call a manual override on the Secret Service. He's calling me back when it's all arranged, but it looks like we're going to be allowed a minimal armed presence – three at the most. They're arranging for a military jet to go into Savannah to pick us up – that's forty-five minutes' car ride from here. The jet'll take us into Andrews Airforce Base. Your Prime Minister arrives there at noon.' Automatically Bond looked at his stainless steel Rolex. It was only eight-thirty. He asked if he could have some coffee. Black. He did not, for once, insist on a brand. Some FBI gofer scurried away to get coffee.

Wolkovsky continued, 'There's a military honour guard at Andrews, and a helicopter to take the PM and party right onto the helipad at the White House.' He glanced down at the notes he had taken. 'No problems thus far. No press at Andrews except the long-range TV people – and I do mean *long*-range. There'll be three helicopters – Number 1, the Presidential, for the Prime Minister and some of the party; Numbers 2 and 3 for Secret Service and three of us. ETA at White House twelve fifty-five. President greets Prime Minister. Six TV crews as usual. No other press. The expected length of lunch and the meeting is three hours. There's a general press photocall, to last for ten – they're saying *strictly* ten – minutes, at two o'clock in the Rose Garden. That's to let all the newspapers get good pictures for late evening and tomorrow's editions.

'The Prime Minister's expected to leave, from the helipad, at between five and six pm. Straight to Andrews. Up-up and away, back to election problems. Your press is screaming that the PM's making election capital out of the meeting. The Prime Minister has frostily announced that the meeting was planned long before an election was called, and you know the PM. When something like a tête-à-tête with the Prez is on the menu not even a General Election is allowed to get in the way.'

Bond looked over Wolkovsky's shoulder, pointing – 'That seems to be the most dangerous time.' His finger rested on the photocall arranged for two o'clock.

Wolkovsky nodded his assent, as Pearlman came back into the room.

'Well?' Bond asked.

'Not really.' Pearlman now looked haggard. 'I have the details, though.'

'Go on.'

'They've been using this stuff that's damned difficult to detect. The dogs haven't latched on to it yet, and it'll go through security screens with no problem.' He paused, wiping his brow. 'If you want to see how they go about it, there's a complete do-it-yourself destruction outfit in the cellars, together with pounds and pounds of the explosive. It's pushed into a sort of large waistcoat, layer upon layer of the stuff, with a master detonator, set into the back. The trigger is in a button, sort of mid-chest at the front. That's operated manually, and can be done very quickly, but Scorpius thought of everything. You have to turn the damn thing and then give it a tug. It takes less than two seconds, but it's safe enough. You can't trigger it accidentally, or by falling or bumping into someone. It has to be a deliberate action, and it *must* be pulled off. Even a bullet through it wouldn't blow the detonator.' He mimed, thrusting his hand into his jacket, turning the hand and tugging hard. 'That's what it takes.'

'And that's what you think Ruth's carrying.'

'That's what I *know* she's carrying.'

Bond told him what they had learned, and, during the telling, the telephone buzzed again. Wolkovsky hurried to answer and returned with the news that everything had been agreed, if reluctantly, with the Secret Service.

'Three of us,' he said. 'Permission to carry one handgun each. We'll have to get ID at Savannah. The jet's leaving in the next half hour.

We'll only just make it in time for the Prime Minister's arrival. So who's it to be?'

Bond looked hard at Pearlman. 'You, David; myself; and Pearly here. It's *his* daughter who's carrying the stuff. If things get really close, it'll be Pearly who'll have to take her out.'

Wolkovsky nodded sadly. 'They've given us an operational crypto,' he said. 'Operation Last Enemy.'

'Last Enemy?' Bond queried.

'Biblical.' Pearlman sounded resigned to what lay ahead. 'New Testament as well. "The last enemy that shall be destroyed is death."'

At Savannah they had their photographs taken in a private room set aside for official personnel. Within fifteen minutes each was provided with a laminated, clip-on ID, signifying that they were attached to White House Security, and should be allowed anywhere without question. There was also a rider saying they could carry weapons. The security officer, whom Bond suspected of being an Agency man, had travelled from Andrews Field in the little anonymous Lear Jet, and he issued all three with standard short-nosed Police Positives, which they carried in shoulder holsters. They signed for the weapons and the ammunition that came with them.

It was just after noon that they landed at Andrews Field, and there was not even enough time for introductions before the Prime Minister's Royal Air Force VC10 touched down on 19 Right, the longest of the two runways.

Bond scanned the whole scene from a jeep moving quietly behind the band and honour guard. The aircraft steps were rolled into place, and the door opened to reveal the familiar figure of the Prime Minister who was closely surrounded by Diplomatic Protection and SB people. The remainder of the secretaries and advisers stayed in the background as the PM stood to attention on the aircraft steps, while the band played the British National Anthem, followed by the Star Spangled Banner. Only when this was over did the party start to come down the steps.

'At least they've got a large team of bodyguards for once,' Bond muttered, holding on to the metal bar as the jeep followed the PM's party up towards the three SH-3Ds waiting for them. 'Could hardly see the PM for the heavies.'

They rode aboard the big choppers in silence, jinking across country to the White House, all three helicopters setting down, one after the other – disembarking their passengers, then taking off for the next flight in – on the White House helipad. The blossom was out, and from the air the city looked spectacular – the Washington Monument, the Reflecting Pool and Lincoln Memorial set like dramatic jewels in the now pink and white parkscape of the Mall. Not for the first time, Bond thought how like Paris the city looked.

By the time the trio reached the ground, the Prime Minister had met with the President, and they had disappeared inside that relatively modest building at 1600 Pennsylvania Avenue.

Wolkovsky contacted the Head of White House Security who was, not unnaturally, slightly suspicious of the arrangements. He had agreed to them, but – as he said – with great misgivings. 'These days, our security is the best in the world.' He looked hard at Pearlman and Bond.

'But we know what to look for in this situation,' Bond said quietly. 'I know you might not believe it, but, I promise you, an attempt is going to be made.' He paused and then seemed to be taking overall control. 'Now, when is the press corps going to be admitted?'

'The TV people are already here. The others will be arriving any time between now and around one forty-five.'

'Which entrance?'

'They'll all have to show White House press passes.'

'Don't worry. This person will have a press pass. You can bet on it.'

'Then you must do what you think best.' The Head of Security gave them a sober look, as if to say he thought they were making too much fuss. 'They all come in by the East Gate.'

By mutual consent, they decided that Wolkovsky should stay up in the Rose Garden – where they all now gathered to take a quick look at the TV crews – while Pearlman and Bond should go to the East Gate. There they would see every person with access to the photocall.

'If she goes through with it . . . if she really tries . . .?' Bond began as they strolled towards the entrance with its own stone and glass booth where passes could be checked. 'Will you . . .?'

'Have I the guts to kill her?' Pearlman asked.

'Well, have you?'

There was a long pause which took them right up to the gate. 'Boss, I just don't know. I've accepted that, bar a miracle, she'll have to die. If I can't do it, you'll know soon enough, and I'll never hold it against you.'

They stood in silence, watching the men and women of the press corps arrive and make their way through the gate, each checked by the guards who seemed to know most of them by name.

The clocks ticked on. One thirty.

No sign of anyone who looked remotely like Ruth.

One forty-five. Still nobody, and the initial flood of photographers had dwindled to a trickle.

At one fifty a young man, dark-suited, and hung with cameras, showed his pass and was cleared through the gate. He was on the plump side, three cameras slung around his neck, short fair hair showing beneath a large-brimmed, flamboyant hat, and a drooping moustache giving the impression that he regarded himself as something of a Bohemian.

'Takes all kinds,' the security officer in the booth called to them. 'That's all, folks, as they say in *Looney Tunes*. Nobody else gets in now.'

'Maybe we were wrong.' Bond did not sound convincing. He felt the tension coming from Pearlman like an electric charge.

'Maybe.' The SAS man looked as though he could drop with stress.

When they reached the Rose Garden, the gaggle of TV and press photographers were setting up their gear, ready for the main event.

They joined Wolkovsky, shaking their heads. Then Pearlman spoke. 'She's here, somewhere. I know it. I can feel it.'

'Would they cancel?' Bond asked.

'No way. Not now.' Wolkovsky took a deep breath. 'I'll stay to the rear. Would you two like to spread yourselves one at each end of the bunch? Watch the photographers, not the President and the PM.'

Bond nodded, and they moved away, Pearlman going to the far left, Bond taking up position on the right.

There was a buzz of excitement from the press, not known for being impressionable. All James Bond could feel was this continued mounting tension, and his own heart like a drumbeat, ticking off the seconds to some dreadful disaster. He began to scan the jostling photographers. There was nobody who resembled Ruth as he had last seen her, at the wedding. A cloud, like bleak, cold fog, seemed to roll over his mind.

He glanced across at Pearlman whose eyes did not stop roving among the press men and women. Then the buzz became a hush as the President and his wife escorted the Prime Minister of Great Britain out into the garden.

It was a cheerful arrival, with the President calling out quips to members of the press he recognised, and making ad lib remarks to the Prime Minister, who looked fit, well and happy, under no strain at all.

Bond dragged his eyes back to the photographers. Perhaps they had got it wrong after all. Was Ruth going to hit the PM alone – even when the RAF aircraft arrived back at Heathrow? He looked towards the line-up again, the President and Prime Minister taking their places together, then turned his eyes back to the photographers, all worried about focus and position.

But this time he knew there was something wrong. In the seconds his eyes had been away from the group it had changed. He couldn't tell how, or why, at first. Then it became clear, fully focused in his own mind.

The young man with the Bohemian look had pushed through to the front, elbowing his way forward. There was something not quite right about him. Another second went by and Bond realised the newsman was not even bothering to handle the cameras around his neck. He wasn't taking pictures. He moved one pace forward, in front of the main crush of photographers, his hand starting to travel upwards, going for the inside of his jacket.

'Pearly!' Bond yelled.

The dark-suited figure seemed to be on the verge of springing. Pearlman had his pistol out, but he hesitated. Too long. Far too long, the SAS man stood there, undecided.

Bond acted without thought – an automatic reflex, his gun coming up, two quick shots, followed by panic and screams.

The first bullet caught the young man in the arm, just as his hand was reaching inside the jacket. The hand was jerked away as the second bullet caught him full in the chest. He was lifted slightly, and fell on his back, with Pearlman running forward, his own pistol, pointing, ready for a *coup de grâce*, should it be needed.

The wide-brimmed hat had been knocked from the young man's head, and with it the fair hair – a wig. Ruth's own red hair seemed to spring from her head, like a grotesque magician's trick. She twitched once, but Bond didn't see her. He had sensed something else.

Turning on the balls of his feet, he traversed the party of VIPs who had been flung into confusion, the Secret Service men and bodyguards moving in front of them to give added protection. All but one. A member of the PM's protection staff stepped free of the group. With horror, Bond saw who the man was, and, in seeing him, everything fell into place.

Detective Superintendent Bailey's automatic pistol was out and coming up to the firing position. His legs were apart, the stance perfect, but his eyes never left his real target. The weapon, an extension of his arms, came to bear low down, onto the Prime Minister.

Bond's swivelling turn was followed through. In that infinitesimal moment he saw everything, knew everything, was assured of how Scorpius had always been one step ahead. Bailey had been there. Unusual, because normally it would have been the Head of Branch. But for the whole of this operation it was Bailey. Bailey, Vladimir Scorpius' man.

The thoughts commingled in a fraction of time, and within that second, Bond pulled the trigger twice more.

The Special Branch man did not realise he was going to die, and could not have known what hit him. His body jerked only slightly as he was knocked off his feet to crumple into the rose bushes.

The Last Enemy had been conquered. Bond quietly holstered his pistol and joined the other security officers in trying to restore calm. One thing was sure, it would be a different kind of job for the bomb disposal people. It was not often they were called upon to render a corpse safe.

'A job well done, 007. A sad one, but . . . Well, one shouldn't dwell on these things.' M did not look his agent in the eyes. It was two days after the incident. There had been a press field day, but the Secret Intelligence Service was not mentioned in any of the reports. The American Secret Service, on the other hand, was taking some stick. Even Congress was giving it a hard time.

The events at Hilton Head Island did not rate a single line of type.

'No.' M was uncomfortable. 'Doesn't do to dwell.'

'No, sir.' Bond was not his usual relaxed self.

'Take some leave if I were you.'

'Just three or four days, sir, if I might.'

'Three or four weeks if you want.'

'I think I should get back to work as soon as possible, sir.'

'Have it your own way, then, Commander Bond. Just sign the slip and I'll pass it through.'

'Thank you, sir.' He rose and began to walk towards the door.

'Oh, and James . . .'

'Yes, sir?'

'The Shrivenham girl. Young Trilby.'

'Sir?'

'She's going to be fine. They've brought her back, and Molony's giving her the once-over. Says she'll be as fit as a flea in no time.'

'Good.'

'In fact, she's asked to see you – only if you wish to see her, of course.'

'Maybe, sir. Maybe in a week or so. I have to attend a couple of funerals in the States first. After that, well, maybe.'

'Good girl for you, James. Good family. Steady.'

'Yes. Yes, I realise that, sir. If you'll excuse me.'

He did not even speak to Moneypenny as he left. Once the funerals were over, he would feel better. Maybe M was right. Perhaps he should take Trilby to dinner or something. One thing was sure, Harry would have approved.